Jean E. Pendziwol is an award-winning Canadian author of books for children. *Once Upon a Northern Night* was shortlisted for a Governor General's Award and the 2014 TD Canadian Children's Literature Awards Book of the Year. *The Lightkeeper's Daughters* is her debut novel for adults. She lives in Ontario in the shadow of the Nor'Wester Mountains near Lake Superior.

You can discover more about the author at www.jeanependziwol.com

THE LIGHTKEEPER'S DAUGHTERS

Elizabeth's eyes have failed. She can no longer read the books she loves or see the paintings that move her. But her mind remains sharp, and music fills the vacancy left by her blindness. When her father's journals are discovered on a shipwrecked boat, she enlists the help of a delinquent teen, Morgan, to read to her. As an unlikely friendship grows between them, Elizabeth is carried back to her childhood home — the lighthouse on Porphyry Island, Lake Superior — and to the memory of her enigmatic twin sister Emily. But for Elizabeth, the faded pages of her father's journals reveal more secrets than she anticipates. . .

JEAN E. PENDZIWOL

THE
LIGHTKEEPER'S
DAUGHTERS

Complete and Unabridged

CHARNWOOD
Leicester

First published in Great Britain in 2017 by
Weidenfeld & Nicolson
an imprint of the Orion Publishing Group Ltd
London

First Charnwood Edition
published 2018
by arrangement with
the Orion Publishing Group Ltd
London

A catalogue record for this book is available
from the British Library.

ISBN 978–1–4448–3777–3

Published by
F. A. Thorpe (Publishing)
Anstey, Leicestershire

Set by Words & Graphics Ltd.
Anstey, Leicestershire
Printed and bound in Great Britain by
T. J. International Ltd., Padstow, Cornwall

This book is printed on acid-free paper

To Richard

So lovely was the loneliness
Of a wild lake, with black rock bound,
And the tall pines that towered around.

The Lake, Edgar Allan Poe (1809–1849)

PART ONE

Endings and Beginnings

1

Arnie Richardson

The black Lab is aging. His arthritic legs stiffly pick their way along the well-worn path, stepping carefully over roots and carrying his stout form between the trunks of spruce and poplar. His muzzle, flecked with gray, tracks close to the ground, gathering the scent of his master's trail.

It is a morning ritual, one that takes them from the cottages at Silver Islet through the woods to Middlebrun Bay — a ritual they have practiced since the Lab was a gangly-legged pup. But even then, all those years ago, the man's hair was white, his eyes framed by crow's feet, his beard dusted with silver. Now they are both slowing, man and dog, wincing at stiff joints, choosing their footing carefully. Each morning when they set off at the first pale orange light of dawn, they greet each other with the simple satisfaction of knowing they have another day to do so.

The man leans comfortably on a walking stick, a length of knotty pine first polished by the waves of Lake Superior and then varnished until gleaming in his workshop. He does not need it, not until the trail begins to climb, and then his grip tightens and the wood becomes a part of him, necessary and integral. He pauses at the top of a ridge. Two paths merge here, the one they

3

are on joining the much wider, more frequently traveled route that is part of the hiking trails of Sleeping Giant Provincial Park. The park is quiet now.

It is a mystical place, this peninsula, jutting out into Lake Superior; chiseled rocky cliffs and worn ridges, mysteriously carved by wind and rain and time, take the form of a giant slumbering in a cradle of icy gray water. Legends speak of an Ojibwe god, Nanibijou, lying down at the entrance to Thunder Bay, his magnificent form turning to stone, eternally protecting rich silver deposits. The story may be myth, but the silver is real. Extracting its riches led to deep shafts sunk well below the surface of Superior, where miners followed the veins of ore under the constant threat of encroaching water. The mine gave rise to the town, no more than a hamlet really — a cluster of wooden houses, a blacksmith shop, a store, all abandoned when the Lake won its battle and buried the silver in an icy grave. After a few years cottagers arrived and dusted off the floors and tables, polished the windows, nailed loose shingles into place, and Silver Islet came back to life, if only for a season each year. For generations now, the man's family has spent the summers in one of the houses, visiting during the winter months for a few days or even weeks when the weather permits. He has walked this path since he was a child.

Man and dog begin their descent toward the shore, the dog's tail painting half circles in the air behind him, the man's stick alternately thumping against damp earth and tapping against hard

4

rock as the trail wanders toward the bay. Lake Superior is beginning to stir, shaking off the mist that settled like a shroud overnight. The foghorns at Trowbridge and Porphyry light stations, now silent, spent the hours before dawn calling out to unseen vessels as they carefully charted their way across Thunder Bay, past the cape at the foot of the Sleeping Giant, out toward Isle Royale and into the shipping lanes of Lake Superior. But the rising sun and the waking wind have chased away any remaining wisps, and instead of the ominous warning of the horns, songbirds serenade the walking pair.

The warning would have been a more fitting accompaniment.

The dog's gait quickens as he senses the nearness of the Lake. His bones are tired and his eyesight faded, but he is a Lab, and the water calls to him. He passes the man and lopes onto the beach of Middlebrun Bay, snatching a stick from the line of debris that was tossed high up above the waterline by waves during a recent storm. He sets off along the shore, the path his paws trace through the sand erased by the Lake as quickly as it is drawn.

The man is not far behind, but far enough that the dog has spotted her before his owner's first footprint appears. The Lab's vision is clouded, but he can sense her presence and discern her shape as it emerges from the rocks and trees and beach and waves. He stands in the water, barking, his stick dropped, forgotten.

She is about twenty-six feet long, her wooden hull splintered and gaping on the port side, her

5

boom swinging as the Lake rises and falls beneath her. Each breath of the water lifts her off the rocky bottom, setting her down again with a shudder. The main sail is still set, but flapping, tattered. She is listing, her bilges breached, the Lake moving through her. The man doesn't need to see the name painted on the stern; he knows that the cursive script reads 'Wind Dancer.'

The beach pulls at his feet as he rushes toward the boat, his prints punctuated by the round end of his walking stick so that his trail looks like a message written in Morse code. The bay is shallow, but there are rocks skirting the far end, and it is there that the vessel lies. He gives little thought to the clamoring of the Lab, calling out instead to anyone who may yet be on board. He stumbles toward the point, splashing into the icy water. Numbness creeps up his legs, clutching him, grasping, but he ignores it, continuing over the rocks, avoiding the crushing gap between boat and shore, and hauling himself into the cockpit where he stands, shivering.

He has never been aboard *Wind Dancer* before, but still the flood of memories threatens to drown him, rushing back as he looks from broken rudder to snapped halyard. He remembers the fort the two of them built together out of driftwood as boys, feels the tug on his rod the time they took the little gaff-rigged boat *Sweet Pea* out fishing in Walker's Channel for the first time alone, tastes the beer they shared, stolen from a picnic basket and carried to the black volcanic beach on the far side of Porphyry Island. He hears the whispering of names,

Elizabeth and Emily.

'Goddammit, Charlie!' He speaks aloud, looking up at the mast and tattered sail, at the silhouette of two gulls soaring high above. 'What the hell have you done now?'

It has been sixty years since they last spoke, sixty years since Porphyry Island went up in flames. He has seen *Wind Dancer* many times, heard stories of her captain, of Elizabeth. Emily. But they did not speak, he and Charlie. Doing so would have given voice to their complicity, however well-meaning, and fed the ache of regret. It has haunted him. Not a day has gone by in all that time that he hasn't thought of them. Not one.

The old man grasps a cleat for balance and peers through the companionway into the cabin below. A seat cushion and a baseball cap float in the pool of water. On the chart table is a stack of books, its faded sailcloth wrapping loose, a twisted pile of twine beside.

He sits on the helmsman's seat. The Lab is silent. There are only birds to interrupt his thoughts, and the quiet chatter of wind and Lake and the creaking complaints of the boat. Charlie Livingstone is not on board.

Wind Dancer is empty of life except for the flickering glow of a kerosene lantern, weakly but defiantly burning, lashed to the boom like a beacon.

2

Morgan

What a fucking waste of time. A bunch of do-gooders, sitting around dreaming up stupid policies. *We're exploring* . . . what did they call it? 'Restorative rehabilitation processes.' They can say they've tried, that they've reached out with compassion to some poor underprivileged soul — *look how brilliant and forward-thinking we are.* Wrapped up in their tiny little worlds with their perfect polite children who go to class and do their homework, and petition to banish junk food and end starvation in Africa and play on the basketball team and never come home high on Saturday night. And they pat themselves on their backs and say, *Look what good parents we are. Look what good citizens we are.* If they only knew.

Let them put a tiny stitch in a gaping wound, set my feet on the right path. I'll apologize, and go through the motions of accepting their compassion. It wasn't my fault, really. It was the system that let me down.

Fucking waste of time.

They searched my backpack. I should have ditched it before I got to McDonald's. Or at least the spray-paint cans. No chance talking myself out of that one. *No, Officer. I was nowhere near Boreal Retirement Home. No, sir. I had nothing*

8

to do with that graffiti. *Those aren't mine. I was just holding them for a friend. Which one? Oh, umm . . . he's not here.*

Assholes. No one spoke up for me. No one. They all kept their eyes down and sucked on their Diet Cokes, their faces plastered with the same condescending looks their parents use. *The poor thing. Can you blame her, really?*

Apparently they could.

When they brought me home, I could tell Laurie was pissed. She gave me that 'disappointed' lecture that made me roll my eyes. I was placed with her and Bill a little over a year ago, and while they act like they care, I can't be bothered. They're not my parents, and I have no interest in pretending they are. I won't be there long. I'm just another foster kid in a stream of foster kids moving through their house.

The bus lurches to a stop in front of a sprawling building and deposits me in front of Boreal Retirement Home before it huffs and drives off. I'm left standing alone on the quiet tree-lined street while the cold wind grabs at me. Here and there, clumps of fallen leaves tumble along the curb. I follow them along the sidewalk to the entrance.

God, I hate fall.

⋆ ⋆ ⋆

The door is locked, and I yank on it a few times before I notice the intercom. Of course it's locked. This place is full of rich old folks, the ones who can afford the private nurses and

9

full-time chefs and river location. As if they could give a shit. Probably can't even remember what they had for breakfast. I press the buzzer, and a voice crackles over the intercom speaker. Couldn't understand a fucking word, but I assume they're asking my name.

'It's Morgan. Morgan Fletcher.'

There's a long pause before the door buzzes and the lock clicks open.

I find the administrative office and pause to knock on the open door. Behind the desk, a middle-aged woman is shuffling through folders.

'Sit down, Morgan,' she says, without even bothering to look up.

So I perch on the edge of one of the chairs and wait. A sign, barely visible among the stacks of papers on the desk, reads 'Anne Campbell, RN, Executive Director.' I suppose she's going to administer my 'restorative rehabilitation.'

'All right.' Ms. Campbell sighs, extending the folder in her hand. 'You're Morgan Fletcher.' She removes her glasses and places them on the desk. 'I see.'

I know what she sees. She sees what she wants to. She sees my straight black hair, dyed so that it shines like midnight. She sees dark kohl circling my gray eyes, my tight jeans and high black boots and the row of silver studs along my earlobes. She sees my pale face that I've made even paler, and my bright red lips. She doesn't see that I am, maybe, just a little scared. I won't let her see that.

I slouch back into the chair, and cross my legs. So that's how it's going to be. Fine.

10

Ms. Campbell opens the folder. 'Well, Morgan, community hours, is it? It says here that you have agreed to clean up the graffiti and assist with further maintenance work under the direction of our maintenance supervisor.' She looks at me again. 'You'll be here every Tuesday and Thursday right after school for the next four weeks.'

'Yup.' I tap my toe against the front of the desk and look at my fingernails. They are painted red, like my lips. Blood red.

'I see,' she says. Again. Ms. Campbell pauses for a moment, and I can tell that she's studying me. I know what's in that folder. I don't want her judgment. Worse, I don't want her pity. I shift my gaze to a spider plant on the top of the filing cabinet. She sighs again. 'Well, then, I guess we'd better get you introduced to Marty.' She leaves the folder containing my past on her desk, and I have no choice; I follow her down the hall.

Marty is old, but not old like the people who live here. He reminds me of a beardless Santa Claus, complete with round belly framed by red suspenders. His eyebrows have a life of their own, the hairs standing out in all directions and curling down, snowy white and bushy. They make up for the lack of hair elsewhere on his head, which is shiny bald on top but has a scruffy fringe reaching from ear to ear. It is the eyes below the runaway brows that I notice most: piercing blue, the color of the sky on a cold winter day.

Marty's sitting at his desk, an old card table

11

shoved against one wall of a stocked supply room. On the table is a pile of newspapers and a book with a painting of dancers on the cover. I recognize the artist: Degas. He's one of my favorites. Our tattered old book had paintings by all the Impressionists, but I liked Degas the most. Marty's probably using the pages to wipe paintbrushes.

'This is Morgan,' says Ms. Campbell.

He stands up, adjusts his suspenders, and looks at me with those icy blue eyes until I can no longer hold his gaze and look down to the spattered tile floor at my feet.

'Morgan,' he says, nodding. 'I've been expecting you. Better put on some coveralls.'

Ms. Campbell turns and leaves without saying another word.

I get a feeling Marty has more to do with me being here than she does.

3

Elizabeth

The tea has arrived with its usual punctuality. It is one thing I admire about this place.

I suppose my proclivity for routine is a carryover from my childhood at the light station. For so many years my life was measured in hours and minutes, broken into fragments of being on duty and off, marked by the time to light the mantle, to wind the clockworks, to check the fuel.

It is beginning to feel like home here. After so many years. How many has it been? Perhaps three now. The days merge; the seasons fold into each other, and I have lost count. It was luck to find this place where I have been able to retain some of the independence I crave yet still access the care that's needed. Besides, it was time to come back, to leave behind the small villa on the coast of Tuscany that was our refuge for more than half a century. We chose it to be near enough to the water to hear the gulls and crashing waves. Even so, I felt that the Ligurian Sea never shared the fickle temperament of the Lake, that it was only a substitute home. We were as happy as can be expected, the odd couple that we were, tucked away from the prying eyes of the world. And we've each left our mark, a legacy, of sorts. Of course mine is not nearly so celebrated;

only a handful of books, some still for sale in gift shops and art galleries around the world.

I am sitting in Pa's chair, the afghan Emily and I knitted draped over my knees. I have the window open, inviting the autumn breeze to roam about my room.

I must be careful with the tea so that I don't scald myself. My fingers explore the tray, running across the small pot, tracing the spout, the handle. My other hand finds the cup. I count when I pour. I know the cup can hold a count of five. They have given me packages of sugar, always two, even though I use only part of one. The spoon is not in its usual place, and I search to find it next to the milk. When I am finished, I lift the cup to my lips, blowing gently, more out of habit than necessity, and take a sip. Sighing, I allow Pa's chair to embrace me.

I have taken to dreaming that I am young again, my hair the color of ravens, my eyes strong. In my dreams, I dance. I am back on the island of my youth, on the black volcanic beach of Porphyry, where the Lake licks the shore and the wind sets the sedge waving. I stoop to gather handfuls of devil's paintbrush and sunny buttercups, adding them to the bouquet of nodding daisies already clutched in my hand. Emily is there, too, beautiful silent Emily, who always had one foot in the world of dreams. We clasp hands, two parts of a whole, and laugh and dance and spin until we fall to the warm ground, breathless, to stare up at the clouds chasing across the summer sky.

But lately, there has been a wolf wandering my

14

dreams. I can see him gazing at us through the gaps between the trees. He slips in and out between the trunks of birch and fir, skirting the shore and watching us dance with his cold yellow eyes. Emily is not frightened by the wolf. She stares at him until he lies down at the edge of the beach, waiting. But he frightens me. I know why he is here. It is not yet time. But each day, I can tell that he is creeping closer, and it takes him longer and longer to settle.

It is one of the reasons I decided it was time to move back to the shores of Lake Superior. Here, in spite of the pain, in spite of the memories it holds, is as close to home, to Porphyry Island and the lighthouse, as I could get. Emily would have wanted that.

I take another sip of tea. Tepid already. The afternoon sun streams in the window, warming me more than the drink. I hold the cup carefully in my lap and turn my face toward the beam so that I can receive its full embrace.

I can hear Marty's voice outside. I know he is the heartbeat of this place. And, oh my, he knows art, nearly as well as I do. Before my eyesight left me, he brought me books with paintings, and as we sipped our tea, he'd turn the pages and we would comment or criticize, depending on the artist. He was an eager listener as I shared tales of my travels and interesting bits of knowledge gleaned during a life spent roaming through art galleries and studying the masters. *The woman in that painting — she was the artist's lover*, as we gazed at the work of Renoir. *This painting, I told him, was stolen from the Jews during the*

Holocaust and found decades later in an attic in Italy. An American bought it, claiming it belonged to his great-grandfather in Holland before the war. Marty and I love the Impressionists most. *This artist hired three people to tend his gardens, great expansive gardens, Marty, full of ponds and pathways and every kind of flower imaginable. Look at all the color.* It was one of my favorite places we visited. We stood on the bridge, touched the wisteria. But the crush of people was too much, there, everywhere, and so we disappeared.

I should have known he would recognize her work, the simple lines, the movement and use of color. His eyes questioned, and mine answered. He is the only one here I have shared stories of my past with. He says little, but he listens. That is enough.

Marty knew, too, when my eyesight began to fade. He didn't say a word. Didn't let on that he saw my fumbled movements, my hesitant steps. He just stopped bringing books and started bringing tapes. Chopin, Mozart, Beethoven. And we sipped our tea and listened, letting the music create the paintings I could no longer see.

I think he understands. I think he knows how much I grieve for Emily, if it can be called grieving. I was Elizabeth and Emily, the twins, the lightkeeper's daughters. It is hard to be anything else. It is hard to be just Elizabeth.

I can feel a cloud pass across my sunbeam, sense the brightness fade with what little is left of my shadowy vision. The breeze is causing the blinds to hum, and I am beginning to get a chill

16

as it reaches cold fingers through the holes in the afghan. For me, autumn is a time of enchantment, when the world is painted with the colors of the masters. So many people dread the season, in all its splendor and romance, seeing it as the door to an end, to a winter of death. But autumn makes me feel *alive*. Autumn is the beginning and the end at the same time.

I reluctantly turn my face from the fading sunbeam and carefully settle my half-empty teacup back on the tray. I fold the afghan, draping it over the arm of the chair. It is time. With practiced care, I stand and cross my room to the door, pausing briefly in the entrance, one hand on the frame, hesitating. It is a daily ritual, one that makes me feel whole, however briefly. I step into the hallway and head away from my room and toward the other wing.

The wolf will have to wait.

4

Morgan

'So you did it all yourself?'

When Marty asks me, he doesn't really seem to be asking. It's a question, but only just.

We're filling up a bucket with warm water at the utility sink in his office. Marty has already loaded up another bucket with a collection of tools and brushes.

'Ya, sure,' I reply. I have to do what he asks, but I don't have to tell him anything more than what I told the cops. I know he doesn't believe that I was the only one here that night.

'Used spray paint?'

'Uh-huh.'

We carry the bucket and tools outside to the residents' garden. It's not a bad place, for an old people's jail. There's lots of plants and pathways and a big patio area covered by a wooden pergola with some chairs and tables underneath. Most of the flowers look like they've finished blooming and have been trimmed back. There are still some purple ones, though. They look like daisies, but not quite. The fence is along the back, separating it from the bike path that runs along the river.

Marty is dressed in a red plaid flannel jacket, and I'm wearing his blue coveralls. We walk around to the back of the fence, the part that's

18

facing away from the building. He sets the bucket down on the lawn, and stands, arms crossed, looking.

'Ain't going to come off by washing,' he says.

'No shit,' I murmur, just loud enough that he can hear.

Marty still stands there, looking at the fence.

'What kind of paint did you use?'

Was this guy for real? 'SPRAY paint.'

'Not very good quality.'

I know that now. It was cheap shit that dripped and didn't cover like I wanted it to. I sit down at the picnic table without answering. I have all the time in the world for his questions.

'Didn't finish?'

'What?'

'You know . . . you didn't finish it?'

I look at my work. Marty's right, it isn't quite finished. 'Nah. Someone must have called the cops, so we . . . I split.'

It was the first time I'd done a piece this big. I wanted to prove to them that I was good enough to be part of their crew, and this was the only way. I did it on my own, but Derrick came along. He was supposed to be looking out for me, making sure I didn't get caught.

I'd met them at a party Derrick took me to. We were sitting around the kitchen table and I was sketching on the top of an empty pizza box, and one of them started watching me. I'd drawn the same thing so many times, over and over and over so it just flowed, and I was barely thinking about what I was doing. I don't know why that one, that picture, but it was always one of my

19

favorites, and I liked to play around with it, change it, make it mine while keeping it somehow still the same. When I saw him looking at the picture, I covered it up with my hand and tried to slide the box away. But he stopped me. He took hold of the pizza box and studied it. He said it was good, real good, and asked me if I'd ever thought of making it big, seeing it up on a wall. I didn't really know what he was talking about. Derrick told me later who he was, that he was part of a graffiti crew. He pointed out some of their pieces around town, and they were fucking amazing.

We ran into them again a few weeks later, and after we'd all had a few beers they invited Derrick and me to go with them to the rail yards. I like to think that it was because they liked my drawing, but I know they never would have asked if it wasn't for Derrick. I didn't give a shit either way; I was just glad to be included. I watched, creeping along with them beside the train near the abandoned grain elevators, my heart racing, my palms sweaty. God, it was such a thrill. To pour your soul onto a wall or a rail car and be able to step back and see your fears and your hopes and your dreams and your flaws. And to be able to walk through the city, to have other people walk through the city, and there's proof that you were there, that you were alive. I wanted to be part of that. I stole some paint from Canadian Tire, started working on my own tag, thinking about my piece, doing small things here and there. It fucking made me feel like Banksy.

Marty's staring at the fence like he's in some art gallery. I wait.

'Huh,' is all he says.

Except for where I was working, the paint has started to peel. It was a stupid place to write, I know that now. Marty walks up to the fence, picks at a flake with his fingernail, and lets it drop to the ground. It looks like it needed a new coat long before I ever came near it with my spray-paint cans.

'Will have to scrape it first.' He hands me a scraper. 'Both sides. Then wash it with a wire brush.'

He turns and walks back to the entrance, whistling.

★ ★ ★

Derrick bought me an iPod and earbuds. He's always buying me things. Well, maybe not always. But sometimes out of nowhere, he just shows up and casually says, 'Hey, I got you something.' And everything's great. We're great. Other times, I don't hear from him for days and I wonder what the hell I've done. I don't care about the stuff. It's nice, but I really don't give a shit.

With my music on, time passes quickly. After a few hours of scraping, the fence looks like a disaster. The places that weren't touched by my bright colors peel off easily and soon the ground and gardens are littered with bits of white and purple and blue.

Marty finally comes back. I haven't seen him since he left me here with the scraper, but I'm

21

not fooled. I know he watched me the whole time. I'm sure Anne Campbell, RN, Executive Director, was peering through one of the windows at me, too.

'It's a start,' is all Marty says.

He picks up the bucket, tossing the water onto a shrub, and heads back inside, so I follow him, carrying the other tools. I peel off the coveralls and hang them up. My boots are covered with flakes of paint.

'You might want to wear different shoes next time.' Marty has his back to me, hanging up his plaid jacket on the hook next to the coveralls. Without turning around to look at me, he adds, 'See you Thursday.'

Fucking waste of time.

5

Elizabeth

I asked one of the support workers to push me outside in a wheelchair. The day is much too beautiful to spend trapped behind concrete walls, the sunlight filtered through glass. I need the fresh air and sunshine to fill my frail body, to sustain me through the long winter months ahead.

I suppose I could have come out here on my own using my walker, but it is becoming more and more difficult as my vision fades to shadowy images that dance in front of me like spirits, refusing to settle into shapes and forms with finite edges. I am dressed for the cold in a warm fleece jacket and have a woolen blanket tucked snugly around my legs. I am wearing the sunglasses Marty gave me in the summer. My eyes are sensitive now, to wind, and to light. It is ironic.

'How is this, Miss Livingstone?' the aide asks, after pushing me beneath the pergola. She is young. I recognize her voice, but she is new and I can't match it to the image of a face stored away in memory. I don't need much help, but when I do, it's nice to know it's here for the asking.

'If you don't mind,' I answer, 'just a bit farther out, where the sun can reach.' She obliges me.

Last night, I was restless. I drifted between sleep and wake, walking the world of dreams where the conscious mind slips into illusory tales. I could not see the wolf pacing this time, but felt his hot breath damp against my cold, dry skin. I cast about desperately for Emily, calling her name only to have it drowned by the sound of waves crashing against the cliffs of Porphyry. My hands, slippery with sweat, tore at the branches, hanging like dark curtains shrouding the forest. When I woke with a start, my heart was racing.

Not yet.

I lay there for a time, just breathing. There was no need to turn on a light when I climbed out of bed. I know every inch of my room with despicable intimacy. The single bed covered by the quilt Emily and I stitched so many years ago out of scraps of fabric rescued from the rag bin or clipped from old dresses. One small dresser against the far wall, containing a lifetime of memories pared down to a couple of drawers. The chair that Pa sat in when he read the paper; the only chair that survived and made the journey from the lightkeeper's house when we left the island. It waited for us, tucked in Maijlis's attic for almost sixty years, while Emily and I wandered the world. There are days when I think I can still smell smoke clinging to the tattered fabric.

Wearing only a cotton nightgown, my feet bare, I crossed the room and opened the window. The breeze, cool and damp, was quick to respond. My hair, now the color of a snowy

24

owl, clung matted to my forehead, pasted there by the roaming of my sleeping mind. As I eased into Pa's chair, the air wandered through me, purging the wispy remnants of the dream. I could hear the clear sounds carried by the night. The clanging of a railroad crossing and shunting trains, their diesel engines complaining with the effort. A siren. Ambulance. Someone was facing tragedy. Cars. Not many. It must have been late. Or very early. There was no wind to engage the trees in conversation. It was then that I heard it. Yes. So faint but there.

A fog signal.

I dozed for a time where I sat until the coolness became too much for my thin gown and I made my way back under the quilt to wait for the halls to stir with the sounds of morning.

But now it is midafternoon; the sun has burned all the dampness from the air and warmed the earth enough that I can smell the richness of the soil. Marty's doing. He knows about compost and mulch. And like the painters in his treasured books, he's an expert in color. The Michaelmas daisy must be blooming by now; lavender purple with a bright yellow center. Perhaps the Japanese anemone survives still. Certainly the mums last as late as this.

I can hear sparrows foraging beneath the picnic table. There is another sound, too. Scraping. And the faint buzzing tempo of distant music, oddly reminiscent of Mozart. Ah, yes. Marty mentioned this to me. A girl, he said, Morgan. Vandalized the fence several weeks ago and set all sorts of chins wagging about the

25

idleness and disrespect of today's youth. But not Marty. He told me, in his cursory way, that her painting intrigued him. But it's the Mozart that intrigues me.

I realize I have been sleeping when I wake to the sound of footsteps heading toward me on the sidewalk. I assume it is the aide, coming to return me to my quarters. What an old lady I am now. Sleeping in a wheelchair, no less, wrapped up like a baby in woolens and fleece. Have I come full circle?

There are three sets of footsteps. Curious. The sparrows continue to chirp, but the steady, rhythmic scraping behind the fence abruptly grows silent.

'Miss Livingstone.' The voice belongs to Ms. Campbell. 'These two police officers would like to have a few words with you. Would you like me to bring you inside?'

I should have recognized the sound of their shoes. They would be black and stiff and polished to a shine. 'No. No, thank you, Anne. I'm sure anything they have to say can be said right here. Please, have a seat.' I nod in the direction of the picnic tables.

'Very well, then. I'll be in my office if you need me.' Ms. Campbell's sensible footwear recedes.

'Miss Livingstone, I'm Constable Ken Barry. This is my partner, Constable Cheryl Coombs.'

I do not offer my hand. I do not wish to be rude, but it has been my experience that officers of the law rarely bring glad tidings.

'We've just come from a meeting with the Coast Guard, and . . . ' Constable Barry sounds

26

like he is fumbling for his words. 'A sailboat was found washed ashore, damaged and abandoned, in Middlebrun Bay near Silver Islet. The boat's name is *Wind Dancer*. It was registered to Charles Livingstone. Your brother.'

I can hear the sparrows. It sounds to me like they are quarreling.

'Miss Livingstone, there is a remote chance that he was able to get to shore. The gentleman who discovered her — a man named Arnie Richardson, who says he knows you — managed to wade out and climb aboard. It is possible that Mr. Livingstone made it off the boat safely.' He pauses. 'It's possible, but unfortunately it's not likely. It would help if we knew why he was out there, out on the Lake at this time of year, and where he might have been going. We could then focus our search. Can you think of anything that could help us?'

There must be more than ten sparrows. They sound like they are in the hydrangea on the far side of the fence, waiting to return to the patio.

One of the officers places something on the table. 'These were found on board. They appear to be old logbooks from Porphyry; we think they may have been your father's. Arnie Richardson thought you should have them. He said he'd heard you moved back to Thunder Bay, that we could find you here.'

The sparrows are moving again; their fluttering wings have carried them to the branches of the lilac bush. They rest for a moment and allow a raven to fill the space with his croaking presence. I am tired. It is time for my afternoon

27

cup of tea. And Marty gave me that tin of shortbread cookies. It is beside the oil lantern. The one that looks like the lamp that was always in the assistant keeper's house at Porphyry Light. The sparrows would enjoy a few crumbs of shortbread. I will have to remember to bring a cookie or two tomorrow if the weather cooperates and I am able to sit outside again.

But they are waiting. They are waiting for me to say something. They have spoken with Arnie Richardson. They want to know about Charlie. They want to know why he was out on *Wind Dancer*. They want to know where he was going. They don't realize he had become a stranger to me. But even at that, I know. There is only one place.

'Porphyry Island. He would have been going to Porphyry Island.'

6

Morgan

I pick up the scraper again, start on another part of the fence. I'm wearing Caleb's work boots this time, which are two sizes too big. He's been at Laurie and Bill's longer than I have, but he's a lazy no-good shit and probably won't even miss them. Between the boots and Marty's blue overalls, I look like a cartoon character. I'm a joke.

The cops are gone, but the old woman is still sitting there in her wheelchair. God, she looks ridiculous in those aviator glasses, her hair long and straight and whiter than snow, falling below her shoulders. She must be at least a hundred years old. I can't imagine what it would be like to be that old, to have no life left to look forward to. And your memory probably gone, so you've lost your past, too. Nothing left but the next breath you take.

I take a breath. Long and deep. The irony almost escapes me.

'Morgan, is it?'

She's speaking to me. She knows my name.

'It seems they've gotten a little busy inside. I'm sure that fence can spare a few moments while you push me back to my room. God knows you keep that up, you'll have scraped right through to the other side. Only so much paint on there.'

She isn't looking at me, but I can't really ignore her. 'I don't think I'm supposed to, um . . . interact with the . . . residents.'

'You always do what you're supposed to do?' It doesn't sound like a question. She's sitting straight in the chair, chin up, gloved hands folded in her lap. I wish I could see her eyes behind those stupid glasses.

'All right,' I say, dropping the scraper into the bucket with the other tools. 'But this will be on your head, not mine.'

'The package,' she says to me, lifting one of her hands in the direction of the table. 'The one they left. Bring it to me.'

I do as she asks. The parcel is wrapped in some kind of faded white canvas and smells of earth and mold. It's tied with twine, but the knots have been loosened and the fabric gapes open so that I can see what's inside. It looks like a set of books, leather covers with rippled yellow pages. I place it on the old woman's lap.

I've never pushed a wheelchair before, so it takes a bit of maneuvering to get it through the door.

'Third room on the left.'

As we pass Marty's office, I can hear him whistling. I don't look at him, I just keep walking, my eyes straight ahead, and my borrowed boots scuffing the tile floor.

The residents' rooms aren't at all like what I expected. They're like one-room apartments. I take a quick glance around as I push the wheelchair through the door. There's a small dining table as well as a bed, a dresser with some framed pictures on it, and a comfortable-looking chair. The bed is covered with a quilt. The pieces are all faded, and I can tell that it's probably handmade, maybe an antique. The furniture, too, is old. Like her. But it's the lantern that catches my eye. We had one like it. It was red, and the glass got smoked up when we lit it, and I used to polish it with an old rag.

The woman sighs. 'That will be fine, Morgan. Thank you.'

'Uh-huh.' I turn to leave.

The woman's hands are moving across the parcel. She lifts it and places it on the table and then begins folding the blanket that was tucked across her lap. 'Did you think the police had come for you?'

I stop in the doorway. 'What?'

'Why did you hide?'

I turn and look at her. 'I wasn't hiding. The cops know I'm here.'

The woman locks the wheelchair into place, carefully stands up, and lays the blanket at the foot of the bed. With one hand drawing along the dresser, she moves toward the old chair and turns to sit. She removes the sunglasses and sets them on the table beside the parcel, her hand resting for a moment on the pile of books.

'Elizabeth. Elizabeth Livingstone.'

I look into her deep brown eyes, sharp and defiant, but at the same time uncomfortably blank.

The old woman is blind.

Something about those empty eyes makes me uneasy, but just for a moment. And then it's

31

gone. It's stupid. I don't give a shit who she is, and I have no interest in starting a conversation with her. So I don't.

'Uh-huh.' I turn and walk out, boots clumping as I head back down the hall.

7

Elizabeth

I'm not surprised and I do not take offense, but it does make me sigh. Fear can turn to anger so quickly; she is afraid of what life can bring and mad at the world because of it.

I absently roll the oilskin between my fingers. The edge is tattered where the fabric has escaped the grasp of the loosely knotted twine. A gentle tug is all that is needed for the rope to release its grip, allowing the musty wrapping to fall open, exposing the leather bindings of the journals. I run my fingers over them gently, exploring the surface of the top volume, pausing for a moment on the embossing in the center of the cover and tracing the raised 'A.L.'

Andrew Livingstone. My father.

The last time I held these journals was after Charlie returned to the island, before the fire. It was the moment I realized that the brother I knew, the brother I saw as an equal defender, as Emily's protector, had been changed by an angry harsh world wrapped as it was in war and prejudice. I should have seen it then, should have known that he was capable of turning against her. Did he live to regret it? I always imagined that he did. It is likely now that I will never know.

They said it was Arnie Richardson who found

the boat. Who thought I should have the journals. That is a name I have not heard for a lifetime. He sent a letter once. We received it years after it was mailed, having chased us around the world, finally arriving tucked into a package from our agent along with correspondence about books and royalties and invitations to events we never attended. It spoke of his return to the island in the weeks after the fire, back to the Porphyry light station to collect what he could from the charred remains of the smoke-stained buildings. Should we come home someday, he said, we could find what little was salvaged in the attic of Maijlis's house. I did not write him back. What difference would it make after so long? It was all behind us. Lives were being lived. It doesn't surprise me, though, that he would know I'd come home. In spite of our seclusion, he would have heard that the few possessions he had stored away for us had been claimed. Maijlis passed away years ago, but her daughter happily arranged the delivery to Boreal Retirement Home.

I have not thought of these journals for many, many years, but I have not forgotten the moment when I saw them last. It was early spring, and Emily was supposed to be bringing in kindling from the woodshed. She had been gone too long, and in those days I was not comfortable having her far from my side, not after what had happened. I found her in the assistant keeper's house. She went there sometimes, perhaps as I did, to remember. She was sitting in Pa's chair, the oilskin wrapping hanging loose, the books open in her lap. I remembered the journals. Remembered Pa sitting at his desk writing, while music played from the radio and the woodstove popped and snapped. They had disappeared when he died, and it hadn't even occurred to me that they were gone. Emily couldn't read the words, but I watched her hand draw across the pages, feeling the letters, hearing his voice, and I was overcome with a longing to do the same. I picked up one of the books, brushed my hand across the top, just as I do now, my fingers tracing the engraved 'A.L.' on the dark leather cover.

The squeaking wheel of the kitchen trolley in the hallway announces that it's time for afternoon tea, and I am drawn from my contemplation. There's a knock at my door.

'Would you like tea, Ms. Livingstone?' the aide asks. I always do. She places a tray on the table. 'Would you like me to pour?'

'No. No, thank you.' I thumb the books. 'I can manage quite well on my own. But if you wouldn't mind passing me the tin of cookies from next to the lantern.'

The aide places it in my outstretched hand. 'Can I get you anything else?'

The metal feels cold. I am back in the assistant keeper's house, my father's journal in one hand. Emily had piled the other books on the table beside her and picked up a metal biscuit tin. She held it out so that it hovered between us. Just as my fingers closed around it, Charlie's shadow eclipsed the door. He paused only a moment, only a brief breath in which he took it all in

35

— me, the journals, Emily, the tin. 'What the hell do you think you're doing?' It wasn't a question. His voice was angry, and he strode across the floor, grabbed Emily, and pulled her out of Pa's chair, shoving her past me toward the open door. The tin dropped from my hand. It fell, bouncing off the arm of the chair, the lid popping open, spilling its contents across the wooden floor like a cracked egg. Time stopped. I couldn't move. It was as though the world ceased spinning. Charlie had never yelled at Emily before. Charlie had never been angry with Emily before. Never.

I still held one of Pa's journals in my hand. He grabbed it from me, and I backed away from a man I didn't know.

'Get out! You have no goddamn business in here!'

Emily had not seen the tin fall; she had her face pressed against the doorframe, looking away from Charlie, away from me, trying, I knew, to understand what had happened, what she had done. She didn't notice the flash of silver escaping from an old piece of white cloth. She paid no attention to the soft tinkling. But I did, oh so briefly, before Charlie stuffed it back in the tin.

I went back on my own a few days later and searched everywhere, but I never found the biscuit tin. I never held the journals again.

Until now.

'Miss Livingstone? Are you okay?'

My hand shakes slightly, so I lay the tin of shortbread down on top of the journals. 'Yes, fine.' I force a smile. 'Thank you.'

Oh, Charlie, what secrets have you kept from me for so many, many years; secrets captured in words penned by our father, Andrew Livingstone, lighthouse keeper at Porphyry Island, secrets so powerful they consumed your love for Emily?

8

Morgan

It's after midnight. I slide the violin case from beneath my bed. It looks like it's been through hell, and there's sticky black tape holding the handle together. I haven't even opened it in months, but I know every detail, every curve of the body, the position of each peg, the number of hairs on the bow.

I lay the instrument beside me and pull out the papers that I found years ago, hidden beneath the lining of the case. They're pencil crayon sketches of birds and insects, and they look so real they could fly off the page. And yet at the same time they're like nothing I've ever seen before. I've studied them, drawn them, dreamed about them, and drawn them again, but I haven't shown them to anyone. They're mine. I like to look at them when I'm lonely.

I scatter them around me on the bed, and the one of the raven catches my eye. It perches on some decaying animal, a deer maybe, killed by a pack of wolves, caught between the living and dead.

I pluck at the violin's strings, and decide to apply rosin to the dry, forgotten hairs on the bow. Tonight is different. Tonight the instrument is calling to me. I answer with a sigh and tuck it under my chin, holding it there while I adjust the

38

tuning. I lift the bow and then lower it onto the strings. It begins to dance.

The notes come slowly at first, as I remember, but gradually build, the music coming from inside me rather than from the movement of my fingers and bow on the strings. I don't need sheet music for this piece. It's one I learned by heart, and we played it together often; me standing beside his chair in the living room with my small violin, watching wide-eyed the way he held his bow, the way he swayed with the rhythm. He played the beautiful instrument that carries my music now.

'You have a gift, Morgan.' He smiled at me, clearly pleased. 'The music has chosen you.'

God, I miss him! It's been six years. Feels like more.

I switch to a reel. It's more upbeat. He made me learn Bach and Mozart, but he liked folk tunes best, and so I did too. Once I'd finished all my scales and practiced fingering and dynamics, we fiddled. His foot tapped the floor, and the tempo grew until I had to stop and all I could do was watch him play. I can see his eyes, crinkling with laughter when I tried to copy him.

He was enough. The two of us didn't need anyone else. We ate potatoes and canned soup and fish he caught himself in the Nipigon River. On dark winter nights, we sat close to the fire and he told me stories about shipwrecks on Lake Superior, and the years he spent fishing on Black Bay with his buddy Jim. And sometimes, when the wind crept through the cracks in the walls and drove icy snow against the windows, he drank whiskey out of an old chipped mug and talked about my mother. 'She loved you, Morgan,' he told me, his accent getting thicker the more he drank. 'In some ways, she reminded me of your grandmother. She was like the wind. Unpredictable. Free. Never knew what to expect from her. You can't tie down the wind, Morgan. It dances where it pleases.' And then he'd take a big swallow, and tell me that my mother had fought. She fought so hard, but she wasn't strong enough, and the wind had carried her away. I was only a baby when she died.

I don't remember her, and I didn't miss her. Not then. He was enough.

Until the day I came home from school and found him sitting in his chair, just sitting there with his eyes open staring at *Jeopardy!* on the TV, the kettle boiled dry on the stove so that the house smelled like hot metal and a choking haze hung in the air.

At first, all I did was play the violin. Wouldn't talk. Wouldn't eat. The kids at the first home I lived in made fun of me, snatching my bow away, dancing around and chanting, 'Morgan can't talk! Morgan can't talk!' until my foster mom made them stop. Let them say whatever the fuck they want, I thought. I heard him speaking to me through the music. That's all I cared about.

I was there for three years. My social worker found a way to put me in music lessons, and every week I went to the music center to study with a fat nun who always wore the same sweat-stained black dress and smelled of licorice. She made me play Mozart when all I wanted to play were his songs. 'You have a gift,' she said, the sweat stains spreading larger and darker as her frustration with me grew. 'You have a responsibility to learn! You must practice and concentrate!'

But the violin seems to like his songs best. They live in the wood and the hollow spaces and echo in my heart. When it became too painful to remember, though, I just stopped playing. At some point, I found my own voice again. Turns out it usually got me into trouble. Once I started high school, I was moved to another home, to parents who took in older kids. Just temporary, they said, until they could find a family for me. I knew better. I knew how the system worked. There wasn't a family out there for me. A few years later, I landed here, at Laurie and Bill's. Just temporary. I get it.

I think of the old woman from Boreal Retirement Home. The way she sat in that chair. Her white hair and weathered skin. And those eyes. Those eyes that can't see, yet somehow made me feel like she was looking right through me. Something in those eyes makes me want to remember.

The door swings open, and the light flicks on.

'What the hell do you think you're doing, shithead! Some of us have to get up in a few hours. Sounds like you're killing cats in here! For god's sakes, shut the fuck up or I'll break the fucking thing!'

It's Caleb. He wouldn't know good music if it hit him in the face.

'Fuck you!' I pick up my hairbrush and throw

41

it, missing him and knocking over the lamp on my dresser. He gives me the finger before slamming the door.

'Asshole.'

The spell is broken. I shove the violin back in its case and close the lid, snapping shut the clasps. My eyes are stinging.

The door opens again, and I'm about to really freak out at Caleb when I realize it's Laurie. She just stands there, in the doorway, wrapping her blue housecoat around her, tightening the belt, fussing with it, like somehow it will hold her together.

'They told me you could play,' she says.

I look at the violin's beat-up case before shoving it under the bed. It's my past, but it's not my present. And I see no place for it in my future. I don't answer her. I don't say anything.

'It's beautiful,' she says. 'The music . . . it's really beautiful.'

The silence stretches between us, but I can still hear the song, echoing about the room. It feels like forever before she finally says good night and turns out the light, quietly shutting the door behind her.

I've forgotten to put the pictures away. I climb into bed carefully, so I don't disturb them, and I lie beneath them. They cover me like a quilt.

★　★　★

Marty looks at me, dripping puddles that collect around Caleb's work boots on the tile floor. 'Too wet to paint today.'

No shit.

I've brought my violin with me. I've been bringing it everywhere now; I don't trust that little piece of shit Caleb to keep his hands off it. Marty points at the shelf and tells me to put my stuff there and then hands me a floor mop, one of those big ones that's used for dusting. 'Run this up and down the hallways. Once we've swept, we'll give it a wash.'

In the few days I've been at Boreal Retirement Home, I haven't spent much time inside. It's not like what I thought it would be, not like a hospital or institution. I guess that's what it's like for old people who have money for the best of everything. It's laid out in a Y shape with the main entrance and a sitting area in the stem. On one side are offices including the one for Anne Campbell, RN, Executive Director. The other side has a dining area, and I can hear the sounds of a kitchen. Marty's office is down a little hallway near the kitchen, close to all the mechanical workings like the boiler and the air-conditioning system. I was down the left arm of the Y when I pushed the old woman back to her room in her wheelchair a few days ago. That's where all the old people live who can mostly take care of themselves but get help with meals and cleaning and shit. At the very end of the hallway is another sitting area with big windows that face the courtyard.

But the other arm of the Y is different. The entrance is locked, like the main doors, and Marty gives me the keypad code. Inside, there's a counter, where nurses work, and the doors to the rooms are open. They're still nice, but I can tell this is where the old people live who need more help. Locked in. Prison.

I enter the code to the other wing, begin at the far sunroom and work my way toward the tile hallway, pushing my line of dirt as I go. The sounds start when I'm about halfway down the hall, reaching through the noise of my headphones and making the hairs on the back of my neck stand up. I pull out my earbuds. The rolling thunder and pounding rain are confusing, but then I hear it again. It's wordless, and haunting, like the cry of a frightened animal, cornered and desperate and heartbreaking. I've heard it before, years ago, coming from a small dark-haired girl kneeling at the foot of an old chair, the kettle boiled dry and the voice of Alex Trebek and *Jeopardy!* in the background.

I watch as the halls come alive with bodies in pink and orange scrubs darting from the nurses' desk and scurrying through a closed door into one of the rooms. I should keep sweeping, but I can't move. I'm invisible, standing here, as aides and nurses scatter and regroup. Finally the cry subsides, and the rain is the only sound remaining.

It's a few more minutes before I resume mopping. The hallway returns to normal, but I leave my headphones around my neck, the music faintly audible. I swivel the mop and head back toward the nurses' desk. As I pass the door where all the activity had been, an aide opens the door and I can't help looking in. I recognize the long white hair of the old woman and look away

44

quickly before she turns toward me. I focus on the mop, the line of dust, the music. But I can feel her. I can feel her standing there. I can feel her watching me. I know she can't see. But if I didn't know better, I'd swear Elizabeth Livingstone was looking right through me.

I'm invisible except to the one person who is blind.

★   ★   ★

I sneak outside for a cigarette, standing under the dripping pergola, my hands shaking from the cold, flicking the lighter until it finally sparks and holds a flame long enough to light the cigarette. I snap it shut and stuff it into my pocket, taking a deep lung full of smoke. I shiver as fat raindrops plaster my hair to my head, trickling down the back of my neck. The clouds are low and dark and show no sign of leaving any time soon.

From here, I can see the part of the fence I've been working on. Most of the peeling paint has been scraped, and it's pretty much ready for priming. The bare sections of wood have been stained dark by the rain, making it easier to pick out the bright colors of my piece. It's not the same as the drawings tucked away with the violin. Those are for me alone. But they inspired me.

Derrick isn't nearly as creative as the other writers. It's not the same for him. If he'd been caught, there wouldn't have been any fucking 'restorative rehabilitation process.' The cops would have been more interested in him than my stupid painting. Way more interested.

My eye wanders over the marks on the fence, resting again on my dragonfly. I love its simple lines, suggesting shape. It's unique. Distinctive.

I think again of the old woman. I don't know why I let her get to me. But she does. Maybe it's because she makes me remember. Things like the lantern. And the pictures. Remembering hurts.

Oh my god! *The pictures.*

I grind the cigarette under the heel of my boot and rush back inside, slipping past Marty's office and down the hall to Elizabeth Livingstone's room, stopping just outside the door. It's slightly ajar, so I push it open all the way. She's back. She's sitting in her chair, eyes closed, asleep, her hands folded in her lap. I step inside, quietly so I don't wake her.

I must have seen them the other day when I was here, but I didn't really notice them; I was too busy thinking about the lantern. There are three of them, framed and sitting on top of her dresser. A bird. Insects. A plant. The artist used a style that's distinctive. It's simple, yet detailed at the same time. I would know it anywhere. I pick up the dragonflies, tracing the outline of the wings, the eyes, the tails.

'Hello, Morgan.'

I drop the picture and it clatters onto the dresser. I try to straighten it up, but it refuses to stand and slides noisily into the other two frames, knocking them over as well. I turn to face the old woman, who's still sitting in the chair, her unseeing eyes now open.

46

I mumble something, nothing. And then it goes from bad to worse.

Anne Campbell is standing in the doorway.

'Morgan?' She looks surprised. I guess she would be. 'I thought Marty had given you some other work to do today.' She steps into the room and stands up the frames on the dresser. 'What are you doing here?'

Her tone is accusatory. I take a few steps back and look down at the floor. I'm dripping puddles. Water is running from my ponytail down my back, and my face is wet. I put my hands in my pocket and feel the cigarette lighter. Fuck! I lift up my head and look her in the eyes.

'I asked her to give me a hand deciphering my father's old journals,' Miss Livingstone speaks before I can. I turn and look at her, relieved, confused, my sarcastic response to Anne Campbell dying in my open mouth. 'My eyes just aren't what they used to be. Marty is busy tinkering with that boiler of his, and I'm sure he won't miss her for an hour or so. Lord knows the halls don't need any more cleaning. If you're going to make work for the girl, might as well make it useful.'

I shut my mouth.

Anne Campbell doesn't buy it. Not for a minute. I can sense that the power struggle is not with me but with the old woman. Thunder rolls far in the distance.

Finally she speaks. 'I see.'

Is that her answer for everything?

'Look.' I figure I better say something. 'I was just — '

'She was just going to change out of her wet boots and bring me a cup of tea on her way back from Marty's office,' the old woman interrupts. 'Run along now, and mind you don't forget the milk and sugar.'

I do as I'm told, slip past Anne Campbell, and hurry down the hall.

9

Elizabeth

I'm not convinced she'll come back, but something drew her to my room in the first place. It is, perhaps, somewhat rash of me to suggest that she help me read Pa's journals, but the more I think on it, the more I like the idea. Marty has been much too busy, and I have been aching to hear Pa's words. I am interested in the secrets I suspect they hold. Secrets powerful enough for Charlie to take that decrepit old boat of his out onto the Lake this late in the season and dig up words that have been buried and hidden, silenced since we were young, since we left the island.

I brush my hand again over the cover of the top book, tracing the *A* and *L*.

Before long, I hear her moving across the room; feel her shadow pausing in front of the dresser before she sits down in one of the wooden chairs at the table.

'Um. Thanks,' she mutters. 'I, ah . . . ' Her struggle to phrase an apology is painful, so I spare her the trouble.

'You can read handwriting?'

When she answers, her tone is sarcastic. It doesn't take much for her to lose her contrite manner. 'No, I'm too fucking stupid.' She thinks she is shocking me.

'Save it, Morgan. Don't waste that self-absorbed attitude on me. I'm talking about legibility, not literacy. Many kids these days can't read handwriting anymore, and it will be a waste of my time and yours if you can't.' I don't let her continue speaking. 'If you are able, then I can use your help. If not, you're welcome to leave. But kindly keep your nose and fingers out of my business and off my things.'

She does not reply, the rain drumming against the window in the silence that stretches between the two of us. Finally she reaches over and picks up the pile of books, placing them on the table in front of her. 'Yeah, I can read handwriting.' She works to untie the twine. 'If you can't see, how did you know it was me in your room?'

It's an easy question to answer. 'You are the only one around here who wears boots two sizes too big.' And then I add, 'Where's the tea?'

10

Morgan

I carefully lift the top book, almost expecting the fragile sheets inside to crumble into piles of dust when I open the cover. They don't. The pages are yellow and the words have faded, but for the most part, I can read them. 'Andrew Livingstone' is written across the top of the first page, and below it:

DAY JOURNAL
22 APRIL 1917
This is not a Government Book

'Who's Andrew Livingstone?' I ask the old woman. She's still sitting in her chair, holding a cup of tea.
'My father.'
'Huh.' That's interesting. I scan the page, working to read the slanted black letters. 'And you haven't seen them before?'
'I've seen them, but I haven't read them.'
And now she can't. Not without help. 'The first one starts in 1917 and goes to 1920. There are more from other years. They're also marked as personal, that they aren't government books.'
The old woman nods, and explains. 'My father was a lighthouse keeper. In 1917 he would have been stationed at Battle Island Light. He only

51

spent one year there before the government moved him to Porphyry Point Light Station. Part of a lightkeeper's job was to keep official logbooks to record such information as when the light was lit, when it was extinguished in the morning, weather conditions. So he had to distinguish that these are his private writings.'

I carefully turn the page to where the lightkeeper made his first entry. 'The year is written at the top, and then there are several entries on each page.' My hand skims over the paper, working together with my eyes to decipher the blotched letters and bring them into words and sentences. 'Along the left side columns there are just letters, W, NW, N, NNW . . . '

'Wind direction. Can you read the writing?'

She seems anxious about whether I'm able to read it. I wonder what she hopes to hear.

Monday, 23 April — I have arrived at Battle Island Light Station, where I will be serving out the season as assistant. Wilson and I have had the light operational for the better part of two weeks, as shipping season is now in full swing. I am learning to man the diaphone at the fog station — a brute of a machine, but I've been told it is a much welcome improvement over the hand-pumped system of the past.

Friday, 25 May — It has been a cool, wet spring. I took the punt around to the fishing grounds and lifted the nets yesterday. I was rewarded with three whitefish, one lake

52

trout, and a sucker, keeping all but the sucker. I have received mail and word of Lil, and have written to suggest she join me for several weeks by catching a ride on *The Red Fox* the next time Captain Johnson makes port in McKay's Harbor. I'm sure the Swede wouldn't mind dropping her here along with the mail and the few supplies I've ordered the next time they're laying nets in our area, which I expect will be in a month or so. I'm learning that many lightkeepers have their families live with them for the season — it makes for happier workers, breaking up the tedium and loneliness. Lil, I am sure, would be as happy here as I am. She is, if anything, better suited to this life than I, having been born and raised so closely connected to the land and Lake.

I look up at the daughter of the man whose words I'm reading. 'Lil was your mother?'

'Yes. My father immigrated to Canada from Scotland in 1914 — chased from the family farm and unable to find work. He came to Canada intent on settling in the west, as so many of his countrymen did, but fell in love with the lakes on his journey from New York. He landed a job working on the mail boats traveling between Collingwood and Port Arthur.'

She fills me in on her family's history. I can read, or she can talk — it doesn't matter to me. So I just shut up and listen.

'The next winter, he decided to try his hand at the fur trade, and moved into an old cabin near

53

McKay's Harbor, or Rossport, running trap lines. He met my mother there and married her in 1915. Her father was Scottish, too. And a trapper. But he was a hard man, from what Pa said, heavy-handed, and strict with his children. Her mother was Ojibwe, and taught her the traditional ways. She learned how to knit snowshoes by attaching sinew to the wooden frame, to skin and tan the animals that found themselves tangled in their traps and snares, and to look to the forest for food and medicine. I suppose there always existed in her a conflict, her half-breed nature never settling easily into being one or the other, and always with that, a sense of pride tempered by shame.'

She pauses. 'By the time Pa was working on Battle Island as assistant lightkeeper, they had brought my brother Peter into the world. Charlie, Emily, and I came along during their time at Porphyry.'

I continue to read. It's a little like a storybook, and the characters begin to come to life on the pages.

It makes me remember, too. It makes me think of my history, my family, of the times we spent in front of the fire on cold winter nights, me sitting in his lap, listening to him talk about the Lake and laying nets and the storms that forced their boats into harbor where they would wait for the weather to change so that they could bring their haul of fish back for processing.

Tuesday, 10 December — Calm seas. I've been told that I will be transferred next spring to Porphyry Point Light Station. It is an older light, without the upgrades seen here at Battle Island, but it is near Edward Island, close to the entrance to Black Bay, and only a day's sail to Port Arthur. Because of the war, and in spite of Borden's conscription, lighthouse keeping has been declared an essential service, and I am to take up my post at Porphyry next season with a view to serving my country.

I look up at the old woman. She seems tired. She holds her teacup in her lap, but it's been forgotten. Her head rests on the back of the chair, yet in spite of that, she doesn't look relaxed. Her lips are pressed in a tight line, and her brow is furrowed. Whatever it is she hopes to hear from her father, it was not written in 1917.

If I'm going to find out about the pictures, I'll need to do more than read.

11

Elizabeth

I listen to the words spoken by the girl. Like the raindrops falling outside, one by one they fill the gaps until the memories pool together and flood through me. I can see Pa moving through his duties at the light, picture him as a young man, resurrected by his phrases. It is an existence he chose, and one to which he was so well suited. The girl speaks, but I can hear his voice, too. It surfaces and floats past, deep and warm. Resonant.

I realize that Morgan has stopped reading.

'Have you reached the end, then?' I ask, and set my teacup down on the table beside me.

'Just the first year.' I can hear her shifting, and the sound of the journal's cover quietly thudding shut. 'Is he dead?'

'My father?' I answer with some incredulity. 'Good lord, child! Long dead. If he had lived, he would be well over a hundred years old by now.'

'No,' she replies. 'I mean your brother. The cops that were here the other day said they couldn't find him on the boat. I overheard them, you know, when they were talking to you.'

'When you were hiding?'

'I wasn't hiding.'

'What are you afraid of, Morgan?'

'You're changing the subject.'

56

'And you're being nosy.'

'So are you.'

A smile tugs at my cheeks. She is spunky. I stand — I have been sitting too long, and my limbs are stiff — and make my way across the room to my bed. Sitting down on it, I bend to remove my shoes.

'I suppose I am. But then again, you were the one sneaking around where you didn't belong.'

'I was just looking at those pictures.'

Yes, the pictures. There are three of them, and I can see them now as if my vision had not faded. They are early pieces, very early, before the world fell in love with her detailed lines and bold colors. I drop my shoes to the floor and swing my legs up onto the bed.

'Why?'

She hesitates before she answers, but it is barely noticeable, and I am not sure I haven't imagined it. 'I like them. They remind me of someone. Where did you get them?'

'I've always had them.'

'Always?'

'Yes, they were painted years and years ago.'

'So they're old.'

'Quite. But who's changing the subject now?'

She sighs. 'Right. Your brother. What happened to him?'

I wish I knew. I am privy to few details of his life after we left Porphyry. He had disappeared by the time I was well enough to look for him, to demand answers. But I'm not sure I would have, even if I could. I heard later that he moved to Sault Ste. Marie and took a job with Algoma

Steel. A few years after Emily and I went to wander the world, he moved back. He worked many jobs, never able to stay long at any one, harvesting wood to feed the paper mill, hammering nails to build houses, even hiring on as a deck-hand with Paterson Steamships. He built *Wind Dancer* himself, and sailed her single-handed for months on end out on the Lake. He knew that boat intimately. The Lake, too. I never could have imagined him coming to this . . . But he was too old to be out on Superior, alone.

'I don't know, Morgan.' My voice has gone soft. 'My brother was a good sailor, but he was also an old man, and the Lake is temperamental. He must have had a really good reason to slip off in the dark of night and head to Porphyry Island to dig these journals out of whatever hiding place they've been in for so many years.'

'Were you close?'

That is such a difficult question to answer. Some of the edge has returned to my voice when I do. 'My brother and I haven't spoken in more than sixty years.'

'So you hated him.' It is the simplicity of youth, framed in black and white, right and wrong, love and hate.

'No. No it wasn't like that at all. I loved . . . I love him, very much. But it's a long story.'

58

12

Morgan

I watch as she settles herself on the bed and pulls the knitted blanket over her legs. Her white hair is tied in a ponytail, but she tucks some loose strands behind her ears and lies back against the pillows. My gaze travels back to the sketches sitting on the dresser. Their lines are so familiar to me, and I want to know why.

Rivers of rain still chase down the window. I don't have to be anywhere. She closes her eyes like it lets her see the images her father's words have brought back to life.

'So tell me,' I encourage her.

'We traveled as a little package of three, the headstrong Charlie with Emily and me trailing along behind in his shadow, more than willing partners in his explorations and adventures. We adored him. My father lived an unconventional life, and by extension, so did we. But we knew nothing different. We thought it normal to live on an island far out on the dark gray waters of Lake Superior, beneath a great beacon that winked at the ships passing in the darkness. We spent our days traipsing through the woods, exploring the channels and bays in a little boat, hunting rabbits and picking wild berries. It was a wonderful childhood.'

'Was Charlie older than you?'

'Yes, by four years. Emily and I were the youngest. We were born on the island, and it was a miracle we even survived. My mother had not anticipated delivering twins. When her labor began, it was more than a month too soon. There were no boats fast enough to gap the distance between Porphyry Island and Port Arthur, and her body was too well acquainted with the rhythms of childbirth, having already brought two children into the world. There was barely time to boil water and fetch Pa. But Mother was a healer; she knew how to care for us. We spent our first months swaddled together in a wooden crate, perched near the heat of the woodstove, thriving on her milk. Emily and I — we were inseparable, Pa told me, two parts of a whole. We couldn't even breathe without our other half. And Charlie, he watched over us.'

The old woman pauses here. 'No, Morgan, I don't hate him. For a time, we were very close. But something came between us, and it has stayed there for longer than I care to remember.'

I pick up the journal, and the sound of my movement brings her back to the room.

'We haven't got there yet, have we? I'm getting ahead of the story. Charlie hasn't even had his beginning. Go on.'

I open up the old book again and flip through the pages we've already read. '1918.'

Wednesday, 3 April — We have arrived as a family this season, Lil, Peter, and I. We traveled aboard the tug the *James Whalen* to Porphyry Island. The light is in immaculate

60

condition, but the dwellings and gardens are in a state of disrepair. Albert Shaw, the former lightkeeper, has retired to Fort William with his daughter. I have been told he is seventy-three years of age. His daughter was serving as assistant for all these many years. Unlike Battle Island, the light tower here is attached to the dwelling, one home shared between the assistant and keeper. The lantern has a catoptric lens, nine feet in diameter, and contains four circular no. 1 lamps with twenty-inch reflectors. The tower itself is thirty-six feet tall, and with it set as it is on the west point of the island on a bit of a cliff, the elevation is fifty-six feet from the Lake. In clear weather, the light can be seen for sixteen to eighteen miles. All the buildings require painting. I have sent a requisition for replacement pine boards for the floor, which I hope will arrive on the *James Whalen* with other supplies. Lil and Peter are settling in.

Tuesday, 23 April — Spotted a caribou cow and her calf swimming between Porphyry and Edward Island while fishing in Walker's Channel. I will return with my rifle. There is a harbor here about halfway down the northwest side of the island, just before the entrance to the channel. It makes Porphyry the envy of other stations, with the shelter it allows for getting supplies or people on and off the island in any weather. It is a bit of a jaunt up to the station through the bog, but

61

the path is well worn. Usually supplies are delivered to the beach near the light and a boathouse has been built on the shore, but it is good to know that there are options when the weather is uncooperative. Assistant George Grayson arrived the week last. He has been discharged not six months from the Canadian Expeditionary Force, where he saw action in the third battle of Ypres, Passchendaele. He bears the wounds of the trenches on his body, his face and arms scarred by the blistering caused by the enemy's mustard gas, which settled like hot kerosene, but burned without flame or means to extinguish it. It is difficult to even look at him. The gas seeped into his lungs as well, his voice raspy and hoarse. He has been placed here as much for the good clean air to heal his lungs as to provide him with constructive occupation. We are splitting the shifts twelve on, twelve off, and are settling into routine. Grayson is a single chap and has set up in his room in the east wing, as I like to call it. We share the common areas. If the family grows any larger, we will need to request the construction of an assistant's house, as space is tight.

Tuesday, 14 May — Repairs to the building mostly complete. Had a visit yesterday from Bob Richardson on the *Margueritte* from Silver Islet. Bob works as a land agent for the government and moves his family into one of the old miner's homes every summer, commuting into town for work. Richardson is fixing up his place so that they can use it in winter as well. There are few who live there year-round, he tells me, just the Cross family, who serve as caretakers, and a handful of others. He brought newspapers with reports from the front in Europe. Grayson has woken in the night several times now in fits of screaming, startling the lot of us. Lil and Peter are both frightened of him. I fear his mind, too, bears the wounds of his ordeal as much as he carries the marks of battle on his body. He sleeps very little, wandering the shores with naught but the moonlight to guide his path.

Friday, 24 May — A toast to the late and most great Queen Victoria was made today by our feeble assemblage amid pouring rain. While April showers may bring May flowers, it is the May rain that will bring the vegetables. We have planted a potato patch by Walker's old cabin and have constructed raised gardens on top of the solid rock ground near the lighthouse, filling the wooden frames with soil and seeding with tomatoes, peas, and beans. We have had no visitors of late, although the up — and downbound shipping lanes into Thunder Bay have been busy with both cargo and passenger ships.

Monday, 19 August — *The Red Fox* arrived with provisions of flour and pork, enough to last us until the close of season, sometime mid-December, when the *James Whalen* is due to return. My concern for Grayson continues, as he has now been disappearing for days at a time. Lil is just as happy not to have him around. His fits only intensify the horror of his disfigured face and tormented eyes. For my part, I find him to be a tortured soul more than he is incompetent, but sometimes he sets off in the little tender and we are left with no vessel should an emergency arise. I have drafted a letter to the Department of Marine and Fisheries, and they inform me that a replacement cannot be found this late in the season. They also advise that positions such as these are to be assigned to veterans and victims of the Great War, and that I am to find ways to work cooperatively, but I find little cause to furnish a portion of the light's budget for an assistant who is absent more than he is present. Lil has been taking on more responsibilities, spelling me on shifts in his absence. We are managing quite well without him, as we must. We have little choice.

Thursday, 10 October — Newspapers are reporting that the Allied forces are gaining ground in Belgium over the Germans. The end of the war is in sight. It has been a war to end all wars. Soldiers are trickling home, some wounded, although there are many who have been left behind, buried beneath the fields of Flanders or lost, their final resting places unknown and unmarked. Our little post has grown quiet, with fewer ships and even fewer visitors, and the gap between the battlefields of Europe and the monotonous routine of filling fuel, lighting mantles, and polishing lenses yawns greater than ever. I have asked Grayson about his time in service, but he shares very little, speaking only of his training in England, of his comrades and dances on the base. When I ask of the battles, his eyes cloud, and I can see the torment the memories bring. I have heard he was one of only a few in his unit to survive the mustard gas, that several of his fellow soldiers died days — even weeks — after the attack, screaming in agony from the burns that blistered their skin and lungs, stealing even their breath while medics and nurses stood helpless. I have heard, too, that there is a scourge crossing the Atlantic, taking passage with the same young men who willingly offered their lives to defend freedom, only to fall ill with a sickness they are calling the Spanish flu. It is spreading wild and has already reached the shores of this great Lake.

Monday, 16 December — The *James Whalen* arrived today to pick up Grayson to return him to the mainland for the winter, but the man is missing. I have not seen him for five days now. He cannot have gone far. The punt was found on Edward Island, but a search has turned up nothing, and I suspect he has fallen into the Lake's grasp. We even went so far as to explore the deserted mine shafts, but there was no sign of him. Lil, the children, and I have decided to winter on the island. We have provisions to last the season, and game is plenty. I have a sufficient supply of shot and Lil her snares and we have begun to cut firewood, enough to keep us warm through the long, cold winter. There is no work in town for a lighthouse keeper, with all the returning soldiers also seeking employ, so it makes little sense to pay rent when there's a perfectly good house right here. And if that weren't reason enough, more and more people are sick and dying of this flu. It is taking the young and strong, filling their lungs with fluid until they can no longer breathe. We shall be safe here, and warm. And should Grayson wander back, God willing, we can attempt to provide for him as well until word can be sent back to town.

I feel like I'm reading a bedtime story, but when I look at her, she isn't drifting off to sleep, but sitting bolt upright. I can't read the expression on her face. I pause for a moment, and I hear her whisper, 'Oh, dear God. It was him. All those years later. Grayson.' She isn't talking to me.

'Is something wrong, Miss Livingstone?' She doesn't answer but tilts her head, thinking.

'Pa never knew what happened to him, never

saw him again. No one saw him. Except Emily and me. And she would have told no one. She couldn't have. And I never did.' She settles back into the bed. 'Go on.'

Wednesday, 1 January — A celebration of the New Year! We had a feast with rabbit soup, boiled beef, sponge cake, and rice pudding. The ice has covered large sections between the islands, and temperatures continue to fall. Before long, the Lake will be solid enough to cross, and we will once again be in touch with the outside world. Peter and I spend long hours looking at books and I read to him often. He is bright, I can tell already. I am grateful for the education I received in Scotland in spite of being a poor farmer's boy. It will allow me to ensure my son receives the same, even if it means Lil and I deliver his lessons here on the island. There has been no sign of Grayson.

Thursday, 27 February — I can feel the approaching spring in the warmth of the sun. Richardson was able to travel with the dog team and sled from Silver Islet, as the ice is solid. He brought with him the mail as well as news and has supplemented our larder with welcome tins of milk. Two of his sons accompanied him this trip, and the children skated for hours on the frozen Lake. Lil made a hearty stew of salted fish, which we shared to keep them warm on the cold journey back.

Tuesday, 4 March — The ice is losing its grip on the Lake, it is being chased out of Black Bay, and the wind is tossing floes up against the shore. While Superior is beginning to shake herself loose, it will still be almost a month before we will see ships in the lanes and have to light the beacon. Peter has been unwell these three days past. So much so that I retrieved my bottle of whiskey from its hiding place in the fuel shed in the hopes that its medicinal properties would be of some benefit. Lil greeted its appearance with disapproval and skepticism, and I had to insist on it being administered. Her father forbade any form of liquor in her home, and his strict upbringing has stayed with her. Instead, she has gathered the inner bark from poplar trees and steeped them to make a strong tea. I fear the insipid venom from the Spanish flu has reached our lonely post, innocently carried by boisterous boys who skated on our shore and supped in our humble home.

Thursday, 13 March — Peter is recovering. I care not whether it was the whiskey or the herbs, our son will survive. Richardson's family, however, has not been spared. We have received word that the eldest of his boys has died.

I stop reading. I can hear Marty's cheerful whistling coming from his office down the hall. I recognize Chopin and start to follow the melody, anticipating the next notes. I can't help myself. It's part of me, a deep, deep part and one that I try to keep buried, but the music stays with me. It's always been that way.

The old woman lies silent for a moment. I think she's fallen asleep, but then she speaks. 'Thank you, Morgan, that's enough. There is only so much memory a heart can bear to hold.'

I close the cover of the journal and place it back on top of the others, taking a moment to rewrap the cloth around the bundle and tie the twine. I place the package on the table near the old woman's bed and turn to head out the door.

'Mind you keep your hands off my things.'

I pause for a moment, looking at the white-haired woman sitting among the pillows, then glance quickly at the dragonfly picture. Without a word, I head down the hall, back to Marty's office.

★ ★ ★

By the time I leave Boreal Retirement Home, the rain has stopped, but there's a damp chill in the air. The streetlights are already flickering on.

Derrick is here, sitting slouched over the steering wheel of his black Honda Civic, and my heart skips a beat. I haven't seen him for a few days, between spending time scraping fences and trying to patch things up at home. Laurie thought I should be grateful that all I ended up with was this restorative rehabilitation crap. It could have been worse, she said. She asked me about the graffiti, about writing, where I got the

69

paint from, who I was with. God, it was like being interrogated. I get it; it's her job. She knows that I've been seeing Derrick. I had him over one night to watch a movie; I thought it would be fine, that it would get her off my back. He has a way with adults where he's all polite and helpful and they think he's fabulous. But not Laurie. I can tell she doesn't like him, so we don't go to my place anymore. That's fine with me. Derrick sees me and starts the engine, pulling up to the entrance. I climb into the front seat and he heads out of the parking lot and we haven't even said a word to each other.

I'm learning that he can be that way. He says he's contemplative, but I told him that was a fat-ass word for being moody. So when he doesn't say anything, I know he's thinking. He's always thinking. Planning shit. He's got so many balls in the air, I can't keep count.

He apologized for taking off when the cops showed up. I had to make my own way to McDonald's, where they caught up with me anyway. I know he had a hell of a lot more on the line than I did. I know it. But I don't feel it. Deep down, in the part of me that wants so desperately to matter to him, to somebody, it hurts. At least he could show that he's grateful, that he appreciates me keeping my mouth shut about everything. He knows that without me, he would have been screwed that night, if the cops had searched him, searched his car, if I hadn't told them I was alone.

He says he doesn't use the hard stuff, and I believe him. I don't either. I've seen what it does to people; how it robs them of their lives.

Derrick's client list is a who's who of the city's spoiled brats, and while he never lets on when he's around them, he hates their 'pretentious goddamn asses.' He tells me he's a businessman, just giving them what they want, what they would find someplace else anyway, so he might as well be the one to take their mommies' and daddies' money. Demand and supply. They look for him at school or text him, and he sets up drops. They pay what he asks without question and come back for more.

I never asked him how he knows the graffiti writers. He hangs out with them, but he never writes himself. I think he likes the thrill of it, that feeling of living a little bit on the edge, of staying one step ahead of the cops, of running around at night, of the messages in paint. It's what drew me to him. For the first time in God knows how long, I feel like I belong. When I'm with him, I feel alive. When I'm with him, I feel.

'Hey.'

He looks at me briefly and smiles. 'Hey,' he says. 'How was school?'

'You know, same old shit.'

He wasn't there today. He's still in high school, even though he should have graduated last year. He's doing a 'lap year,' a second grade twelve. Usually it's the jocks that go back because they want to play another year of football and raise their average by retaking courses they flunked. But Derrick has other reasons. He wants to stay close to his clients, pass them in the hallway, chat with them at lunchtime, and make drop plans in the parking lot. He's small-time. Nothing too big or dangerous. And he never does deals at school. He's too smart for that. Unlike me, he's passing all of his classes, even though he isn't there half the time. Derrick is the kind of kid who doesn't have to try hard. Everything comes easy for him. He gets what he wants.

'I got caught today in the old lady's room,' I said. I don't tell him why I was in there. I don't tell him about her pictures. The one that looks like my dragonfly. 'So I had to help her read her father's journals.'

'No shit?' He actually sounds interested. 'Why?'

'She's blind. Can't read them herself.'

We speed down the street heading toward the waterfront. Derrick is chewing his bottom lip, his forehead creased in a scowl. Thinking.

He reaches over and rubs my leg, grabs my hand.

We met last year at a party. He's two years older than I am. We go to the same school, but our paths never crossed in the halls. We didn't move in the same circles. Not then.

I met Alyssa in grade nine, and we started to hang out. Then I switched foster homes last year and I had to switch schools too. I didn't know anyone at the new school except Caleb, and he's just an asshole.

Then, one weekend, Alyssa heard about a party at a gravel pit out on Highway 61 and called me. She found us both a ride, showing up at my door just before midnight with a two-six of rye and a few beers, and I slipped out without Laurie knowing. She's had kids in her home for a long time before I came along, yet she's too stupid to realize that it's easy to pop open the bedroom window and climb out.

By 2:00 a.m., Alyssa and I were both drunk, and I was sitting in Derrick's lap. A half hour after that, the cops showed up. Derrick and I ran into the bushes at the edge of the pit, sliding down the embankment and lying together, giggling, while flashlights blinked, sweeping across the field in search of partygoers passed out in the grass. We lay there gazing at the stars overhead, the earth spinning beneath us, until the cops left and we could creep to Derrick's car and slip into the backseat. Derrick grabbed a beer from a cooler on the floor, opened it, took a sip before he passed it to me.

I drank. The beer wasn't cold anymore, but I was thirsty. We passed the beer back and forth a few times.

'God, you're beautiful,' he said, his hand touching my face, tracing my eyes, my nose, my chin. 'How come I never noticed you before?'

I started to laugh. It was the beer. I wasn't beautiful, but let him think I was. When he kissed me, his lips were moist and tasted of the warm beer. I didn't feel like laughing anymore. His hands wandered beneath my jacket and then my shirt, tracing the length of my spine to the top of my jeans. I shivered. He slipped open the clasp of my bra, sliding his hand beneath the pink lace to cup my breast. I tensed and drew back, looking into his green eyes, barely visible in

73

the dark interior of the Honda.

'It's okay,' he whispered into my ear. 'Trust me.'

He bent down and kissed my eyes until they closed, then found my mouth again. This time, my lips parted, and I let him in.

Derrick always gets what he wants.

I thought I'd never hear from him again. It pissed me off that I wanted to. A week later, he called me up, and we went to the party where I met the writers. That was when I first realized what he did, how he made the money to afford the Honda and the designer jeans he wore and the booze he always seemed to have in endless supply. I didn't give a shit, not really. None of that matters. For me, it's all about the writing.

The car speeds along Water Street, the radio blaring some country trash that I've never learned to appreciate, but I don't say anything. And I don't change the station.

We turn into the marina and follow the road along the waterfront, pulling into a parking spot overlooking the harbor and the looming grain elevators. The wind has stirred up a choppy swell, the waves crashing against the rocky break wall. There's a freighter swinging at anchor in the bay. Derrick cuts the motor and turns to look at me.

'I've been thinking.'

The way he says it, I'm not sure I want to know what he's been thinking. I pull out my cigarettes. I offer one to Derrick, even though I know he doesn't smoke and that he doesn't like me smoking in his car. That's about as defiant as

I ever get with him.

'Yeah? About what?' I flick the lighter until the cigarette catches and take a long haul.

'You getting caught and doing community hours in that home is maybe a good thing. It's an opportunity.'

I really don't see how it could be a good thing.

'Babe, those old folks are taking painkillers by the bucketful. That place has got to be full of drugs we could sell — oxy, Percocet, you name it. You just need to get your hands on them.'

I almost choke on the cigarette. 'Are you fucking insane, Derrick? It isn't like they leave pill bottles lying around.' I look at him, staring into those hypnotic eyes, but he doesn't seem convinced. 'And what the hell do you think is going to happen if something goes missing? The first person they're going to come looking for is me! I've gotten into enough shit already.'

'Just look at how you got into that lady's room today. We find a way. We look for a loophole. Get cozy with the old folks. The staff. Get them to trust you.'

He leans over and plucks the cigarette from between my fingers, sending it out the crack in the window, and leans down to kiss me.

'You can do this, babe. You can do it for us. We can build a future together, me and you. It'll be fucking amazing.'

I like the sound of that. His mouth closes over mine. Damn him.

13

Elizabeth

I am sitting in my wheelchair, snugly wrapped in blankets, sunglasses on, parked in the courtyard. It is nice to be outside again. The rain fell persistently for several days but has finally retreated back into the clouds to be carried to other destinations. The air is cool and damp, with a promise of shorter days and the coming winter season. I can hear the girl working on the fence. She is plugged into her music again, the tiny speakers leaking a faint rhythm that wanders over to where I sit. It is familiar, but I can't quite place it.

'What are you listening to?'

The sounds of scraping stop, briefly. 'Music.'

'Aren't you witty.'

'Aren't you nosy.'

'The time will pass much more quickly if you have someone to share it with.'

Silence. Except for the scraping. And the hint of melody.

'Why don't you take a page from Tom Sawyer, convince someone else to paint the fence for you.'

'Who's Tom Sawyer?'

I shake my head. 'What are they teaching in schools these days?'

'Stupid things. Waste of fucking time.'

I can't decide whether to laugh or sigh. She is naive. In spite of her hard shell, I know more about her than she would ever admit to. Her parents are either dead or absent and her home, whatever that is, has little appeal. She covers up her fear and loneliness with anger, and in a desperate attempt to belong, makes stupid choices and misinterprets what she thinks is love. Judging from her reaction to the police, I would wager she has aligned herself with some sort of disreputable characters, who likely abandoned her at the first sign of trouble. But there is something about her. Something unique.

'So, this is a better use of your time?'

'Can't think of anything I'd rather do today than paint a fence.' Her tone is sarcastic, but I sense that the facade she is working so carefully to build is fragile. There is a need for her to reestablish herself after the vulnerability of being caught in my room, of having to be rescued by an old lady. And a blind one at that.

'I think it was my least favorite thing to do. Not that I painted fences, per se. But whitewashing. There was always whitewashing. Every summer, whitewash the cottage, white- wash the fog station, and whitewash the light tower. God, I hated it.'

The scraping continues.

'I'm listening to Epica,' she says.

'Never heard of it.'

'Them.'

I can just make it out. I lean back in my chair, listening to the strains of violin and cello and the haunting voice that accompanies them. It takes me back. It was winter. Emily and I lay on the carpet in front of the woodstove, the Lake outside frozen silent while a million stars pricked the inky ceiling over the hushed stillness. Pa sat in his chair, smoking his pipe. Mother was mending. Our Zenith radio was tuned to the NBC station in Michigan, the signal drifting across the subdued expanse of the Lake to our isolated island, transporting my ten-year-old self far from the boreal forest to a magical world. I sat entranced, listening.

The music changes now, abruptly, as drums precede what can only be an electric guitar. It is unusual, to say the least.

'Good lord, what type of music is that?'

'Symphonic metal.'

'Interesting.' I've never heard such music; an odd combination of classical and some sort of angst-riddled approach to contemporary noise. I can see why it appeals to her.

Morgan tosses the scraper into the bucket and sits down at the picnic table. She lights a cigarette. I make no comment. I am sure she expected one.

'Have you heard anything about your brother?' she asks.

'No.'

I rearrange the blanket that covers my legs. The girl intrigues me.

'Look, Morgan. When I told you I hadn't seen my brother in over sixty years, I wasn't being completely truthful.' She does not respond, but continues to smoke her cigarette. 'He has not tried to contact me in all that time, but two days

78

before his boat was found abandoned, he came here. They brought him to me outside in the garden, and he didn't say a word. After a few minutes, he left.'

The smell of the cigarette hangs in the air, damp and heavy.

'Morgan, those books may hold answers to questions I have about my past. I can't read them. But you can. And if I'm not mistaken, you have the time.' Marty would read them eventually, I'm sure. I could ask him. But I ask her instead, 'Perhaps we can make a trade? You keep reading me the journals, and I will give you one of those paintings you find so interesting.'

I can hear her grinding the cigarette beneath the heel of her boot, but she is silent. She must have removed one of her earbuds, as the strains of Epica are more easily discernible, mingling with the chattering of sparrows and the rustling of the wind through the hydrangea.

'Can I pick which one?'

It is an interesting response. There are three sketches. One is a dragonfly, the other a hummingbird, and the last a detailed study of beach peas. Common themes repeatedly transcribed from various angles. Some critics suggest that a series of the same subject could almost be compiled to create a three-dimensional image, as though each interpretation adds a layer that expresses a slightly different perspective, yet immediately associates with the others. Even as sketches, they are each worth a tidy sum. But I don't think that is the appeal to her. What does she see in one of those pictures?

'Yes.'
'All right, then. Let's get started.'

14

Morgan

Derrick's voice whispers to me when the old lady suggests I continue to read her father's journals. Maybe this is the chance I need.

But we don't go to the woman's room. We sit in the sunroom at the end of the hallway, looking out on the courtyard and gardens. The coveralls hang in Marty's office, and I've left the oversize boots there, too. My own are black, and lace up the front almost to my knees. They are much quieter when I walk down the tile hallway and across the wooden floors. I'm dressed all in black, like a raven, except for a scarf I got for Christmas last year from Laurie, bright cobalt blue with threads of silver, which I have laced through the belt loops of my jeans. I've heard that ravens like shiny things, just like magpies. I keep my eyes open.

I place the journals in a pile on the table, and the old books look strange and out of place on the modern furniture here. I'm almost afraid to open them, they're so fragile. But I have no choice, and carefully turn the pages until I reach the last entry I read.

'Now where did we leave off?' I ask, skimming the words. 'Your parents moved into a lighthouse on some island out in the middle of Lake Superior. The Spanish flu was killing people.

Some guy named Grayson went off the deep end and drowned or something.'

'He didn't drown,' the old woman replies.

'What happened to him, then?'

She hesitates before answering. She's sitting in a chair, her hair combed and pulled into a tight braid that falls down one shoulder, and she's taken off her sunglasses. 'I find sometimes it's better not to know the end before the beginning.'

So I continue.

'All right, then. Nineteen nineteen to nineteen twenty.'

Friday, 13 June — There was a glorious full moon last night that attempted to outshine the light itself. I took Peter out in our little boat, circumnavigating our island home by moonlight in the wee hours of the morning. There are times this Lake behaves as a civilized and proper lady, gentle and well-mannered, and I am almost fooled into complacency. But I am learning. She is temperamental and prone to fits of rage, working herself into a tempest at the slightest suggestion, throwing herself at us for endless days until her fury subsides again, and she is once again tranquil. I approach our relationship with caution.

Lil and I planted vegetables in our raised beds at the light, and I have expanded our potato patch in Walker's Channel to include beets and turnips. *The Red Fox* has been visiting every few weeks on their way between Port Arthur and their fishing grounds and bring with them the mail and papers, and we are well in touch with the outside world again. There are many still ill with the influenza, and while I have made several trips into the city, Lil insists on remaining here at the light with Peter. I cannot fault her for that.

Wednesday, 23 July — I continue to marvel at the knowledge and skill of my wife. She is teaching me about the land between the work of keeping the light and tending our gardens. Our pot is often filled with the rewards of her snares, and she has begun already to prepare foods to sustain us through a winter of isolation — salting fish, preserving berries, and drying herbs. I have been out a few times with the Niemis on their tug, helping them to bring in nets and gut their harvest of fish that they bring to Kemp Fisheries for processing. They live in Port Arthur but base their summer fishing operations from a camp in Walker's Channel. I find the work hard and only leave when the weather is fair and Lil is able to manage the chores of the light alone. We have not put in for an assistant. Lil and I have been able to share the workload, and the Department seems happy with the arrangement.

On the pages, summer turns to autumn, autumn to winter, and still I read. It's repetitive in places — the same listings of visitors and how much fuel they went through and food they ate, but I'm not bored. Not really. It's better than scraping fences, and I'm finding it easier now to figure out the handwriting. I suppose I'm getting used to it. I pick up the next book and begin 1921.

Tuesday, 5 April — The *James Whalen* arrived today, and construction has begun on the fog station. We have assembled the structure a few yards from the main lighthouse building, and the diaphone system is being installed. The crew is staying over, and it is just as well that Lil and Peter have taken a rare trip to visit with Lil's cousin, who recently married and moved to Port Arthur. The timing is fortuitous, as Lil's date of confinement is approaching.

Thursday, 14 April — *The Red Fox* arrived today with news of Lil. She was delivered of a boy yesterday. Will return with the Swede for a quick visit while Sutherland's nephew covers the light. Named him Charles.

'Your brother.'
I do the math in my head. My god, he was over eighty years old. He was fucking nuts to be out on that boat alone.
'Yes.'
We continue like this for almost an hour. In a weird way, I'm helping her see her past again, and parts of it she probably didn't even know about. Like that Grayson guy. Her brother must have read the books before; I can tell she's trying

84

to figure out why he went back to get them. Why now. We're both looking for answers, but for me, I don't even know what the questions are.

It's getting dark, and the lights come on. The quiet noise of the home continues in the background, as my voice fills in the days of life on the island in the years before the old woman was even born.

I read to the end of 1924. 'That's it,' I say, 'that's the end of this book.'

'Are you too tired, then, to go on?'

'No. It's just . . .'

I'm sorting through the books, stacking them up.

'The next one isn't here.'

The old woman sits up. 'What do you mean it isn't there?'

'The one that starts in 1925 isn't here. There's a book missing.'

She leans back in her chair and sighs, sounding like she's in pain, and I know that this is where she expected to find her answers.

'What happened in 1925, Miss Livingstone?'

Her voice is barely a whisper. 'Emily and I were born.'

15

Elizabeth

Here I sit at the end, my living mostly behind me, and I don't have a beginning. The Lake has conspired to keep the truth from me. The Lake and Charlie. The tattered books don't hold any answers to my past. They have shed no light on what motivated my brother's actions, set his boat on the water with a course charted for Porphyry. He has seen to that. After all these years he still holds that power over me.

I can feel the girl watching me. Waiting, I suppose, for a response.

'And the next book?' I keep my voice flat, not wanting to convey the emotion that is coursing through me. 'What year does it begin?'

'Nineteen-thirty. Do you want me to start on that one?'

There are other voices in the room. Mr. Androsky and his family are here. I can hear the excited chatter of his granddaughter, a tiny slip of a child who is perhaps four or five years old. They come every week to visit. It is a ritual I've observed for months and can now re-create for my sightless eyes; the son pushing his father's wheelchair to the sunroom, where they eat takeout off the coffee table, the old man happily soaking up the boundless energy of the very, very young. Between French fries, the child propels

86

the most recent movie character in an array of acrobatics around the room. 'No, Nemo, Grampy needs the wheely chair cuz his legs are tired of work. Quick! Hide in the bushes so the sharks don't get us!' Every week, they bring Mr. Androsky a chocolate milk shake, which he sucks on happily, while the girl's father runs interference between the child and her grandfather, tirelessly directing the tyke to the tepid package of chicken nuggets that I know is spread out on the wax paper wrapper, and asking the same slate of questions and getting the same slate of answers from the old man.

'How are you this week, Dad?'

'Still on the right side of the grass. That's all that counts, I suppose.'

'How's the food?'

'Can't complain. Nobody'd listen anyway.'

'Do you need anything?'

'Good shot a whiskey in this milk shake would do me a world of good.'

And so on. They stay only about half an hour, and then the nuggets find a resting place in the garbage pail beside the sofa, the latest toy is dropped into the Hello Kitty backpack, and Mr. Androsky is wheeled back to his room, slurping up the last few sips of milk shake. It is a ritual I dismissingly tolerate, but secretly envy.

I have no family to come visit me. No weekly offerings of barely digestible fast food, no cards on my birthday, no one asking if I am well that week or need anything. It is only when I hover on the periphery of Mr. Androsky's life that it occurs to me that I am missing something. Emily was my life. Yes, there was Charlie, too, for a time. But I could not bring myself to reach out to him. I could not forgive his misguided actions or contemplate an apology from him, should he even have wanted to provide one. And I could not be sorry for those things that he would not forgive. So we lived in mutual exile from each other. He was never acknowledged, never present, but always a shadow that hovered just beyond our existence. We had been so close, the three of us; he our champion and we his adoring followers. But darkness swallowed us, and when I had to choose, I chose Emily.

So, Charlie, you took the book — 1925 to 1929. What happened during those years that drew you away from your cabin in the woods, to slink into my new home after all this time, after all that has been left unsaid, only to stand in a corner and remain silent? You could return to the Lake, to Porphyry. You could speak to the wind and waves and face the ghosts that walk the rocky beaches to pull secrets from the past, unearthing Pa's silenced words. And yet you could not speak to me.

The girl interrupts my thoughts. She has been waiting for me as I allow the realization to settle. 'Do you want me to keep reading?'

'If it's all the same to you, Morgan, I think that's quite enough for today.'

I stand. 'Mr. Androsky.' I nod a greeting in his direction, forcing my lips to smile.

'Miss Livingstone. There's no need for you to leave. Plenty of room here for the lot of us, supposing you don't mind saying hello to

Becca's new fish friend.'

'That's quite all right, Mr. Androsky. We're finished — we were just leaving anyway. Enjoy your visit.'

16

Morgan

She's trying not to let it show, but the missing book's upset the old lady. I collect the journals back into one pile and rewrap the fabric around them. The little girl climbs up beside me, settling back into the seat.

'You read us a story?'

'Maybe some other time.' I collect the bundle and stand up.

'Your grampy want some French fries?'

I look down at the girl. Her wispy brown hair has escaped from butterfly barrettes and hangs in her eyes. Her feet are tucked underneath her, and she holds a plastic Nemo in one hand and a soggy fry in the other.

'My grampy?'

'Yeah. Daddy says Grampy can't eat French fries. His tooths all falled out and now he can only have chocolate milk shakes. Maybe your grampy wants somma my French fries? Or did her tooths all fall out too?'

I look at the old lady, already stiffly walking down the hall, one hand gripping the rail that runs the length of the wall. I can't read the expression on her face. She's hidden her disappointment and appears indifferent, but I know better. I bet she was a handful when she was younger. Before her hair turned white and the wrinkles carved her face. Before those unsettling brown eyes grew cloudy.

'She isn't my grampy,' I reply. 'And her teeth are just fine. In fact' — I lean in close to the little girl, whispering — 'I think she might really be a shark. Big old teeth inside that mouth.' I shiver. 'Better hide Nemo!'

She squeals in mock terror and runs behind her grandfather's chair. I catch up to Miss Livingstone and fall quietly in step beside her. There's a hint of a smile tugging at her lips, and she leans closer to me, whispering, 'Nemo is such a small morsel. He would only whet my appetite.'

Damn, she can hear everything.

In spite of myself, I think I'm starting to like her.

17

Elizabeth

'A woman is sitting in a chair at the beach. Her face is hard to see behind a thin veil. The wind is brisk, blowing the skirts of her dress, forming whitecaps on the waves and filling the sails of a boat on the horizon. She's holding a parasol.'

'Is her parasol tipped backward, or does she hold it above her head?' I ask.

Marty is sitting at the table in my room, sipping coffee. This is a game we have been playing of late, when he has the time to leave his tools and spend a few moments with an old lady, bringing color back to the gray vision of her sightless eyes.

'Backward.'

'Monet, 1870. *Camille sur la Plage de Trouville*.'

He flips a few pages.

'A large gathering, couples dancing outdoors, and the sunlight coming through the trees makes interesting patterns of light and shadow. The focus of the painting is not the group, but a young couple dancing. You can almost see the woman's skirts moving as she twirls.'

'Renoir, 1876. *Bal du moulin de la Galette*.'

'A haystack — '

'Please, Marty.' I don't let him finish this one. 'Don't patronize me.'

'Yes, yes, of course.' He flips more pages. I know he is smiling. 'Here we go. Rhythmic swirling patterns, painted with short brush-strokes of blue, indigo, and violet with circles of gold and the sliver of an orange moon. A village is in the valley below, the church spire slim, white.'

It is one of my favorites for many reasons, and I can see it clearly from his description. 'Isn't it a shame that artistic genius hovers so near insanity?' I reply. 'Does it require a tortured soul, Marty, to capture beauty? To see and speak truth?'

I am lost for a moment, wandering around in my thoughts, and we both sit, silent.

I have learned that most of us . . . we are merely life's spectators. Those who have allowed their demons to inhabit their lives — to sleep with them and wake with them and let them whisper in their ear — they are the architects of life, constructing the world as we know it. But at that, and maybe because of it, they tread a thin line between being reviled and revered. Who decides when they've crossed from tortured to talent, to be embraced and immortalized? When we like what our eyes see and our ears hear? Genius and insanity. Which brings the other?

Marty is patient and does not push me. He knows the demons I have dealt with. And he knows I know this painting. 'Van Gogh, 1889. *Starry Night*. Painted while an inmate at Saint-Paul Asylum.'

He closes the book softly. 'He perceived his illness as a gift, Elizabeth. Used it — you know that.'

'It killed him.'

'Yes, undoubtedly. But you cannot separate one from the other. It made him who he was.'

He collects the book and coffee mug and stands up, heading out the door just as Morgan arrives. He pauses in the entrance and turns back toward me, speaking softly. 'It made her who she is too. You cannot blame yourself. You did what you had to.' And then the joviality returns to his voice, and he turns to the girl. 'A little bit early, aren't ya?' He doesn't wait for a response. Needs no explanation. Without another word, he heads down the hall, whistling.

Morgan drops what I assume are her bags on my bed, and then flops down beside them. 'What was that all about?'

'It's a game Marty and I play,' I reply. I'm not sure how much she heard of our conversation, but I sidestep the question. It is difficult for me to talk about, especially now that Charlie is missing and my memories are being refreshed by the journals rescued from the wrecked *Wind Dancer*. 'He tests my visual memory by describing the artwork of famous painters to me, and I guess them. Correctly, I might add. He hasn't been able to stump me yet.' I feel around on the table in front of me until I find what I am looking for. 'I had Marty pick you up a little something.'

Morgan takes the book from me, flipping it from front to back.

'*Tom Sawyer?*'

'Thought you might find some inspiration for your fence painting,' I say, trying to make a little joke between us. Perhaps she does not get my humor.

'Umm. Thanks?'

'You're welcome.'

It lands on her pile.

'So . . . ' She lets the word hang in the air between us, hoping I will pick it up. She is early. We had not planned to read today, and I wonder what has motivated her to come.

'So?' I reply.

'Apparently I'm early.'

'Apparently.'

'So I thought we could continue where we left off.'

'Yes, yes. I suppose we could.' By my calculations, she should be in school right now. Perhaps there is something she seeks that cannot be found within the brick walls or among the groups of children that cram the hallways and classrooms in contrived society, pressured toward futures when their youth still hovers so lightly on them. I can speculate, but it is not my place to judge. 'What year does the next book start again?'

She has already collected the pile of journals and is removing the cloth. She sets them down on the table near me, and selects one to bring back with her, kicking off her boots, which drop to the floor with a double thud, and settling on my bed. 'It's dated 1930 to 1933.'

And we begin.

Saturday, 25 January — Day three of a nasty storm that has brought with it strong winds

95

from the SW. The Lake is open to the south as waves continue to roll across the fetch between Isle Royale and Porphyry. Peter and Charlie have been hard at work on their lessons, although it may be many days, if not weeks, before we can find a way to have them delivered to their instructors in Port Arthur. Peter is showing great aptitude. I have some concern for Charlie, whose mind tends to wander, who leaves tasks half accomplished. He is marvelous with the twins, however, and I am grateful for that. Lil has retained some vestiges of the illness that swept through our family several years ago. She does not share the same joy in the twins that she did before. It is understandable, given all that has transpired. I have begun reading with Elizabeth, and she seems to have an excellent grasp of language, even though she is not quite five years of age. Emily much prefers to amuse herself and remains silent as ever. I fear she will never learn to talk, let alone read. It matters little, as Elizabeth is her constant champion. She seems to understand her every nuance, every unspoken thought. They share a silent language that seems to make it unnecessary for our little Emily to acquire any words of her own.

Thursday, 30 January — The winds of last week have abated, and we have settled into a low-pressure system that brings with it cold temperatures and bright skies. I have cleared the ice surface in the bay on the NW side of Porphyry Point, and we have been skating almost every day.

Monday, 10 February — Richardson arrived by dogsled from Silver Islet. He will be staying with us for several days, as he has offered his team and his help to harvest more wood. We will be cutting on Edward Island and will stay in Walker's old shack while we complete the work. Peter will come with us, but Lil and the youngsters will remain at home. Charlie threw a fit of temper at being left behind, but I feel he would still be more of a burden than a help. Besides, if I took him along, who would entertain the girls? He was consoled when I said that I needed him to be the man of the house in my absence. His chest puffed out like a partridge, and he nodded, accepting the responsibility.

He did entertain us. Then and always. Whittling crude dolls out of pieces of cedar for us to play with. Fashioning bark boats that we piled with loads of twig-size firewood and sailed across the wooden floor for the little village we built beneath Pa's chair. Pulling us around the point in the sled. Stumbling through a chapter of a novel. And Emily and I adoring the attention. Mother, efficient, practical mother, always in the background.

Morgan and I settle into the quiet routine of reading, and the months continue to unfold.

Time passes quickly on the pages, with spring nudging out winter. Pa's words are fluid, articulate, almost poetic. They enhance the great contradiction that he was, belying his humble beginnings in Scotland and his decision to spend his life responsible for the machinations of a navigational aid on the largest inland lake in the world. What was it in his past that led him to settle deep in the heart of Canada, married to a woman who was half Ojibwe, far from the shores of his native Scotland and far, it seems, from a background steeped in classics, the novels of Austen and Carroll, the music of Mozart and Beethoven? And more so, to instill that passion in his children amid the pine forests of Canada and expansive waters of Lake Superior?

Friday, 21 March — Vernal equinox and the first day of spring. I explained it to the children using a large canning jar still filled with preserves and the kerosene lamp to simulate the sun. Peter began to apply math principles, calculating the number of days until the solstice. He is bright. I see a future for him that will take him beyond the island.

Tuesday, 8 April — Lit the lamp for the first time. The season has officially begun. I took Charlie and the girls on a boat ride around the islands in *Sweet Pea*. We spotted a large sow on the east shore of Edward Is., near the entrance to Walker's Channel. She had three cubs with her. The *James Whalen* stopped briefly to offload provisions en route to Number 10 Light and Battle Island with the returning keepers. Ross Sutherland and his wife are again stationed at Battle Island. Lil will continue to serve as official assistant here, and Sutherland has made the same arrangements for his station. The Department of Marine and Fisheries has recognized that keepers are much happier to have their families with them and that wives often serve better in the position of assistants. That suits me well.

Monday, 5 May — Discovered the remnants of an encampment on the NE shore of Edward, near the mining shafts. Layers of pine boughs, scorched earth delineating a campfire, and a collection of rabbit bones. It is likely someone has been setting trap lines in the area. It is unusual that they have not stopped in to say hello. The Niemi brothers have returned to their camp on the north shore of Porphyry Island in Walker's Channel and have begun to lay nets. They continue to work with Kemp Fisheries, harvesting whitefish, herring, and trout. They have begun construction of a Finnish steam bath. I hope to have the opportunity to try it.

Friday, 27 June — Ran the foghorn for two days solid as the Lake was draped in a curtain so thick the birds themselves refused to fly. Peter kept me company on the evening watches, waking me every two hours to wind the clockworks. It is not his calling, I can tell, even at this age, but he put in a valiant effort.

Thursday, 21 August — Received word today that Sutherland is dead. He was found, drowned, washed ashore after his boat capsized. His wife will carry on as keeper to see the season out.

The girl yawns and stretches. 'Sounds like it could be a dangerous place out there.'

'You have no idea,' I reply.

'Do you remember any of this?' she asks. 'You were, what? Five years old?'

'It does waken some long sleeping memories.' The names and places. The snapshots of life. They are my past. They are my youth. They are my home.

18

Morgan

I keep reading through to the end of 1930 and move on to 1931; the year when the mantle on the light burned out three times, when the ice came in early but New Year's was spent in a snowstorm. That summer, Charlie asked to go to school in town. I was surprised to read that his father told him no, and wrote that a boy of eleven still had much to learn at home.

School's a fucking waste of time in my opinion anyway. So many stupid rules, and the teachers rarely give a shit. Being shut up in a stuffy classroom all day, fed facts and dates and names, expected to regurgitate them like some goddamn bird feeding its young — it teaches us fuck-all about what we can become, and more about who, or what, we aren't. I know what I'm not. I don't need that reminder day in and day out.

I think I might have liked growing up on an island, all that freedom, being outside in nature and shit. I haven't had that since Grandpa died. I think I would have been happy there.

In 1932 they started raising chickens. They were Charlie's responsibility, the lightkeeper wrote, but Elizabeth and Emily helped. The twins were always with their brother. He spent most of that summer building a coop.

I'm near the end, four years of the old

woman's childhood condensed down into this one book, when I turn the page and find it. It's resting there, waiting to fly. It's much simpler, but it's unmistakable. I trace the lines with my finger, the body of the insect, the wings, the eyes. Someone has drawn it on the blank pages at the back of the book.

I realize I've stopped breathing.

It's my dragonfly.

'Miss Livingstone?' A woman in pink scrubs is knocking on the door, opening it as she does, looking around the room, at me, at the old woman. She appears upset, frustrated maybe. 'I'm sorry. You're needed. We've done all we can. Can you come?'

The old woman sighs as though she's tired, like she is dealing with a young child. 'Yes, yes, of course.' She turns to me. 'I am being summoned, it seems, and I'm sure your fence is calling to you.' She stands, slowly, moving toward the door, but something stops her. She turns, tilting her head in my direction. 'What is it, Morgan? Is something wrong?'

I can't have paused for more than a few seconds. She can't see me. I know she can't. But my heart is racing, my hand hovering over the image in her father's journal. 'No, I'm fine.' I make sure when I answer that my voice is calm, even though I'm not. I slide off the bed, pulling on my boots, my hair falling over my face. I can feel the deep flush starting at the back of my neck, spreading to my ears and cheeks. I don't want the nurse to notice — she might ask questions — so I keep my head down and fiddle with my boots. 'I'm sure Marty's ready for me by now. I'll see you later.'

She turns and follows the nurse down the hall, gripping the railing as a guide.

I stand up, collect the journals, and stack them on the table. I'm about to retie the fabric, but I don't. I can't. Instead I look at them, the years piled one on top of the other. One of them holds my dragonfly, the dragonfly that's connected to my past, my memories, drawn in pencil and pressed like a leaf between the pages of a book that was meant to hold the memories of someone else. The same dragonfly was tucked behind the velvet lining of the violin case, this time drawn in the pastel of colored pencil. And then it landed, my dragonfly landed, on the old lady's dresser, a watercolor sketch, the shapes bleeding together, the image framed in brown wood. I can't just put it away. It's tugging at me.

I turn to the violin case that I've tossed on the bed, flick open the clasps, and lift the lid. I ignore the instrument, instead sliding my hand behind the lining to pull out the pictures that are tucked there, spreading them on the knitted afghan that's draped over the bed. I take 1930 to 1933 out of the pile, open Andrew Livingstone's journal to the last page, and lay it beside the others. In some ways, they're different; the quality of the drawing, the proportions, the material used — but like with the framed paintings on the old lady's dresser, the artist is unmistakable. They're different. But they're the same. I turn to the watercolors, snatching them up one by one, and study the scrawled signature at the bottom. I can't read it. I can only read the date — ''56.'

I collapse into the chair Miss Livingstone always sits in.

Who the hell is the artist?

I'm unsettled. Agitated. I put the journals back, carefully re-wrapping them and leaving them on the table. I also arrange the pictures on the dresser. As I'm about to leave the room, I catch my reflection in the mirror. Black on black. Gray eyes looking back at me. There's something in those eyes I haven't seen before. For a fraction of a second, I'm not sure who I'm looking at.

I need to get a grip.

The halls are quiet, like they usually are at this time of day, so I step into the old lady's washroom and rifle through the medicine cabinet. There are no meds tucked away on the shelves over the sink, no oxy tablets rolling around in the drawers. I move back to the main room and check the bedside table, finding only a tube of Burt's Bees lip balm, some hand cream, and a stack of CDs. Derrick has no fucking idea how these places run. I don't know how he expects me to get my hands on narcotics in here.

I'm about to leave when I hear footsteps coming down the hall. I close the door. Miss Livingstone coming back already? No. Whoever it is walks quicker and with more purpose. A staff member, maybe. I can feel my heart in my ears. Then I realize that they wouldn't know what I've been doing, that I've been looking through drawers and inside cabinets. So I'm in the old lady's room. I was invited in here. Who gives a shit?

I look in the mirror again. This time, I see the raven.

I grab my violin and step into the hallway, turning toward Marty's office and the old work boots and paint-spattered coveralls waiting for me. Anne Campbell, RN, Executive Director, is walking in the other direction. She pauses, looks at me.

'They just came for Ms. Livingstone,' I say, then turn around and walk away from her. I don't look back. I just keep walking.

Marty gets me set up with primer and brushes. It felt like all my work scraping and washing and sanding weren't making anything better, that I was just making a big fucking mess. So it feels good to finally be painting. The white covers all the tired, faded parts, making them bright and smooth. I actually feel like I'm accomplishing something.

I'm thinking all the while of the dragonflies hidden in my violin case. There are seven paintings, but the dragonflies are my favorite. There are two of them together, one larger and one smaller, the same as the old lady's painting, and I like that. I stop when my paintbrush and primer come close to my piece, hovering on the bottom right side of the fence. I only painted one, using lots of blues and purples, the wings simple suggestions, like it's still learning how to fly. I stare at it. I didn't paint eyes. Mine can fly, but it can't see. It seems incomplete now, without a partner. It glares at me, sightless, and I feel like I'm being told off. Within seconds, the white primer covers the image. I drop the brush into the pail and head back inside.

★ ★ ★

Derrick is waiting. After tossing my violin in the backseat, I climb into the Honda, lean over, and kiss him, a long and lingering one. He is warm and open, and as I pull away, he smiles at me.

'You're in a good mood,' he says.

I want to forget. I don't want to think about old ladies and islands and dragonflies that travel through decades to land in my life. They're like ghosts. And I'm being haunted.

'Let's go back to your place,' I say. 'Play some Xbox, order pizza.' Derrick is my present. He's my reality.

He flicks the steering wheel with his thumb in time to the music on the radio as the Honda pulls away. 'Yeah. Sure. Just gotta do something on the way.'

He pulls up to Pizza Hut and hands me some cash. 'Why don't you run in and grab something? I just got to make a few phone calls.'

When I come back to the car I grab a slice out of the box and slide the rest of the pizza in the back next to my violin. Derrick's still on the phone.

'Look, there's no problem, I hear what you're saying.' His voice is calm, reassuring, almost condescending. 'There's nothing to worry about. I've done this before. It will be fine.' He's making weird faces and crossing his eyes, so I know it's a client. He sounds sincere, but he really thinks they're assholes.

It makes me laugh.

'I'll see you later.'

He starts the car, dropping the phone into the cup holder of the console, and drives toward downtown, turning up Bay and then onto Banning Street. We pass a mailbox that's been tagged. I notice these things now and try to see whose it is, but can't make it out. He pulls the Honda to the side of the road and cuts the engine.

'Wait here.'

He takes a bite of my pizza, and then he's gone, slamming the car door and heading up the sidewalk toward a sagging two-story house. What a dive. Derrick's clients don't usually live in places like this. He glances up and down the street before opening the door and entering the porch. I slouch in my seat, watching, eating my deep-crust Hawaiian. A tabby cat creeps out from beneath the crumbling concrete steps, slinks along the wall before disappearing into the long grass around the corner. The windows of the house are dark, all covered by boards or thick fabric, except one that's draped with a Leafs flag that droops at the top corner. One of the wooden shutters has rotted through, loosening the hinge so that it hangs, crooked. Derrick hasn't quite closed the door to the porch, and the wind shoves it open farther until it bangs against the front wall.

I'm just about to reach for another slice when I notice, barely visible beneath the front peak over the porch, a small camera, trained toward the front yard. And then I realize with a pounding heart where we are. It's a dealer's house. Derrick's never taken me on a pickup before.

I look up the street and see a young couple walking hand in hand. They look like they are deep in conversation, heading slowly toward me in the Honda. A black car pulls into the driveway across the street, but nobody gets out. I don't like this. I slouch lower in my seat. I'm just being paranoid.

Derrick's phone buzzes. I watch the tabby cat slink across the lawn of the house next door, then dash across the street. The phone buzzes again. The young couple reaches the car and keeps walking, turning at the corner and heading down the hill toward the shops and cafés on Bay and Algoma Streets. I can't see anyone in the car across the street, but I know damn well no one got out. Derrick's cell buzzes again.

I look at the number. Private caller. Whoever it is seems desperate to get in touch with Derrick. I don't know if I should pick it up. He doesn't like me to answer his phone, but he normally doesn't leave it behind, either.

'Yeah, Derrick's phone.'

'Listen quick, babe, 'cause there isn't much time. There's a couple of bags in the glove box. Take them and get out of the car. Get out of the car and walk away.'

'Derrick?'

'Do you hear me, Morgan?' His voice sounds calm. I don't think he is.

108

'Derrick, what the hell's going on?'

And then I know he's not. 'Jesus Christ, Morgan, get out of the fucking car.'

I drop the phone and open the glove box, grabbing the white bags before climbing over the seats and falling onto the floor. I open my violin case, stuffing them inside before snapping it shut again. When I peek out the window, I can see that the same couple has returned, still deep in conversation, but this time heading in the other direction. They pass the car, their backs to me. I ease open the door on the opposite side, slipping out, crouching beside the car, clutching my violin. I shut the door, but not completely, trying to be quiet so they don't hear me. Their backs are still toward me, so I carefully stand up and walk away. At first my pace is slow, measured. I don't want to be noticed. It's taking all of my self-control not to break into a run, and it feels like an eternity until I reach the corner of Bay Street and start to head down the hill. As I turn, I casually glance behind me. The street's empty. Completely empty. The couple has disappeared. I can't see anyone inside the black sedan. And Derrick hasn't come out of the house.

I quicken my pace, embracing the violin case in both arms, not daring to look behind or to the side, keeping my eyes down. I've walked one block. Two blocks. I won't run. I won't look behind me. There is only one more block before I turn onto busy Algoma Street and join with other people heading to restaurants or window-shopping. I reach the intersection and press the button to change the light, waiting.

'Hey!' The shout comes from behind me, a man's voice.

I fear the worst and drop the violin to one hand, dangling it at my side. I turn, slowly.

'Hey, you're Miss Livingstone's granddaughter! How are you?'

If he hadn't said the old woman's name, I never would have recognized him. Mr. Androsky's son is smiling at me, holding a cup of coffee in one hand. 'Becca was asking about you on Wednesday. We didn't see you there.' He's reaching out a hand to me. 'I'm sorry, I've forgotten your name.'

My heart is pounding inside my chest and echoing in my ears. I shift the violin from one shaking hand to the other, then reach out and take the man's hand. 'It's Morgan.'

★   ★   ★

Derrick shows up at my place around midnight to pick up the drugs. I sneak out of my bedroom and sit in his car, smoking a cigarette, not even bothering to open the window. I can't bring myself to say anything. This whole thing scares the shit out of me. It was hours before he called and said to meet him outside. Hours of not knowing if someone was going to come knocking on my door. Hours of not knowing if he was okay.

'Hey, I owe you one,' he says as he takes the packages from me and puts them back in the glove box. 'They got nothing on me. Searched my car.' He laughs. 'Shit! That was a close one.' He's very casual about it all. Everything always works out for him. He always gets what he wants.

It's not something I'm familiar with.

He reaches out to put an arm around me. I'm still shaking. I'm not ready to go back to normal. This isn't writing. This isn't a little bag of weed passed to some high school kids in the McDonald's parking lot. I'm angry, I'm scared, I'm hurt. Fuck, I don't know what I am. But I'm not ready to pretend like it's all okay. I flinch and back away, and this pisses him off.

'Aw, come on, Morgan. Nothing happened.'

I smoke my cigarette.

'You're okay. I'm okay. Nobody got arrested, and we haven't lost anything. It's a win-win all around.' He's using the voice that he uses with his clients. The one where he sounds all calm and matter-of-fact, but his eyes are rolling. It makes me feel cheap. I thought I meant more than that to him.

I think of the drugs, sitting in my violin case, tucked up against the only things I have left from my past, the only pieces of my family that I can touch. It feels like someone shit on them. I think of my dragonfly, borrowed and altered but still the same dragonfly, the purple spray paint against the peeling wooden fence. It all sickens me. I feel like I am losing something, like I'm giving away a piece of me that wasn't mine to give. Something I didn't even know I had. Something beautiful and wonderful and precious and me.

I turn and look at him. He's scrolling through the playlist on his iPod. Like he doesn't give a shit.

'I don't need this crap.' I finally find my voice. 'I don't need to sit in some fucking car on some fucking street wondering if you're going to come out of a fucking dealer's house alive and wondering whether the cops are going to come knocking on the door to haul my ass off to jail.' My shaking hand brings the cigarette to my lips. 'God, you're such a hypocrite! You think you're above it. You think you're better than everyone else. Just because you don't use the stuff doesn't mean it isn't controlling you.'

He just sits there, fiddling with his iPod.

I snub the cigarette on the dash. I know I'm crossing a line, but it gets his attention. 'I didn't sign on for this, Derrick.'

'What the hell has gotten into you lately?' He finally looks at me. 'You think you're above it all, Morgan? If it weren't for me, you wouldn't have shit. You think you'd have that iPod and cell phone? Where do you think that came from?' He reaches over and grabs me by the back of the neck, pulling me toward him. I've never seen him angry before. I'm a little frightened. 'You think you'd be asked to go along to the rail yards? You're nothing without me. This is who I am, so get used to it. You, you're a fucking nobody.'

I slap him. It is a stupid thing to do, but I can't stop myself.

He lets go of me and sits back in his seat. 'I don't recall signing you on for anything. You want out, get out.'

'I never wanted in, Derrick.' I just wanted him, but I don't say that. I don't know how.

'Out of my car.' Derrick's eyes flash. I can't

believe he's serious, but he reaches across me and opens my door. 'I can have that seat filled again before the night's over.'

He starts the engine. I grab my stuff and get out.

'Prick.'

I sit on the curb, watching the red taillights of the Honda disappear down the street.

19

Elizabeth

I wake with a start. As the fog of sleep recedes, strains of music filter through the darkness, dancing into my room. It has been years, many, many years, since the notes of that song lifted into the air, and I begin to weep at the memory come to keep me company. I lie back against my pillows and let the sounds wash over me.

We were on the beach, the black volcanic sand warm beneath our bare feet. The Lake was calm and chatted quietly as it breathed between the rocks. Emily was there, but it could have been just the two of us; he with his violin and me braiding the purple beach-pea flowers into a garland for my hair. He was standing on the point, his brown hair tousled by the wind, his canvas pants rolled to the knees, fiddling like an ancient Greek siren, drawing not sailors but the young lightkeeper's daughter under his spell. It was a tune I hadn't heard before. Sweet, airy. The song was captured by the trees, filtered by the sand, and shared with the waves, but I didn't mind. My pulse quickened with every phrase.

'Do you like it?' He flopped down on the sand beside me, resting the instrument on his knee, grinning.

I looked at Emily. She was lying on the rocky outcrop, staring into a pool of water that had

114

collected in a crevice. White pearlwort nodded in the breeze, clinging to the exposed, lichen-stained surface with a tenacity that never ceased to amaze me. I knew the pool would be teeming with tiny insects; mosquito larvae, water beetles, pond skaters. Emily was completely absorbed in her world, surrounded by the living creatures that sustained her.

I looked back, squinting against the late-afternoon sun into his tanned face. His bright blue eyes were twinkling, mischievous. 'Yes,' I answer. 'What is it? I haven't heard it before.'

'It's new. I just wrote it.' He took his eyes away from mine; cast his gaze out over the water. 'I call it 'Lizzy's Song.''

So long ago. So very long ago. I allow the tears their freedom; feel them emerge hot to escape down my cheeks, arriving as cool puddles that fade into my pillow. What nonsense, this, after all these years. But the music continues. It has not dulled with the world of dreams, but remains sharp and persistent. I climb out of bed and cross the room to my window, sliding it open. The music comes from the garden. The melody is unmistakable. 'Lizzy's Song' — my song — played with the same intonations, the same catches in each phrase, the same resonant tone. There is only one person who can play it.

My bare feet make little noise on the cool tile floor as I follow the handrail along the hallway to the entrance that leads to the courtyard. I am drawn by the music. I push the door open and step out onto the flagstone walkway, stumbling sightless into Marty's garden.

115

20

Morgan

I'm standing on the picnic table. It's a stage. My hair is floating loose, and the wind pulls at it just like it does the few leaves that remain clinging to the trees. My god, it's fucking cold out here. I can see my breath hanging in the air in front of me, and my fingers are stiff on the bow. I know this, but I don't feel it because all I can do is play. When I'm playing, I don't feel anything except the song. The same song, over and over and over. It was his favorite.

I don't remember it being foggy when Derrick drove away, but it's foggy now. Everything is blurry. My face is hot and wet, my forehead damp. Through the mist, I can see a ghost in the garden, walking toward me. I'm being haunted. The ghost is white on pale, translucent. I consider whether or not I should be frightened of the ghost. I pause, my bow hovering above the strings. Perhaps it's death, coming to visit me. Death with white hair. Death dressed in a nightgown. Death walking in bare feet. Death stumbles.

Death is blind.

I start to laugh and collapse onto the table. I'm such a fool. Such a fucking fool. 'Oh my god, Miss Livingstone. You scared the shit out of me!'

The vision stops and speaks. 'Morgan?'

I jump off the table and don't quite land like I planned — my feet are unsteady — but even though the ground beneath me moves, I'm able to stand up. I spread my arms open wide, my fiddle in one hand and bow in the other, and start to laugh. 'Miss Livingstone, I thought you were a fucking ghost!' I can't stop laughing. I'm laughing so hard I catch my breath, and then I realize I'm not laughing, I'm crying. I can't stand up anymore; the ground reaches up for me, and I embrace it, the tears streaming down my face. 'I thought you were a ghost . . .'

21

Elizabeth

I reach out, my hands searching for the form of
the girl who lies crumpled on the sidewalk at my
feet, weeping. I can smell the whiskey, strong and
pungent. I can hear the commotion behind me;
the faint pinging of the alarm, the scatter of feet,
the shouts between members of the staff. The
door opening would have set that all in motion,
but I pay it no heed. My hands find the fiddle
first, and I linger, briefly, so very briefly, before
reaching the face of the girl. I wipe the tears
away, sweeping the loose hair off her face and
tucking it behind her ears. I try to hold her as
she sobs, cradling her head in my lap,
whispering, 'I thought you were a ghost, too.'

*　*　*

Marty's footsteps make their way down the hall
and stop at my door, his round frame blocking
the small amount of faded light that suggests the
entrance to the open door of my room. I am
sitting in Pa's chair, the afghan wrapped around
my legs and a thick woolen cardigan draped over
my shoulders. Dawn is still a few hours away;
they must have called Marty in. He will know by
now that he is listed as my next of kin. He knows
more about me and my life than anyone. I

suppose they didn't know what to do with me. I insisted they let the girl stay. It is my room, after all. In spite of the safeguards and administrative structure supporting this place, I am a tenant, not an inmate. I had to remind them of this. I asked them to put the violin in Marty's office, along with the bottle of whiskey. She cried herself out — something, I suspect, she has not allowed herself to do for quite some time — before falling into my bed. I can tell by the rhythm of her breathing that she is asleep.

'She can't stay here, Elizabeth.'

'She can and she will.'

'Her family — '

'Has been informed.'

'What happened?'

I shrug. 'She was drunk. She was babbling on about this and that, but the gist of it is, she got dumped.' I don't bother to mention the part about the drugs and the cops and that 'goddamn fucking prick' who always disappeared when there was any sign of trouble, leaving her literally holding the bag. 'Not the first time a young person drank too much after getting dumped.'

Marty comes all the way into the room and pulls out one of the chairs from the table. By the way the air moves past me and from the sounds of feet on the carpet, he has turned it around and is straddling it, leaning over the back as he often does. He has something in his hands. Papers.

'No. I got that. I meant you.'

I shift, pulling the cardigan closer around my shoulders. The staff has not spared him any

119

details of the night. 'I heard her.'

Marty and I have come to know each other well these past three years. He realizes that I am not being forthcoming, but still he does not push. I can hear him shuffle the paper he holds.

'There are two dragonflies, one slightly larger than the other. The artist has used a lot of color and bold swirling lines to create a distinctive image. The background is a complex pattern suggesting water and rocks and trees. The eyes on the dragonflies are riveting.'

The silence stretches for minutes, punctuated only by the soft breath of the sleeping girl. My mouth has gone dry, and I can hear my own heart beating.

'Where did you get it?' My voice breaks.

'It was in her violin case. There are others.'

I lean forward, whispering, not wanting to break the spell that hovers in the room, lingering on the notes of the now-silent violin. 'Emily Livingstone, 1943. *Sisters in Flight.*'

22

Morgan

I wake to daylight brightening the room. My mouth feels like old shit, dry and furry, and a dull throb beats a steady rhythm behind my eyes. I roll onto my back, groaning, and squint up at the white ceiling, memories of the previous day slowly seeping back. Derrick. The cops. The drugs. The fight. The rye. The violin.

The violin.

I bolt upright, struggling free from the tangle of sheets and quilt, and land, my bare feet cold on the tile floor.

'Good morning.'

I spin toward her voice, and the room around me registers. The old lady is sitting in the chair, a silhouette against the window, wrapped in a blanket. I realize I'm dressed in a flannel nightgown, the kind grandmothers wear. My clothes are folded at the foot of the bed.

'What the hell?'

I sink back onto the bed.

'I trust you slept well?' she asks.

I bring my hands up to my face, rubbing my eyes and then running fingers through my hair. It's still damp. The last few pieces of the puzzle settle into place. Crying in the old woman's arms, babbling on — the whiskey did a great job of loosening my tongue, and I've made a stupid

121

ass of myself. She brought me inside, with the help of some staff; tearstained, snotty, and empty. She made me shower. I let the hot water wash over me, peeling away the streaked makeup, the pain, the loneliness, and then passed out in her bed.

What a fucking idiot.

'Look, I'm really sorry about last night,' I mutter. 'I was an assho — I mean . . . ' I look up at her. 'I was way out of line.' I grab my pile of clothes and stand up, heading to the washroom. 'I'll just get out of your way.'

'Who are you, Morgan?'

This stops me. What the hell kind of question is that? It makes me laugh. It's like everything that's happened in the past two weeks has been screaming that same question. Who *am* I? I can tell you my name: I'm Morgan Fletcher. But after that, all I am is a bunch of memories that are mine alone. To everyone else, I'm a few pieces of history bullet-pointed in a folder and stored in a social worker's filing cabinet. I'm a child without a mother and a father no one knows anything about. A delinquent teen, living in a foster home, the now ex-girlfriend of a drug dealer, sitting in a borrowed nightgown, hungover, in the bedroom of a fucking senior home. Who am I? I'm just like Derrick said.

I'm nobody.

But I don't say this. 'What do you mean?'

The old woman sighs. 'Marty found the pictures.'

I know right away what she means by the pictures, and this makes me angry. It doesn't occur to me that it's my own fault for getting wasted and leaving my violin case for just anybody to rifle through. But it pisses me off anyway. I turn and face her, clutching my clothes to my chest, like they're my violin, like I'm protecting them. 'What the hell are you doing going through my things?'

'Do you really think you're in any position to ask that?' She snorts. 'Fine question coming from someone who felt perfectly at liberty to poke around in mine. Twice.' I guess she knows I went through her medicine cabinet. 'For god's sakes, Morgan, you're lucky those pictures didn't blow away last night when you were carrying on like some tragic spectacle, holding a pitiful drunken midnight performance for a building full of old folks. What on earth were you thinking?'

'I don't need this shit.' I sit back down on the bed and start pulling on my jeans. 'A building full of old folks — blind, deaf, and mostly dead. I obviously wasn't thinking?'

'Cut the crap, Morgan. You came here for a reason.'

'Your words, old woman. Your words.'

'I may be more than half blind, but that doesn't mean I don't see things. And while death prowls, my feet are still firmly planted in this world, and with each breath I take, I am *living*. What I heard last night was not happenstance, a return to the scene of your graffiti crime. You came *here* for a reason. What are you looking for, Morgan?'

I continue to struggle into my clothes.

123

Her voice loses some of its edge. 'The pictures. The violin. The song.' She pauses, 'Who taught you that song?'

I stop, one black boot in my hands. It had been his favorite. He never taught it to me, but I heard it many times and found it easy to pick up the melody, copying it from memory. He usually played it on nights when whiskey was in the tin cup, the wind howling around our little cabin while the woodstove popped and crackled in the background. After I was tucked into bed and he thought I was sleeping, he would tune the violin and play. It was light and upbeat, but still it always seemed so sad to me. And the pictures; they were hidden for years. He never spoke of them. I had never seen them when he was alive.

'Morgan, who is he?'

I look at the journals, still on the table where I left them yesterday, the dragonflies sleeping between the yellowed pages.

'My grandfather.'

23

Elizabeth

I close my eyes and lean back against the threadbare fabric of the chair. He had a granddaughter.

24

Morgan

I drop the boot and collapse back onto the bed. My hands find their way back to my face, and this time, I leave them there. The tears start again; I can't stop them. They seep out from between my fingers. It's a release. But still I want to hide. I'm ashamed to be so vulnerable.

'Did he draw the pictures?' I whisper.

Miss Livingstone stands and walks to the dresser, her hands exploring the items arranged there until they find the framed paintings. She picks one up, the dragonflies, and turns back to face me. 'No.' She crosses the room and sits down on the bed. 'No. They are Emily's.'

I wipe my face with my sleeve. 'Emily's?' I sit up. Emily. That explains their appearance in the journals. That explains the collection on Miss Livingstone's dresser. But it doesn't explain how they ended up tucked behind the velvet lining of a violin case belonging to an old fisherman who lived in a rundown shack with his granddaughter.

Emily. Emily Livingstone.

Who are you?

25

Elizabeth

I run my hand across the top of the frame and over the glass. I can see the image as clearly as though my vision never paled. I can pick out every brushstroke; I know every color and shadow. Of all the work that Emily completed, of all the paintings that hang in galleries and prestigious offices and expensive lofts around the world, none speaks to me so completely as this image of two dragonflies, one larger, one slightly smaller, not quite entwined but connected through the swirling patterns in the background, the subtle correlation in shading that creates movement. I have named it, as I have all of Emily's paintings. I call it *Sisters in Flight*.

The girl gets up off the bed and returns with the stack of Pa's journals, rifling through the pile.

'I found them,' she says, 'here.' She lifts my hand, placing it on the page. The lines are barely discernible, merely suggestions of the images floating beneath my fingers, captured by the same innocent hand, an imprint left long, long ago.

My Emily. My dear, sweet Emily.

Who is this girl? With his violin and Emily's pictures? With the music that beats in her heart like it did in his, with his blood coursing through her veins? Does she know that the story that has its roots in the pages of these journals is as much hers as it is mine?

I slide my hand out from beneath hers, leaving the lines of the image, but resting for a moment on the girl's fingers, hesitant but full of question. 'Would you like to know how your grandfather knew Emily?' I ask quietly.

She answers with silence, but I can feel the yearning in the soft hand beneath mine. I realize that we have both loved the same man. He holds a place in both our hearts that gapes empty.

'Perhaps we need to adjust our little arrangement,' I offer. 'Perhaps I should take a turn as the storyteller.'

I have no idea when I begin to speak, giving life to the story of the lightkeeper's daughters, that she will be the one to find the beginning long after the end has been told.

PART TWO

Ghosts

26

Elizabeth

The story of your grandfather and Emily begins a long time before he stepped onto the black volcanic shores of Porphyry Island. You see, my sister was extraordinary; she didn't fit easily into the conventions of society. At first I was not aware. To me, Emily was just Emily; beautiful, wonderful, silent Emily, my sister, my twin, an extension of me. Until one night I overheard a conversation between my parents, and it changed my life. And it is there this story has its roots.

It was late August 1935. The Great Depression gripped the world, but we barely noticed, settled in our home beneath the light far out on Lake Superior, with a roof over our heads, fed and content. It was my favorite time of year on the island, and we were busy with preparations for the long, cold, isolated months that stretched in front of us. Mother preserved vegetables from our garden. She picked and chopped and packed and sealed, and the green- and yellow-tinted jars joined the lush tomato red on the bursting shelves in the dugout cellar beneath the stairs. Braided onions hung from the rafters. Potatoes, pulled from their beds, were mounded into baskets and settled close to the cool earthen floor. Bags of flour, tins of canned meats, oatmeal, salt, and sugar were purchased and stashed away for the months when we could not get off the island, not by boat and not across the ice.

In a few days when Mr. Johnson aboard *The Red Fox* dropped anchor and nosed into shore off the point, both Peter and Charlie would climb aboard and head to Port Arthur. Thunder Bay wasn't a city then — and it wouldn't be for years — but the name defined the expanse of water between the Sibley Peninsula and the mainland where the communities of Fort William and Port Arthur had sprung up in close proximity to each other.

Peter had already spent a few winters in town, studying with other children his age, and now, Charlie was to join him. They would live with the Niemi family, one of the brothers who fished from the camp on Walker's Channel in the summer and lived in a little blue house on Hill Street in the winter.

Mother thought it was time that I go to school in town as well, which was unusual, given her disregard for most of society. Pa disagreed. He preferred to teach us at home, and felt I was too young to be away for such long stretches of time. Besides, there was Emily to consider. Any decision of Pa's became the rule of the household, always, and this was no exception. I know this because I heard them whispering about it one dark summer night when the rest of the house slumbered, weary from the chores of the light and the efforts of bringing in the gardens and putting food by.

I remember the conversation clearly. In itself,

the discussion of my schooling is not memorable. It should have faded, one of hundreds of inconsequential exchanges inadvertently overhead. But I remember it because of the other words my mother spoke in reply, words that settled deeply on my soul, words that opened my eyes and charted a course for my life. Pa was pulling on his boots to complete some last-minute chores before turning in for a few hours of sleep. I had been up to use the chamber pot we kept in the corner of the room and had just crept back under the covers, my body cleaving to Emily's. My parents' voices floated against the stillness of the evening, when even the Lake slept quietly beneath the pinpricked ceiling of the late summer sky and refused to join the conversation. 'We've done a fine job teaching her all these years,' Pa said, so soft I could barely hear. 'I don't see a reason to stop now. Besides, it would not be right to send one and not the other. And we cannot send the other.'

Through my sleepy, half-closed eyes, I saw Mother's shadow pass the doorway as the light swept its eye across the house and back out over the still, black water.

I was not concerned. I did not want to leave the island, although I enjoyed our rare trips to town and admit to entertaining thoughts of school and classmates and lessons. But I loved the freedom, the sound of the Lake, the wind in the trees. And I had Emily. I drifted, sleep reaching up and wrapping itself around my sister and me.

I heard Mother laugh. It was not a happy,

amused sound, not one of contentment. It was a sad, remorseful one, which hovered close to a sigh. I wanted to close my ears and stop listening, but I couldn't. My sleepy eyes opened wide, and my ears sharpened. I heard the ticking of the clock on the mantel, the squeak of a mouse beneath the wooden floor, and Emily's breath, soft and regular.

'We . . . you should have let her go. You should have let her die,' came my mother's voice, angular and ragged. 'What good is it? We have damned them both. Emily will never be right.'

Time stopped. The clock ceased ticking, and the mouse was silent. There was only Emily breathing, steady and rhythmic like the light.

You should have let her die. Emily will never be right.

I'm sure my heart stopped cold inside my chest and paused, waiting, not daring to interrupt what I so desperately wished I couldn't hear, and dreaded with every unmarked beat. I could hear Emily's breath grow as big as the room and spill out the door to fill the space between me and my parents. The light swept through the room again, jumping as it moved past the doorway to reach the other bed where my brothers lay, asleep, and then quickly ran out the window. I placed my hands over my ears.

Pa's voice, rarely sharp, reached my muffled ears with little strain. 'Never again, Lil. You will speak of this no more. She's our daughter. We owe her life. Not a word. Not ever.' He moved toward the door. 'And Elizabeth will stay on the island.'

134

I remember slowly releasing my breath as the screen door banged shut, and hearing Pa's tread crunch along the path toward the fuel shed. Emily had not stirred, but a lock of her black hair, so like mine, tumbled onto the milky white pillow. The light's beam took another run through the room, and I studied my sister's peaceful face; her black-lashed sleeping lids shuttering gray eyes so unlike mine, her gentle mouth that had never once spoken a word, but always appeared to be holding a secret. Mother's footsteps creaked closer, and I squeezed my eyes shut, feigning sleep. She stood above our bed a long, long time, so long I finally fell asleep and never heard her leave.

I realized then that all those things that I thought of as just being part of who Emily was were those same things that meant she would never settle easily into a world outside the small one we had created on the island. We had always been Elizabeth and Emily. The twins. We were inseparable. We were one. I could not imagine Emily thriving in town, sitting in a classroom. And so I could not imagine it for me. That my mother would choose to separate me from her was unthinkable.

As autumn progressed, it was Emily and I who helped with the chores at the light and in the kitchen, bringing in the garden and filling up the pantry. When the days turned cold and wet, my mother had our lessons waiting, and we sat at the kitchen table under the gentle glow of the kerosene lamp with grammar books and math problems. Emily never learned to read or write or figure out addition and subtraction. She spent her time covering pages with pencil drawings of butterflies and birds instead of working out sums or marking nouns and verbs. Mother said nothing, her lips set in a tight line as she collected the pages and tucked them away in a drawer in Pa's desk.

Mother knew there would be many cold, dark months ahead of us; when the late autumn days dawned mild and sunny she let us run out of the house, abandoning our schoolwork on the table. I missed Charlie's conversation now that our trio had shrunk down to the silent Emily and me. But my sister and I shared something different; a language that needed no words and rested on easy familiarity. We relished the silence of the island, the routine of a keeper's life, and the freedom to fly as free as two gulls.

Pa seemed content to have Emily and me help him out with the chores now that the boys were gone. He would hand us both cleaning rags and show us how to polish the light's lenses in larger and larger circles so we didn't leave streaks. I made sure that I always went after Emily so that he wouldn't see the marks she left behind. Mother had us gather driftwood off the beach and pile it in the woodshed to use as kindling in the stove during winter. Emily came along to help, wandering along the beach, picking up sticks and moving them a few feet before placing them back down again. I tried to get her to fill her arms, having her stretch them out as I lay one bare and bleached limb over the other, making sure I didn't give her more than she could handle. We set off together, but I always arrived alone, Emily having stopped along the way, distracted by the buzzing of a bee in a late-blooming dandelion or the musical dance of a goldfinch announcing its passage through to warmer winter destinations. I always made sure the pile of kindling in the woodshed was more than we needed.

I never forgot Mother's words. With each wave that crashed against the base of the cliff near the fog station, I heard the Lake echo: *You should have let her die. Emily will never be right.*

Once I caught her watching Emily, when she didn't know I was watching too. Emily was in one of her trances, her face lifted up to the sky and mouth open, forming unintelligible sounds, talking to the wind as it picked up a handful of golden brown poplar leaves and chased them around her billowing skirts. She stood on the headland of the island, her raven-black hair whipped into a tangle, in conversation with the sea. And then, with the wind her partner, she began to dance. Mother simply turned and tossed a basin full of soapy wash water into the bush before heading back inside.

Emily. My other half. My sister. Our lives and hearts and very beings so entwined that each could not exist without the other. She was a spirit, haunted by the Lake, lingering between two worlds, fragile and vulnerable. And so I was surprised to discover that it wasn't Emily but I who was the ghost.

27

Elizabeth

The autumn that Charlie left the island, Emily began to roam. One moment she was there under my vigilant, watchful eye, and the next she was gone. At first her wanderings threw my parents and I into a panic. We entertained visions of Emily absently stepping off one of the cliffs that framed stretches of the shore, or startling a black bear, or drowning in the icy grasp of the Lake that fascinated her so completely. We fanned out from the light station, one of us first checking that she hadn't set off in *Sweet Pea*, which was kept on the beach near the light, pulled high up beyond the grasp of the waves. We searched the boundaries of the coastline, along the paths that traced our route to the sheltered bay where the boathouse was, through the bog where we picked cranberries in late summer. We called her name, our voices swallowed by the thick cushion of moss that carpeted the forest floor or the mocking laughter of the Lake as it rolled onto the rocky beaches or slapped against the bluffs. We knew she would not respond. Emily never did.

As often as not, we found her, oblivious to our concern, absorbed as only Emily could be absorbed in the activities of a hill of ants or watching a red squirrel move her kits to a new nest. I once observed her for what must have been hours simply looking at the blossom of a columbine. She sat in the sun on the dry earth, legs crossed, head resting in her hands, staring at the nodding flower. She didn't move, didn't touch it or smell it. She just looked. I called to her, but my voice mingled with the sounds of the forest, and she paid it no more heed than she would the call of a jay or the buzzing of a cicada. So I sat, too, legs crossed, head resting in my hands, and watched Emily while the sun marched across the sky. After a time she stood, brushed the bits of twigs and leaves off her skirt, and walked to me, smiled, and took my hand to help me to my feet. I realized that she was aware of my presence the entire time. I sat in her world. I was part of it. I just wasn't the part that mattered right then.

My father had newspapers delivered to the island. They arrived a week or more at a time, and he devoured every last word, sharing stories with us around the dinner table, or in the evening by the fire. That year, 1936, the papers carried news of parched farms, of crops withering in fields, of livestock suffocating, their lungs filled with soil carried by the wind. By stark contrast, the winter was cold, remarkably cold, so cold that we all slept together in one big bed, dressed in our long underwear and piled beneath stacks of woolen blankets and quilts stuffed with down. It was a cold snap that stretched from December to February, holding a nation of weary and troubled people in its icy grip.

Emily and I spent much of that winter huddled around the woodstove, warmed by Mother's soup, flavored with herbs she had harvested and hung to dry in the pantry and rich with the meat of freshly snared rabbit. I escaped from the little island to the pages of *Jane Eyre*, *Pride and Prejudice*, Shakespeare's plays, and *Tom Sawyer*. I wallowed in stories of adventure and romance, resisting Pa's attempts to draw me to the articles in the *Times Herald* newspapers stacked sequentially in abundance in the rafters, endeavoring to stretch my interests and broaden my perspective. Emily, on the other hand, spent hours with her pencils and paper, working sometimes for days on a single drawing, rendering from memory a moth or columbine flower and filling it in with vibrant pastels or colored pencil. At times she sat, captivated by the dancing flames inside the woodstove, so completely still that I wondered if the wind creeping between the siding boards had frozen her into a statue.

It was late that February when Emily once again disappeared. The red on the thermometer barely stretched above its bulbous base, and the air itself hung sharp and crystal cold. It was much, much too bitter for a little girl to be wandering aimlessly in the woods. A scrawny ten-year-old, fearless and determined to be her sister's protector, I did not then think of myself as a little girl.

Pa was splitting firewood, Mother peeling potatoes, so it was I who donned my coat, wrapped a thick scarf around my head and neck and took Mother's fur-lined mitts to keep my hands warm, and embarked on yet another quest to find my twin. My breath hung in the air, little puffs of smoke, as I strapped on snowshoes, quickly fastening the buckles before stuffing my hands back into the soft rabbit fur. The snow was deep. In places the days-old flakes had drifted to over several feet, and the distinctive tracks of other snowshoes patterned the ground around the cottage and outbuildings. Emily had at least had the foresight to wear snowshoes, and I could detect her trail as it diverged from the well-worn paths and headed out onto the Lake.

Superior covers such an extensive area that it rarely freezes over completely. Day after day of cold temperatures and calm waters can, by February or March, mold the ice into a solid expanse that stretches from island to island and island to mainland. Sometimes even then the wind will tease up waves, sending them over and under and through, jumbling the frozen surface into floes and open water. But that year, the Lake was solid. My ears hurt from the muffled silence as I stepped away from the shore, my snowshoes following Emily's prints.

As my feet wandered, so did my thoughts. The snow-drifted surface of Lake Superior turned into the desolate English moor, and I slipped into the world of Jane Eyre, romantic, tragic, stumbling toward my destiny, until a shuddering, cracking boom froze me in my tracks. My heart pounded and my skin prickled. The romance of the moor disappeared, replaced by the isolation of the undulating mounds of snow-covered Lake and the silent forests along the shore. Another bang rang out as the plates of ice shifted and adjusted. *It's just the Lake speaking,* I told myself. *Like an old woman settling into bed.* I stood about half a mile from shore, near the entrance to Walker's Channel, the ominous cliffs of Hardscrabble Island catching and releasing the groaning of Superior.

I saw her then. She stood still, a black silhouette, tiny and vulnerable in a world that stretched great and white and silent from horizon to horizon. She was not alone. I could pick out five from where I stood. Three of them were pacing along the jumbled mounds of broken ice that defined the shore; the other two were tracking, their noses to the ground, switching back and forth as they loped through the windswept snow, their gray fur full and glistening in the late-afternoon sunlight. Emily was between the two groups.

Her name caught in my throat. I lurched forward, clumsy in my snowshoes, stumbling as I attempted to run. The wolves were working together, circling, edging closer and closer to my sister's silent form. My mother's mitts, too big for my childish hands, dropped off and landed in the snow, but I pressed forward until I too, tripping over the wooden frames strapped to my boots, landed in the snow. When I raised my head, I was close enough to see the yellow eyes of a large male as he glanced in my direction before returning his focus to my sister, circling as a unit with the others in the pack. Emily turned slightly and crouched down, catching those piecing yellow eyes with her striking gray ones, fearless in her round, pale face. I lay still in the snow, my bare hands prickling from the cold, not daring to move. The wolf stopped. Their eyes locked. The other wolves stopped too. I could hear them whining, see them pacing in tight patterns while they waited on the alpha. Minutes passed before Emily moved again, and then she simply stood, turned and walked past the brute toward me. And as she had done the day I watched her absorbed in the columbine, she smiled, took my hand, and helped me to my feet before collecting my rabbit-lined mitts from the snow.

She didn't look back. But I did. I watched the animals regroup, bounding away from us across the bay toward Edward Island.

It was then that I saw him for the first time. He was barely visible, blending into the trees in his deer-hide coat and thick black beard, a fur hat on his head. He held a rifle in his hands, and I saw him empty the chamber and lower the weapon to his side before disappearing into the shadows.

I followed Emily back to our little cottage beneath the sleeping light. As with most journeys, the return trip felt much shorter, but even still, the sun hung low in the winter sky by the time we rounded the point and saw my father.

Emily trudged past him, barely acknowledging his presence.

'She was around Walker's Channel,' I said. 'A pack of wolves had wandered out onto the ice, and she was . . . ' I have never been one given to superstition, but I was certain something had passed between the wolf and my sister, some agreement forged there in the snow-blanketed passage between Edward and Porphyry Islands.

'She was watching them, and they were watching her.'

My father fell in step beside me, and we continued in silence for a while. Emily was a few feet in front of us, methodically placing one snowshoe in front of the other. 'She does have a way,' he said very quietly.

'There's more,' I continued.

Emily halted.

'I thought I saw — '

Emily turned quickly and looked at me, her eyes dark and fierce and pleading. In silence, she asked me not to tell, not to speak the words that struggled to take shape. Not that. Not now. It was to be our secret.

'What, Lizzie?' my father prodded.

Emily continued on her path. She knew I had understood and would honor her unspoken request.

'I thought I saw caribou tracks. I'm sure the wolves were on their trail.'

My father grunted in approval, and I knew he would head out the next day in search of the herd. The wolves had come out onto the Lake to track something; I hoped it was caribou. I hoped he found them.

That night, tucked snugly into bed, a sliver of moon shining bright on the snow outside, the Lake grumbling and popping in complaint

144

against the confines of winter Emily and I heard the wolves howling. My parents were in quiet conversation around the fire, and the moonlight made a window-shaped puddle of silver on our covers, Emily and I two tiny bumps beneath. She turned toward me and, in a gesture so unlike her, reached over and traced my face with her slender fingers, across my forehead, around my eyes, down my nose, over my lips to my chin. And then she rolled over. I snuggled up tight against her, sharing her warmth, listening as her breath became soft and regular and she fell asleep.

It was some time before I was able to drift off. The nighttime chorus both thrilled and terrified me as I thought of the wolf and his yellow eyes staring intently at Emily while the rest of his pack paced, waiting. I thought, too, of the man I had seen. I tried to convince myself that he was merely a figment of my imagination — an apparition conjured by the white snow and the presence of the prowling wolves. But Emily had seen him too. She had known he was there, just as she had known that I was.

Emily had seen him, and she didn't want my father to know.

28

Morgan

I'm sitting on her bed, leaning back against the wall, my knees pulled up against my chest and my arms wrapped around them, listening. I've been carried to her world, back through the decades. She talks in a way that makes me feel like I can touch the snow, see the stars, and hear the crashing waves. She picks up the framed picture of the dragonflies, and as she does, the blue veins beneath the skin on her hand jump with the movement of her fingers, and I try to imagine her as a little girl. In some ways, it's impossible. But then there's something about her that makes it not. She slowly gets up, walks to the dresser, and stands the picture back up with the other two.

The journal sits on the bed, open still. I close the cover and let my hand rest on the raised letters, tracing the *A* and *L*. The lightkeeper never wrote about the bearded man. He mentions the wolves and the caribou, which he did find, and Emily wandering off, but not the strange man who hid in the trees and watched. It's a secret kept by a ten-year-old girl.

'He was my grandfather,' I say. It's not a question.

Her back is still toward me as she arranges the pictures. I see her straighten, but she doesn't turn around.

146

'Good lord, child, no!' She turns toward me, her vacant eyes desperately seeking to connect with mine. 'He was the man your grandfather killed.'

In the moment it takes her to tell me that, my whole childhood shatters.

29

Elizabeth

I don't need to see her face. She is stunned. Of course she is. Why did I expect that she would know? He would have told no one. To protect us. To protect Emily. It was much too complicated. And yet I ask a redundant question: 'You didn't know?'

'No, actually, it never came up.' I sense a tremor in her voice. She is upset. But she is quick to raise the mask again, and her next words are laced with sarcasm. 'But then again, it's not the type of thing that someone would just drop into conversation with their ten-year-old granddaughter, now is it? 'Oh, my dear, did I happen to mention I killed a man? Would you like some more mashed potatoes?''

'Ten?'

'Yeah. He died when I was ten.'

He is gone. Of course he is. Morgan would still be with him if he weren't. All those times I permitted myself the luxury of memory, to picture him, imagine where he was, what he might be doing, whether he had loved again. Whether he thought of me. He is gone. It pains me to hear it spoken into reality, but in truth, I have known for many years now. A heart recognizes when part of it has died, and he's carried a piece of mine since the day we slipped away to the north end of the island along Walker's Channel and lay together on a bed of moss. I take a deep breath and allow my mind to register the loss, to piece together the imagined pattern that was his life and allow the seam to close. There will be time to grieve later — if there is any grieving yet to be done.

'How?'

'A stroke.'

'And your parents?'

'My dad was never in the picture, and I don't remember my mom. She died when I was about a year and a half. She got cancer when she was pregnant with me and refused treatment. Refused to terminate, even though the doctors said she would die if she didn't. Grandpa took care of both of us.'

I sense a tenderness for this mother she never knew, a longing for the woman who chose to give her child life instead of keeping her own. It is remarkable, the human capacity for love. To have such a deep and profound connection to someone you have in essence never known. The sentiment doesn't last.

'I never really gave a shit anyway — didn't need them. Didn't need either one of them. He . . . we had each other.'

Again, I hear the longing in her voice.

'He was the only parent I ever knew. After he died, they tried to find out about my dad. They never did. I bounced around between foster homes for a few years. Landed up where I am now. Shitty, but hey, that's life, isn't it? I'm doing fine. I get by just fine.'

Like you did yesterday, I think, but I keep it to myself. She is so young. There may be time yet.

It is so like him to raise the girl. He would have been good with children, just like he was good with Emily. Most people never understood Emily, and what they couldn't understand, they mocked or feared. They refused to look past her muteness, her fixations and trances and peculiar ways. But not him. He loved Emily just like I did. And in the end, it ruined our love for each other.

'He wasn't a murderer.' I hope this consoles her some. 'But it is a long story.'

She settles back, gathering my quilt around her, the quilt Emily and I made. 'I'm listening.'

30

Elizabeth

Emily wandered no more that winter.

By March, soaring temperatures created havoc as the mountains of snow that had fallen during the worst winter on record melted. Ice-choked rivers burst their banks, bringing an end to the cold with horrendous flooding. It was the beginning of what was to be the hottest summer on record. In a paradox of nature, a heat wave stretched across the Americas, stealing back all that moisture, sweeping the fertile land of the prairies into the air in the peak of what became known as the Dirty Thirties. We read all about it in the newspapers my father hoarded, mercifully spared as we were from the heat, fanned by the cool breezes off the Lake — temperate offerings drawn from the water's icy depths.

Only Charlie came back to the island for the summer, once school let out. Pa made sure to keep him busy at the light, saying a boy of fifteen should be working, not gallivanting about in boats or running carefree through the forests. He was grooming him for the life of a keeper. Peter, Peter was destined for bigger things, but Charlie was at home on the Lake, and Pa knew that. Emily and I were put in charge of the chickens and helped out in the vegetable patch, but the chores of the lighthouse, which my mother and I shared during the months of April to June, shifted to Charlie. He would spell my father off overnight, especially when the foghorn sounded and the light swept across the darkness, conversing with the captains of passing ships, repeating, 'We are here, we are here, we are here.' He was tasked with whitewashing buildings, tracking the levels of kerosene in the fuel tanks, helping to unload provisions and supplies when they arrived. On days when the sun shone, the chores were complete, and the foghorn sat silent, I was able to convince Charlie to slip away and take Emily and me out in *Sweet Pea* for a little adventure.

Charlie was always a good sailor. He took to it naturally, like gulls take to soaring on updrafts, high above the water, swooping with the gusts and tacking with the shifting breeze. He could read the wind and the waves and seemed happiest with the boat's tiller in his hand and the Lake air filling the canvas sails of the little gaffrigged vessel. And while I possessed enough skill to navigate the waters around Porphyry, Charlie took us farther, across into Black Bay or down past Shaganash toward Swede Island. We sought out and found bigger and better berry patches and spent hours picking the plump, juicy fruit to be dried or preserved for the long, cold months of winter. Or on days when the wind was still and the sun blazed down, we drifted aimlessly, the sail flopping, while Charlie worked the sheets, easing them off and then bringing them back in again, trying to tease any speed at all from the boat, enjoying the challenge of it.

Emily and I lounged lazily, our fingers dragging along in the cool water.

Early that summer, he took us to Silver Islet for Dominion Day, to celebrate Canada's confederation nearly seventy years before.

The end of school always heralded the arrival of families at Silver Islet who settled in for the summer months, and it felt like civilization moved just a little bit closer to our island home. For a season, the place flourished. The shelves in the general store were stocked with dry goods and an assortment of penny candy, the beach at Surprise Lake on the edge of the community was raked and opened for swimming, and evenings saw the shoreline dotted with bonfires. The impending celebrations for Canada's birthday only made the adventure even more appealing for me. Charlie had gone the year before, and he had told Emily and me all about it — the games, the food, and the fireworks — especially the fireworks. Even then, when half the country struggled to put food on the table, someone had managed to furnish fireworks.

After fastening *Sweet Pea* to the wharf, we headed to Arnie Richardson's place. Charlie and Arnie had become good friends at school, and his parents had invited us to stay with them, assuring us that they had plenty of room, since Arnie's brothers would not be there. Mother eventually conceded. Pa didn't want us sailing home after dark, and I was not about to forgo seeing the fireworks.

Arnie was the youngest of five kids, all boys, with his nearest brother almost six years older.

153

His father often came out to the island during the winter, but the family moved out officially when his mother stepped off the tugboat onto the wharf in June and set up housekeeping for the summer.

'You going to win this year?' Arnie asked. We had collected a group of kids as we wandered along the dirt road from Arnie's toward the beach at Surprise Lake. Charlie had just missed out winning the hundred-yard dash last year to Doug Owen from Fort William. He was determined not to do so again.

'Yup,' said Charlie. 'I'm taking home that trophy.'

'Doug's here again,' Arnie said. 'Staying with his cousin.'

Charlie kicked a pebble, sending up a cloud of dust. 'I can beat him.'

I knew he could. He had been practicing and was the fastest in his class, training all winter in the gym at Port Arthur Collegiate Institute.

We spread out our blanket alongside many others, seeking shade where we could find it. I eagerly soaked up the atmosphere, watching the little children running in and out of the cold water of Surprise Lake, listening to the laughter and conversations of their mothers. This was a different world from the one I knew. My mother rarely had the luxury of idle conversation or idle hands. She would not have felt comfortable here.

Charlie and Arnie entered every event they could; the three-legged race, the sack race, the wheelbarrow race; they ran them all and won most of them. Emily and I watched, me

154

cheering, she silent as always, preferring to stand back, away from the crowds and the noise, more interested in the plants and bugs than in the people who tried to engage her in conversation. Charlie and Arnie even convinced me to enter the sack race, which I didn't win. I didn't mind, though. I couldn't remember ever having laughed so hard, stumbling across the finish line in next-to-last place, spending almost as much time falling to the ground as I did hopping forward.

There was a scavenger hunt, too. Emily helped me with that. We scattered with the other children into the bushes to find pine cones, moose maple leaves, seagull feathers, four-leaf clovers, heart-shaped rocks, and reindeer lichen. We found most of the items on the list, winning a little brown bag of candy that kept Emily busy for the rest of the afternoon.

Finally, it came time for the hundred-yard dash.

Charlie, Arnie, and Doug lined up with the others. I left Emily on our blanket in the shade — she had her sketchbook and candies and seemed perfectly content — and gathered with the other spectators alongside the course. When the pistol sounded, the crowd erupted in cheers. This was the last event of the day. The rivalry between Charlie and Doug was well known, at least among the younger crowd, and it was the race everyone had been waiting for.

Doug took an early lead, but Arnie and Charlie were right on his heels.

'Go, Charlie!' I yelled. 'Run! Faster!'

Charlie pumped his arms, his face a picture of focus and determination. He passed Arnie within a few steps and was quickly gaining on Doug. It was going to be close, and for a moment, I doubted Charlie — doubted that he could make up the distance between them. Seconds became minutes, but with each step that Charlie landed, he moved closer and closer to Doug. The hundred-yard dash is not a long race. It's over in a few heartbeats, but it seemed to me to last an eternity. By a toe, by half a foot length, Charlie crossed the finish line first. The trophy would be his, just like he said.

But Doug thought that he had won. He raised his hands into the air, dancing around the finish line while Charlie and Arnie recovered their breath. Charlie wasn't about to stand for it. It was a fault of his, I suppose. Instead of waiting for someone else to fill him in, Charlie stepped in front of Doug and tapped him on the chest.

'I beat you,' he said, still winded, panting. 'I won.'

Doug dropped his hands, squared himself to my brother, stood toe to toe, eye to eye, and leaned toward him. '*I* won.'

The crowd grew silent. I could see Charlie's jaw working, his fists clench.

'Come on, Doug,' said Arnie. 'Charlie won. Fair and square.'

'That's bull.' Doug still kept his eyes level with Charlie's. He didn't look at Arnie or at the faces of the hushed crowd. I could feel the tension building. 'You don't even belong here.' He spat on the ground. 'You and your retarded sisters.'

156

Doug never saw the fist coming, but he felt it. It knocked him right to the ground. Arnie was quick to grab Charlie's arms and hold him back so he couldn't take another swing, and by the time Doug had scrambled to his feet and wiped the blood from his nose, someone had grabbed him, too.

The starter stepped between them. 'That's enough.' His voice was firm and authoritative. 'We'll be having none of that. Get on out of here.'

Charlie struggled against Arnie's grip, but not for long. Then he turned and walked away from all of us.

That night, Emily and I climbed into *Sweet Pea* and pushed off from the wharf. It was still and calm, and I only had to pull on the oars a few times to maneuver us out into the channel between Silver Islet and Burnt Island where we floated, drifting on the inky surface of the Lake. The moon, nearly full, was climbing the sky, and it provided us with all the light we needed. I could hear the music. I knew there was dancing. I knew Charlie and Arnie would be there. All the young people were. Except Emily and me. I convinced myself that we weren't old enough to go anyway. Next year, Charlie would bring us. Next year we would go to the dance. We lay in the bottom of the boat, wrapped in our picnic blanket, hands clasped over our ears, while fireworks burst against the indigo backdrop of night.

When we sailed back to Porphyry the next day, the trophy did not come with us.

31

Elizabeth

The summer continued hot and dry. Sometimes, when the heat became unbearable, we swam. Superior holds the cold of winter deep, deep in her dark depths and refuses to let go, and that year was no exception. The blue waves that lapped at the shore were tempting, and we occasionally stripped to our undergarments and slipped into the water's grasp, the chill quickly reaching the center of our bones, leaving us shivering and aching and sated. Emily never swam. Even on days like that, she would only wade to her ankles before retreating to the shade of a tree to watch Charlie and I gasping at the cold, splashing each other and laughing.

On other days Charlie took us out on the Lake, where the breeze tempered the blazing sun. It was on such a day, hot and dry, that Charlie, Emily, and I boarded *Sweet Pea* with a canning jar of cold sweet tea to drink and a half dozen biscuits wrapped in a towel and headed around Porphyry Point, past Dreadnaught Island and down Magnet Channel between Edward Island and the Black Bay Peninsula. The wind was light, but strong enough to fill our sail and send a trail of ripples out from the stern. The sea rolled, large, lumpy waves that heaved across the still surface and tumbled little *Sweet Pea* about like a cork. We could only come this way on clear days; the hands on Charlie's compass would spin wildly about as we neared Magnet Island, and we knew how the place got its name. We decided to take our picnic into Pringle Bay, to sit on the beach and dabble our toes in the water.

I brought a book with me and lay in the shade, quickly traveling far from the shores of the Lake to distant lands with a man named Gulliver, devouring the fascinating creatures imagined to life on the pages. Emily had brought along a sketchbook that Peter sent back for her, and she had her pencils, rendering the beach peas onto the pages. Charlie headed off to explore, slingshot in hand.

I must have dozed off, with visions of Lilliputians scurrying over my legs as I lay in the sand, restrained by imagined threads, drifting between Swift's land and my own in a dreamy world populated by scurrying black ants and the waking dreams of afternoon naps.

'Well, well, good afternoon, young ladies. What a surprise this is! Out in the middle of nowhere, no less.'

I startled awake, quickly glancing about me, as was habit, for the whereabouts of my sister. She sat as she had when we arrived, capturing every detail of the beach pea's purple flowers and curling tendrils, and the slender pods that were just beginning to form. She had not appeared to notice the man and woman who were walking toward us along the beach. I knew better.

I jumped to my feet, smoothing out my light cotton skirt and squinting up at the young man, whose voice sounded foreign, as though he had stepped right out of the pages of my book. He stood well over six feet but was slender, with long arms and long fingers and closely set hazel eyes. He was shaven, except for the dark hint of a beard that suggested his razor hadn't been used that day. His cotton pants were slightly stained at the knees, his shirtsleeves rolled up; a wide-brimmed hat sat on his head, and a satchel was slung over his shoulder.

A few paces behind him walked a woman so slight that I would have thought she was a girl except for the way she carried herself. She was picking her way along the beach, her face flushed from the heat and sun, her nose and cheeks liberally patterned with freckles, her hair pulled back and tucked beneath a wide-brimmed hat, not unlike her companion's. She wore trousers, rolled up at the ankle and cinched in at the waist with a piece of rope. She was no taller than I, with inquisitive green eyes and delicate hands.

The man stretched out one long limb, offering his hand in greeting. 'I'm Alfred.'

I shook his hand.

'This is my wife, Millie.'

'Elizabeth. That's my sister, Emily. She doesn't talk so much,' I added, hoping to avoid the awkwardness that often followed someone meeting Emily. 'My brother Charlie is around somewhere.'

I gazed toward the woods, thinking Charlie might hear our conversation and emerge. I wasn't frightened, not at all, but the appearance of these two strangers on an otherwise isolated island far out on Lake Superior had unsettled me, especially since I'd just emerged from the dreamland of *Gulliver's Travels*.

Alfred turned and was examining *Sweet Pea*. 'Did you sail here?'

Sometimes adults ask the oddest questions of children. I bit back a sarcastic reply that we had actually flown the vessel there, harnessed to a flock of cormorants. Of course, he was simply making conversation, thinking, as he must, that he had traveled to the far edges of civilization, beyond the reach of children appearing on deserted shores of remote islands in a little wooden boat. So instead I replied, 'Charlie is a very good sailor.'

'Have you come far?'

'Not so far. Porphyry Point Light Station.'

'Ah, yes, around the other side of Edward Island,' Millie said. I saw her looking intently at Emily.

Alfred circled *Sweet Pea*. 'She's a pretty little thing, isn't she?'

I nodded. 'We use her at the light to ferry provisions on and off the supply boat. And to go fishing. Pa bought a motor that can be mounted on the back, and the mast can be stepped when it's not needed. But Charlie prefers to sail her.'

I watched Millie watching Emily as Alfred inspected the 'pretty little thing.'

I remembered my manners then, and made the appropriate inquiries in return, keeping one eye on Emily.

'Do you have a boat here?'

Alfred removed a handkerchief from his

pocket and wiped his brow and neck. 'Just a little canoe, a wood and canvas thing. It serves its purpose. Millie and I have to provide the propulsion. No sails or motors. Just us and our paddles.'

Somehow Alfred didn't strike me as the boating type. He didn't look like he would be terribly comfortable or confident out on the wide stretches of a lake the size of Superior, especially given as it was to squalls and fog and summer storms that kicked up waves taller even than he was. And while canoes occasionally stopped at the light, they were usually paddled by someone who appeared to have more experience.

'Awfully big lake for a canoe.'

Emily had moved on from the beach peas, her colored pencils and sketchbook sitting on a rock while she crawled through the sand, following a black beetle. The insect scurried over pebbles, then flicked its legs, digging itself into the beach until it disappeared beneath the hot sand. Emily watched where it had gone, waiting.

Millie watched Emily.

'Quite. Yes.' Alfred stood looking at *Sweet Pea*. 'Oh! Yes, right! We came out on a tug, from Port Arthur. The *James Whalen*, I believe she was called. Strapped the canoe to her deck. Dropped us off two weeks ago, and they'll be back in another two. We're just using the canoe to explore the island.'

Emily's sketchbook had caught Millie's attention. Before I could call out a warning, she stooped down to pick it up. Emily's hand shot

162

out and snatched it, clutching it to her chest.

'Please, Mrs . . . ' I was at a loss for words. We were not in the habit of calling adults by their first names, as young people do these days, but I did not know Millie's last name. 'Mrs. Millie, Emily . . . my sister, she's a little . . . ' I didn't want to call her odd, although most folks thought her so. I didn't want to call her different. She was. 'She's special. She doesn't take kindly to — '

Millie reached down and touched Emily on the shoulder.

Emily screamed. She flung her arms wide, knocking the woman to the ground. I ran to Emily. Alfred ran to his wife.

Charlie appeared then, clambering over the rocky outcrop at the far end of the bay and sprinting along the beach. 'What the hell?'

Millie rejected her husband's attempts to help her to her feet. 'I had no right. No right at all. I apologize. My fault. My fault completely.'

Her hat had come off, releasing her hair from its confines, and it tumbled in red-gold waves around her shoulders. I had never seen such hair, the color of the evening sky. Emily noticed, too. She pulled from my grasp and walked toward Millie, taking a lock between her fingers, twisting it.

'Emily!' Charlie's voice was as firm as his stride.

'No, please.' Millie's words belied the tension in her body. 'It's quite all right. Let her be.'

Emily let the coiled hair drop and moved her fingers to the freckles on Millie's face, her gray eyes wide and inquisitive as she traced a pattern from spot to spot. She took Millie's hand, pushing up the sleeve of her top and rubbing her fingers up and down her arm.

'Really, now!' Alfred had moved a step closer to his wife.

'Alfred.' Millie's tone stopped her husband.

Emily continued to explore, gently, until her scrutiny came to rest on the green eyes. Millie held her gaze. It was very unlike Emily to seek out and hold the eyes of someone, anyone, other than me.

I realized I had been holding my breath when Emily turned away from Millie, and I released it with a sigh.

She sat down on a rock and held out her sketchbook. Millie sat beside her and took the book into her hands. She examined each page, each image, at length before continuing on to the next. Charlie, Alfred, and I were outsiders, watching the two of them. Emily, of course, said nothing. Neither did Millie. She just studied the pictures, page after page. When she reached the last one, she closed the cover and looked at Emily.

'Extraordinary.' She turned to her husband, her eyes shining. 'Quite simply extraordinary. The detail is remarkable. Alfred, she has a *Listera borealis* and a *Polygonum viviparum*. There are plant species in here that are native flora of arctic terrain, never recorded in these parts. But this' — she opened the book again, flipping through the pages until she stopped at a drawing of a plant I am quite familiar with

164

— 'this is the most extraordinary.'

We called it devil's club. It was large, growing as tall or taller than me. Its leaves resembled those of the maple, and it produced bright red berries that Mother told us we must never, ever eat. But the most distinctive feature of the plant was that it was covered, from stem to leaves, with long, sharp spines.

Millie turned toward Charlie and me. 'Has she traveled elsewhere? West, perhaps? Or to the far north?'

'No, ma'am,' Charlie replied. 'She's barely left the island.'

Millie stood up. 'You must take us there, show us the plants, where she found them.'

She moved as though she were ready to leave right then, to set off in little *Sweet Pea* or trudge straight through the woods. I had never really examined Emily's drawings before. Never paid them much attention other than to note that they were lovely and detailed and full of color. But something had ignited Millie.

It was Charlie who spoke up. 'What's listeri boreali?'

'*Listera borealis*,' Millie replied, her excitement palpable. 'It's an orchid. A lovely delicate green flower shaped like a little tongue, very rare. Oh, it's not nearly as showy as the Cypripedium family, with flowers that look like delicate little moccasins. I've been searching for this particular species for some time now. But the *Oplopanax horridus*, the devil's club, is it nearby?'

Over cups of tea at their sparse campsite, we learned that Alfred had studied botany in

165

England, specializing in peat and wetlands. Millie was a student at the University of British Columbia, working on her thesis about orchids. She had studied under the eminent naturalist John Davidson, and had spent time as a field assistant in the ancient forests of the west coast, where devil's club was common.

'We met a little over a year ago,' said Alfred. 'At the university.'

'He was giving a presentation about sphagnum moss,' added Millie as she handed us a tin of biscuits. 'Orchids are one of a few species that flourish in the low acidity of mires, so we quickly found something in common.'

They married only a month before their research set them on the shores of Lake Superior, with a speculative list of orchid species rumored to be on the islands of the north shore and their cobbled-together collection of camping gear.

After we shared tea on the beach, they relocated their campsite to Edward Island near the old mines, where it was closer for them to paddle their green canvas canoe to the boat harbor or around the point to the light to join Emily and me on excursions. Charlie, committed as he was to the light and chores, observed our budding relationship somewhat grudgingly as we led the couple from bog to fen, Emily in the lead, and I acting as intermediary and interpreter.

We showed them the patches of devil's club. It was a plant Mother had turned to many times, carefully avoiding the dangerous stems to dig up the shallow roots, which she used to make tinctures and poultices. I failed to appreciate their fascination with it, but it pleased Millie, so it pleased me.

That summer was dry, but still the mosquitoes tormented us as we mucked about in the wetlands. Millie wore netting that hung from the brim of her hat, keeping her delicate face free from bites, but Emily was particularly bothered by the insects and often refused to venture into the bogs in spite of Millie's pleading. On those days we sat on the beach where the breezes off the Lake chased away the pests. Millie always found something to look at, hauling out her field notes and guidebooks and writing observations in her journal. She was incredibly patient with Emily, but I still always felt that I needed to be there, a protective shadow, one part of a whole.

Millie fascinated me, with her burnished golden hair and tenacious passion for science. She was young and beautiful, but she was also smart. And she wore men's pants. She was not like any woman I had ever met. We filled the silence around Emily with conversations about books, and she promised to send me copies of her favorite novels when she returned to Toronto in the fall. She laughed often, and when she did, it was as refreshing as a summer rain.

They spent some time visiting at the light. While Millie and Emily sat together with sketches and notebooks, Alfred and my father lit their pipes, settled into wooden chairs in the shadow of the beacon, and debated politics, the rising tension in Europe, the drought on the prairies, and the economic depression that had left young, capable, and eager men unable to feed their families.

Alfred was a conservationist, long before it was common to be one. He was critical of the popular approach to wildlife management, which, to his dismay, tended toward the routine elimination of animals considered to be vermin. Animals like wolves, he argued, played a vital role at all levels in what he called natural society, and indiscriminate culling would disrupt a balance necessary for the preservation of even the most humanized and valued of wildlife.

Pa disagreed. It was not the way of woods, he argued, but the way of scientists, far from the shores and forests and creatures, far from reality. He argued that wolves had devastated the caribou population and, without control, would lead to their disappearance from the forests of the Great Lakes. But I noticed, even as he argued, a twinkle in his eye. He enjoyed this debate. And I don't imagine that Alfred, when he and Millie set off in search of elusive orchids, had anticipated finding such insightful and lively scientific deliberations from a lighthouse keeper on a remote island. I sat silently at my father's feet, listening and learning.

My mother did not stop and sit with us. She didn't like Millie's pants and wild hair, or the way she entered into conversation with her husband and Pa, often disagreeing with one or the other. She scoffed when the young woman praised Emily's talent, when she suggested that she had a future with her sketches and paintings.

I knew Mother had little tolerance for idle hands and idle minds. Emily had not learned to cook or skin rabbits, to clean or mend clothes, to knit socks or chop wood. Emily did not have the skills Mother saw as necessary for a future.

A red fox made Porphyry home that year, likely having wandered over on the ice the previous spring, her belly already swelling with a litter of kits. Emily and I spotted her many times over May and June, prowling around the perimeter of our yard, her teats long and black, her eyes sharp and darting, ears pricked as she hunted food for her young.

Eventually Emily came across her den, a well-concealed entrance behind a pile of rocks, and brought me there to show me. We spent several lazy midsummer days watching the fox's offspring, four of them, tussle with each other in a little clearing within safe distance of their burrow. Emily could approach them, moving slowly, clicking her tongue and lulling them with her gray eyes into calm curiosity, so that they touched their sharp black noses to her fingertips.

Millie could spend hours as we did, simply watching the antics of the growing kits, marveling when they wandered close enough to tug on Emily's skirt. My mother was always busy, washing or mending or weeding. And while she was quite capable, I never saw her read for pleasure. Never saw her stop to consider the shape of the clouds scudding across the sky or pick a bouquet of wildflowers. I wanted to have Millie's untamed red hair. I wanted to wear pants that made it easy to crawl through the woods. I wanted to engage in deep, meaningful conversations. I wanted to laugh often and freely.

The *James Whalen* returned on schedule to collect Alfred and Millie, who loaded up their green canoe, securing it to the deck for the journey across Thunder Bay to Port Arthur, and stashed their tent and crates below. They took with them samples of plants, in little bags painstakingly marked with dates and locations and the names of genus and species and family.

We did not see Millie and Alfred again on the island. We kept in touch, an intermittent correspondence connecting the wilds of northern Ontario, the academic institutions of British Columbia, and the battle-weary towns of England. But when I needed them, when I had to fight for Emily like I had never fought before, they were there.

32

Elizabeth

Peter did not come out to the island that year, not once. He had plans to become a doctor, a dream the meager salary of a lightkeeper could not provide for. But my brother was determined. At the height of the Great Depression, he was able to secure a job in a government-sponsored work camp, earning a meager wage along with room and board, enough to keep him out of the soup lines and still have a few coins left over to tuck away. I was proud of him; I admired his dreams to go to school and how hard he worked toward achieving them. He was much older than I, and so I regarded him with a measure of awe. He was handsome, tall, and dark, with the heart of a poet, a little mysterious and very smart. Charlie, on the other hand, was fair-haired, like Pa. He was more at home with the water and the wind, full of noise and chatting conversation and always spoiling for a fight. My brothers were as different as ravens and gulls, and I loved them both dearly.

Mr. Niemi had been kind enough to let out a room to Peter when the government program ended. Perhaps, Charlie hinted to us as he prepared to return to Port Arthur at the end of summer, it was because of their daughter, Maijlis, who was just a year younger than Peter.

Maijlis was plump and blond, with round blue eyes, and could gut a fish as fast as any of the men. But she stayed back from their fishing camp that year, taking a job in the kitchen of the Hoito in the basement of the Finnish Labour Temple, where she served hot home-cooked meals to members of the Finnish community and brewed pots of strong black coffee in the evening for Peter to drink while he studied by the light of an oil lamp.

By late summer, there was only one fox kit left. I named it Heathcliff, only to discover later that she was female. She was big and dark and sinewy, beginning to outgrow the clumsiness of youth, but still not yet an adult. Emily was like another of her littermates, and she bounded along at her heels with teenage exuberance or curled up in the shade of a tree while Emily drew and I read. I like to think Heathcliff's mother and siblings left the island swimming nose to tail across Walker's Channel, relocating to the much larger foraging grounds of Edward Island. I like to think that, but I know they began to disappear right after our chickens did, when Pa walked off in the early morning with his shotgun.

Labor Day crept up on us, the hours of sunlight slowly shrinking, the air becoming cooler because of it, bringing some reprieve to the oppressive heat. For the cottagers at Silver Islet who escaped city life to enjoy weekends and holidays in their summer homes in the old mining community, it marked the end of the season. It was an opportunity for one last adventure, one last thrilling boat ride across the cold green water of the Lake, one last afternoon playing hide-and-seek in the woods and lying on the warm black beach while the seagulls rode the breeze overhead. They spilled onto the shores of Porphyry with their baskets full of ham sandwiches and potato salad, carrying woolen blankets to spread on the ground.

With Charlie already back in Port Arthur, it was just Emily and I who greeted their boats as they floated into the harbor, catching their ropes and fastening them to the cleats on the sagging wooden dock. The adults set to work building a fire on the shore, heating up water for coffee as the children scattered into the woods and across the short trail to the east shore of the island. There were two boys in the group that I hadn't met before, Everett and his brother Jake, cousins of Arnie Richardson, visiting from Toronto. They were new to us, and unlike the others, who made the trip out to the island many times over the years, they were new to Emily, and Emily to them. Emily did not look at them — but then, she did not look at anyone. She followed along some distance behind the rest of us, part of the group and yet not, Heathcliff having disappeared into the cover of trees and shrubs before the animated crew arrived.

We sat on the beach, sifting through the sand and black pebbles for beach glass, broken shards that had been polished by the waves and lay like glittering jewels, waiting to be discovered and plucked from their transient home.

'What's wrong with your sister?' the boy named Everett asked. He picked up a flat stone,

173

tossing it into the water so that it skipped across the surface, six, seven, eight times, and then smugly turned to look at me as though his accomplishment should garner my devotion. Emily was sitting off from the rest of us, looking out at the waves, out at Dreadnaught Island and the ship beyond that was steaming toward the middle of the Lake.

'There's nothing wrong with her. She's just shy, that's all,' I replied. It was all the explanation I wanted to give. All that was needed. I picked up a stone, too, and with a flick of my wrist, sent it jumping across the Lake eight, nine, ten times. It was probably the wrong thing to do.

Everett turned away from me and declared to the group he was bored. 'This place is stupid.'

Arnie had been out to the island many times. He knew the secrets the island held. And he knew how to intrigue a boy from the city. 'I dare you to walk through the cemetery,' he said.

Everett took another rock and threw it into the water. It didn't skip once. 'I walk through cemeteries all the time. There's cemeteries all over the place in Toronto.'

'Yeah, but this is an Indian cemetery — right, Elizabeth?' Arnie looked at me, eyes twinkling. 'Her ma's ancestors have known about this place forever. It's haunted. It's old, older than Silver Islet even, from before white man even came here. Only the greatest warriors are buried there. They say it's sacred, an opening between the world of the living' — he paused, lowering his voice so that we all had to lean in closer to hear his next words — 'and the world of the *dead*.'

174

This was the first I had heard of the tale, but I didn't dare contradict Arnie's account. Our Indian culture was not something we celebrated, and I knew very little about my mother's family.

Our youthful imaginations were fertile soil. Arnie continued to sow the story.

'The warriors drift between the two worlds, their faces and bodies streaked with red and black and yellow war paint. They dress in bearskins, still dripping blood, draping them over their shoulders like living capes, and they wear giant headdresses made from the feathers of mystical black ravens, spirits of the underworld. Their screams, eerie bloody screams, call out into the night, a warning to the living or a battle cry to the dead.' Arnie paused, our rapt attention feeding into the fabric of his tale. 'They wait to paddle the newly deceased to the underworld in birch bark canoes, possessed canoes, haunted . . . If you go there during a full moon, you can see the ghosts through the trees.' His voice grew quieter yet, and he glanced over his shoulder. We all did the same, checking, I suppose, for the telltale flash of a bear hide or the glimpse of a raven feather. 'But if the ghosts see you' — Arnie paused again, looking at each and every one of us — 'they will snatch you and drag you to the underworld with them. And you can never, ever . . . ever escape.'

Emily and I had taken Millie there, to show her the patch of devil's club that grew thick and tall in the open spaces between the trees. And sometimes Mother would send us to harvest the plant's roots. To me, it was a quiet place,

175

peaceful and reverent. I did not think of it as a haunting ground for spirits. I did not think of my ancestors. We did not dwell on our heritage, for we had never experienced the prejudice that could have accompanied Mother's blood.

Until that day.

'A baby could do it,' Everett pronounced.

That was all that was needed for the dare to be taken. The adventure was to happen at dusk, after the evening meal, just as the light began to sweep the Lake but before the boats set off for their moonlit ride back to Silver Islet. Everyone would take a turn, walking the breadth of the cemetery, risking capture by warrior apparitions and a fate of certain misery, wallowing for all eternity as a living being in the land of the dead.

As the sun eased into the west, we crept off, away from the crackling campfire and the conversations of the adults, our path lit by a convenient moon that conspired to heighten the mood. Emily did not come with us. She'd left some time before, silently disappearing. It was her way.

We were full of bravado — giggling from the girls and cheeky talk from the boys. There were no paths to the cemetery. I led the way between the trees and through shrubs until we came to the site and stopped. I'd begun to have reservations, to hesitate. I was not the only one. The giggling had ceased. The boys, silent. And then Everett stepped forward.

'You're all a bunch of goddamn sissies,' he declared, and headed into the trees. 'I'll see you

176

on the other side.' The dimness cloaked him as he walked into the bush.

The call of a vixen is haunting. It is the sound of a child, caught between a cry and a bark and a scream. It is also the sound of an undead Indian warrior, reaching from the grave to snatch children into the land of the damned. I knew it was Heathcliff right away, but still the hairs on the back of my neck stood on end as the sound ran up and down my spine. It is possible we became even more still and silent, not a breath raising our chests as tense seconds passed. The darkness had completely swallowed Everett.

'Is it the ghost?' Jake whispered, trembling. We did not answer.

'Shall we go after Everett?' It was Arnie. Though he knew that the story he told held not a single morsel of truth, still he stood, immobile as the rest of us, gazing out across the ancient resting place of the people who walked this land and paddled the great Lake hundreds of years before the night we stood on its edges while the voice of Heathcliff rose into the air.

I saw Emily before I heard Everett. She was moving through the trees, her white dress luminescent in the moonlight, her black hair flowing loose over her shoulders. She was walking away from us, toward the sound of Heathcliff, and before I had a chance to call out, Everett began to shriek. His scream was laced with terror, and I knew that he had seen her, too, his vision clouded by tales of dead Indian warriors and obscured by the tricks of shadow and light. He was running through the woods, crashing and stumbling about in the semi-darkness, reckless in his panic.

Arnie called out to him, 'Everett, over here! We're over here!'

'Oh my god! Oh my god!' came his desperate reply. 'Help me! Someone help me!'

I called to Emily, walking toward her, carefully picking my way over fallen logs and around the patches of devil's club. She did not look at me but continued toward the sound of Heathcliff's cries. Moonlight glowed blue, revealing Everett darting away from her, glancing over his shoulder as he went, and I watched him stumble and fall, landing in the prickly grasp of devil's club, where he floundered, his focus no longer on the specter moving toward him as the thorns grabbed at his flesh. Emily stooped down, pursed her lips, and clicked her tongue as she did to call the fox, and Heathcliff emerged from the shadows, slinking past the boy to her side. She turned and looked at Everett, her gray eyes piercing, with an intensity I had never seen before.

Arnie and the others reached Everett and helped him to his feet. His face was scratched, and tiny welts covered his arms and hands where the spiky stems had punctured them. The front of his pants were stained, wet. He shook off the arms that supported him, wiping at his face with the back of his hand, and turned to walk away. I wish he had kept walking, that the others had just followed, but after only a few steps, he stopped and spun around, glaring at Emily, at the fox cowering at her feet.

'You're a goddamn Indian witch,' he said, his voice hoarse, almost a whisper. 'I'll get you for this.'

And he did. Oh, how he did.

33

Elizabeth

The days became shorter as winter approached. The cottagers did not return to the island after their Labor Day excursion, but Heathcliff visited frequently. Emily and I concealed pieces of venison or bits of pork rind beneath our skirts and delivered them to a large flat rock beside the woodshed. She grew full, her coat shiny and her tail lush, and our simple offerings became unnecessary but welcome additions to her diet of mice and birds. Pa ignored her for Emily's sake, and I loved him all the more for it. Even Mother took to setting aside bits of kitchen scrap in an old dented pot and giving it to Emily to bring outside after dinner. There were no more chickens to tempt the fox; our few remaining hens had stopped laying and had found their way into the soup pot. But I feared for her fate when the seasons changed and the coop was again alive with feathered clucking.

I needn't have worried.

I will always remember that winter for two reasons. One was the wreck of the *Hartnell* in November. The other was the death of Heathcliff.

It was Heathcliff who alerted us to the disaster that was playing out on the icy, wind-tossed waters of the shipping channel between Isle

Royale and Porphyry.

I was asleep in the bed that Emily and I shared. The light was running, its barely discernible rhythmic hum a steady, unregistered backdrop to the angry conversations of wind and waves as an early winter storm worked its way across the Lake. I woke with a start. Something had stirred me, reaching into my dreams. I gazed about me, shadows settling into shape and substance in the darkness. And then I heard the bark of a fox.

Instinctively I reached for Emily, my hand sweeping across empty bedding, feeling only a residue of warmth.

Heathcliff called again, and I knew Emily had gone to her.

Mother and Pa were asleep. It was rare that they both slept at once, especially when the weather was foul. They usually took turns throughout the night, checking the light, monitoring the fuel, measuring the wind, and chronicling it all in the logbook. I can only assume that exhaustion had overcome them. But the light was blinking, and I could see nothing amiss. I slipped into my boots and pulled on a jacket, the noise of the storm drowning the sound of the door banging against the wall of the house in the wind. I pulled it shut behind me, and looked at the sweeping ribbons of light shining out across the dark water. The beam danced against wind-driven snowflakes, creating a sparkling curtain around the island.

A sloppy layer of snow covered the ground. It was enough to brighten the darkness, and I could make out the path that led down to the point. The rocks were rough, black, and porous and I picked my way carefully. The wind whipped up a tempest on the Lake, and the waves crashed spectacularly onto shore, a frigid shower that mixed with the falling snow.

Emily was standing on the point, looking out across the heaving black sea. Heathcliff was far back from the reach of the waves, pacing along the ridge above the beach, her ears flat, pausing intermittently to call out her warning.

I was weary of my sister's wanderings, self-absorbed behavior that left me chasing about on nights such as this, risking health and limb to drag her back to the warmth of our home and the safety of our bed. It was the first time I can remember ever being angry with Emily.

'Emily!'

My voice was caught by the wind and drowned in the water that hung in the sky, sleet chased by the gale.

'Emily!'

She turned when I called, looked at me, and then turned back to the Lake, lifting one arm, pointing out into the blackness. The light's beam swept pathetically against the wall of mottled darkness, and I caught a faint glimpse of a boat, listing dangerously, being carried by the waves toward the black volcanic rock of Porphyry Point. Its engine was silent, the crew likely struggling to control the vessel, if they hadn't already abandoned ship.

I left Emily, a white figure, standing on the black rock beneath the beacon. Within minutes

I'd called for Pa, and he'd launched *Sweet Pea*, the little outboard motor roaring to life as he nosed out into the heaving swell. Mother stoked the fire and set pots of water to boil.

The wait was interminable. Emily refused to come inside, so I joined her on the point, where we stood wrapped in woolen blankets, watching the disjointed images as the drama unfolded, dramatically illuminated by the light. The *Hartnell* was a cargo vessel, likely making her last voyage of the season from Duluth, and how she had blown so far off course I could only speculate. Had she been seeking shelter, running from the fierce winds and pounding waves of a classic November gale, hoping to tuck in around Isle Royale and the shelter of McCargo Cove? Perhaps. If she had, something had gone wrong, terribly wrong, and the revealing eye of the light showed her drifting aimlessly, pushed by the wind and waves, until she grounded solidly, her metal hull buckling as she came to rest in the shallow waters of Porphyry Shoal.

I heard shouts in the darkness and the sound of the outboard motor. Emily and I, lanterns in hand, met *Sweet Pea* onshore. There were five men crowded into our little boat, wet and shivering, their faces pale and eyes darkly ringed with shock and fear.

'Take them to your mother. Get them warm.'

Pa remained in the stern of *Sweet Pea*, the beaching waves lifting the boat and tumbling it around, drenching him with each pass.

'There are still three missing, including a woman.'

183

My heart clenched. It was not unusual for the wife and sometimes the children of a boat's owner or captain to travel aboard. I lost sight of Pa long before the sound of the motor was swallowed.

Mother had the men strip, wrapped them in warm wool, and steeped strong black coffee. They sat in shocked silence, their teeth continuing to chatter long after their skin pinked and the hot drink was consumed.

Once the men had been tended to, Mother turned her attention to Emily and me. We had changed into dry clothes and sat with our hands stretched toward the warmth of the fire. But still Emily shivered. Mother took Emily's face in her hand, her thumb lingering for a moment on the pale cheek until the gray eyes looked up at her and held her own for a very brief moment. Then she sat down and brushed Emily's hair until it shone like a raven's feathers.

The story unfolded, pieced together by the men as they found their voices. The *Hartnell* had lost her engines two miles off Passage Island, a little before twenty-two hundred hours. Monstrous waves broke over the deck, tearing at the hatch covers and flooding the engine room. She was rigged with a mizzenmast, and they hoisted the sail, altering course to tuck in behind Isle Royale, where they could wait out the storm and then head in to Port Arthur for repairs. But the waves became too much and they lost steering around midnight, left to the mercy of the wind, which set them straight onto the rocks off Dreadnaught Island. They launched the lifeboat,

184

and were beginning the process of abandoning ship. The first mate was aboard the raft to assist as the captain's wife clambered in. Just as they did, a massive wave descended, tearing the boat from the side of the ship and sending their three passengers into the dark grasp of Superior.

I knew enough of the Lake to comprehend their fate. Once someone was in her icy clutch, Superior was not inclined to let go. I could tell by the faces of the men perched on chairs in our humble dwelling, huddled beneath blankets, that they knew the same.

Pa was gone for what felt like hours. The wind continued to howl, easing up slightly only as the sun appeared, its diffuse glow futilely attempting to shed light and warmth on the snow-covered island. He appeared at the door in the early hours of the morning, and wordlessly shook his head.

The men stayed with us for three days. Pa was able to get word to the Coast Guard, and the *James Whalen* came out to collect them. A salvage boat arrived shortly after that, and the *Hartnell* was hauled off the rocks and towed to the shipyards in Port Arthur, her hull battered and beaten and twisted.

Emily spent those three days walking the shore. Bits and pieces of the *Hartnell*'s cargo washed up on the beaches — wooden crates, tins, buoys, and pieces of torn fabric. Heathcliff was never far away, from dawn until dusk, her faithful companion as she paced a pilgrimage, occasionally stopping to turn over a piece of flotsam, searching. I couldn't understand her obsession, but there was much about Emily I could not understand.

We found her on the fourth day, sitting next to the woman's body.

Pa stopped when he saw them — Emily so small and fragile, crouched beside the dead woman — and called to me. Emily had removed her red woolen scarf and draped it over the body. One end trailed in the water and moved with the waves, like a living thing, and all I could think about, all either my father or I could think about, was getting Emily away from that cold, bloated form. 'Get her the hell outta here, Lizzie. Dammit, take her home.'

I did as I was told, but not before I noticed that none of it made sense. The woman had come ashore on the east side of the island; she lay on the beach beyond where the Lake could have placed her. She should not have come ashore there, not with the direction the wind had been blowing for days. And Emily, dear little Emily, could not have carried nor even dragged the corpse and positioned it as it was. I realized that someone had moved the body. Someone had brought it where they knew it would be found. Someone who knew the wind and waves. Someone who knew that the lightkeeper's daughter had been wandering the shore, searching. Someone who was able to hide his presence from all of us. Except Emily.

And I knew who it was.

As Emily and I walked away, I looked around me, searching the trees for a glimpse of his dark beard and deerskin coat. Was he watching us even now? I shivered and pulled Emily closer to me.

34

Morgan

I have the journals spread out around me on the bed, following along as Elizabeth speaks. Her memories echo on these pages.

'It was Grayson, wasn't it?' A few of the pieces are coming together. 'The assistant lightkeeper who went missing.'

'Yes,' she replies. 'I didn't know it then. At the time, I thought he was . . . I'm not sure who I thought he was.'

'What happened to Heathcliff?'

'Ah yes. She stopped coming some time in February. I assumed she had moved on, crossed to another island on a causeway of ice in search of a mate. Emily did not appear concerned. It was the way of nature, and while we both enjoyed our time with the fox, she was still very much a wild animal. Sadly, however, that was not the case.

'I accompanied my father to town that winter. We traveled to Port Arthur by dogsled from Silver Islet across frozen Thunder Bay, the looming Giant slumbering beneath a blanket of snow. It was an exciting excursion. While we were there, we stopped in at Sewchuck's Brokerage, a storefront on Cumberland Street that served the needs of trappers who exchanged pelts in trade for traps and tools and shot. While we were there, a man came in with a bundle of fur and stood in the shadows while Pa completed his business. He was wearing a deer-hide coat and fur cap but had his back to me. I thought I recognized him, but couldn't think from where. He felt my gaze and turned, looking down at me. His face was hideously scarred, the marks barely obscured by a full black beard, and I stepped closer to Pa. I had seen him before. Only once, but I had seen him, hidden among the trees on a cold winter day, a lone wolf, cast off from his pack.

'At the top of his pile of pelts was that of a fox, darker than most, rich and full. My hand reached out to touch it. I knew without a doubt that it was Heathcliff. Perhaps she had wandered inadvertently into a trap, set to catch lynx or marten, complacent in her tameness. Perhaps. The man's eyes met mine, briefly, and when he looked away, disappearing into the shadows, I saw in them shame and sorrow. I never forgot those eyes, dark, haunted. And I never told Emily.'

I say nothing for a few minutes. I can tell she's lost in thought. She's putting pieces of a puzzle together as much as she's remembering.

'But that wasn't what you were looking for in here — to find out who that man was? That's not why your brother went out to Porphyry on his sailboat to get the journals?'

'No. Charlie never knew about him. No one did. Aside from Emily and me. And, eventually, your grandfather.'

'Right, so what does all this have to do with

my grandfather?' As much as I find Miss Livingstone's story fascinating, there's no connection to the man whose violin and collection of Emily's pictures started it all. It has nothing to do with me.

'It is all important, Morgan, but it is not simple or even easy.' Miss Livingstone hasn't moved from her chair. 'Your grandfather played a small but vital role much later in this drama.'

My mouth is dry. A raging hangover is simmering, and I can feel the rye in my throat. I have no idea what time it is. The room is getting brighter, so the sun must be up. The door isn't quite closed, and sounds drift in from the hallway; the routine of life goes on, the shuffling of footsteps, doors closing, voices talking. Marty whistling far, far away. I can smell coffee and food cooking. I think of Laurie, wonder if she's noticed by now that I'm not in my bed.

'I should call someone and let them know where I am.'

'They've been called,' she says, then adds, 'hours ago.'

I only feel guilty for a moment.

I get up and help myself to a glass of water. The old lady says nothing. I can tell that she's waiting for me, that she follows my movements and knows what I'm doing. She seems to sense that I'm eager to hear the rest of her story, to find out more about my grandfather, and how he knew Emily. I brush my dark hair back off my face and pull it over one shoulder, working it into a thick braid.

I walk back to the bed, flipping through the

190

scattered journals. I stack them up in order, with the first years at the bottom, the ones I read aloud, and the newer ones on the top. There is only one more book.

'Where are the rest of your father's journals?' I ask. 'These only go to 1943. What happened to the others?'

'There are no others,' she replies, folding her hands in her lap. 'There could not have been. If there were, your grandfather would not have been a part of this story. He would not have come to the island. He would not have met Emily. He would not have killed Grayson, the man I called the lone wolf.' She pauses for a moment, then adds, 'He would not have been needed.'

I climb back onto the bed and wrap the afghan around my shoulders, flipping through the pages of the last journal. 'Why?'

35

Elizabeth

Peter and Maijlis married in June of 1939. It was a small wedding, a simple ceremony, quickly organized, at Immanuel Lutheran Church on Pearl Street. Pa wore a suit and tie. He pulled at that tie throughout the day and removed it as soon as the pastor and his wife left the reception. Mother and Mrs. Niemi made platters of sandwiches and fried fish cakes and strawberry tarts for the guests who gathered in the church hall after the midmorning ceremony. Maijlis looked beautiful and carried a bouquet of lilacs, tied with a piece of blue ribbon.

We couldn't afford new dresses, but Mother made sure that we were scrubbed clean and our clothes were mended and pressed. She braided our hair that morning, twisting the long black coils around our heads so that we looked like princesses. She wore purple, and seeing her without an apron around her waist, I could picture what she might have been like when she and Pa were married. She gave me strict instructions to keep an eye on my sister, to make sure that Emily didn't cause a commotion or wander off into the streets of town. She didn't need to tell me.

Peter wore his uniform. With no money for medical school, he had enlisted in the army and had just completed his training. A young girl of fourteen, I thought the wedding so very romantic, steeped as I was at that time in the novels of Jane Austen. But Mother, I suspect, did not share the sentiment. She was proud, so proud, but she was giving up her son, to Maijlis and to the army. I can remember her straightening his tie for the photographs, her hand lingering on his lapel as she stared up into his dark eyes, and I wasn't sure whether she was sad or happy. Peter, I could tell, had never been happier. He leaned down and kissed the top of her head then rushed off to join Maijlis on the steps of the church for pictures. It was a moment of tenderness so rare and poignant, it has stayed with me always.

Peter and Maijlis moved to Winnipeg, where my brother served with the Winnipeg Grenadiers. That September, Canada declared war, and by the following May, Peter's unit was sent to Jamaica for garrison duty, and Maijlis moved back to the little blue house on Hill Street.

Charlie found work at Port Arthur Shipbuilding. The company had been idle during the long, hard years of the depression, but the war that carried with it death and destruction ironically breathed life into the industry when they secured contracts to build warships for the Royal Canadian Navy. He boarded at a roominghouse in Current River and only made it out to the island a few times that summer.

The war was on everyone's mind; it filled conversations around the dinner table, on the docks, and in the streets. Young men were recruited and trained and dispatched across the sea, full of idealistic righteousness, the kisses of their sweethearts warm on their lips and their mothers' love knitted into woolen socks.

I had a letter from Millie. She wrote that they would be leaving soon for England, if they hadn't already departed by the time her note reached our Island. Alfred's father was unwell, so in spite of rations and restrictions, and the uncertainties of German bombs, they felt it best to leave their work in Canada and return to his home. She was preparing to publish a paper, she wrote, about the orchids of the boreal forest and wondered, might she include some of Emily's sketches that she had taken with her? She sent her love to all, paper and pencils for Emily, and books for me.

Peter wrote to us frequently, his letters sometimes delivered five or six at a time. My replies to him filled pages and pages: I wrote of routine happenings at the light, of Emily's latest creatures, of the story lines of the newest book I was reading. I sealed them up and sent them off on *The Red Fox* to a war that seemed so very, very far away, across vast lakes and an even vaster ocean, but also touched so very, very close to home.

Peter came home briefly in the fall of 1941, but we did not get to see him. He shipped out again a few weeks later, and I began to take more interest in Pa's newspapers, which continued to arrive with regularity. We read them aloud in the evenings. They carried stories of the politics of war, of battles won and battles lost and the number killed and wounded.

The spring of 1942 marked the beginning of what I think of as the year of three deaths.

The first was my own.

The season started early, with the shipping channels open and the light operating by the beginning of April. Pa took great satisfaction at being able to set the light shining and the mirrors spinning before any other keeper had even been able to reach his station. The freighters that had hibernated in Thunder Bay harbor nudged their way out onto the Lake in the wake of the icebreaker and set off, their holds brimming with cargo, for the locks at Sault Ste. Marie and Welland, and Pa was there to mark the first leg of their journey.

Spring was the season to collect gull eggs, which we boiled or used in baking, a delicious alternative before our own hens could provide us with a steady supply. Emily and I headed to the seagull rookery on Hardscrabble Island to gather them, my sister for the first time trusting my boating skills to transport us safely over the black waters of the Lake. We pushed *Sweet Pea* out in early morning, not bothering to step her mast, but instead each taking one of the oars and working together to cover the expanse to the steep cliff face on the south shore. We could see down Walker's Channel, past the Devil's Thumb, a sacred rock formation Mother called Shamanitou, which stood at the entrance. I've heard it is no longer there, the Lake having pried it loose with frozen fingers a few years after we left the island. Behind it, I could see *The Red Fox* in the distance and could tell by her position that she was heading for the Channel and would likely stop at Porphyry.

We rowed to the cobbled causeway that connected the two parts of the island and would provide enough shelter to pull *Sweet Pea* up out of reach of the waves. I secured the painter to a tree as an added precaution, as it was not unusual for the wind to stir up a swell with little warning. Emily and I took our baskets and worked our way through the dense shrub toward the top of the cliff.

Our presence had the expected response. Gulls rose to the air, filling the sky with discordant squawking and the shrill screams of panicked birds. They circled above our heads, swooping down frighteningly close, attempting to chase us away from the nests where their brown speckled eggs lay, exposed and vulnerable. Emily shrank from their assault, crouching, hands over her head, her eyes clenched tight. The noise and flurry were too much for her. I should have known that.

I pressed forward, leaving Emily beneath the trees, selecting one egg from each nest that had two, just as Mother had taught me. They would lay again, she said, just like the hens. I placed them in my basket gently, ignoring the flash of white wings near my face and the spinning turmoil in the sky above me until my basket was full. I knew Emily would not fill hers.

'Go back to the boat!' I told her. Her basket lay on the ground beside her, and I picked it up. 'I'll meet you there.'

196

In minutes I had filled Emily's basket. I gathered both in my arms and set off, cautiously picking my way to the shore below.

Emily was not at *Sweet Pea*. The boat was still moored tightly to the tree trunk, so I placed the baskets in the bottom and sat down to wait. Coils of mist began to float along the far shore of Edward Island. It was a gentle fog, not the thick impenetrable screen for which the Lake is so infamously known. But it was enough for me to consider our short row back with more urgency. I needed to find Emily.

I began to push my way along the shore, thinking that she would have put some distance between herself and the screaming birds. In places, the vegetation grew right down to the water's edge, and I had to blaze a path around, scratching my arms and legs on the prickly branches of wild roses and raspberries. As I rounded the north side, the ground gave way to a low knoll, relatively clear of trees. I had never come this way before.

Wisps of fog had climbed the hill as well, drifting like a stream around the island and settling in the shallow vales and along the shores. I gazed out across the Lake. From here, I could see Porphyry, beginning to float in and out from behind the gauzy curtain, although the light tower itself rose clear above the low-lying cloud. I looked around for Emily.

Instead, I found a cross — a simple wooden marker, its gray surface weathered. I knew without question I had stumbled upon a grave. The romantic in me was intrigued. Whose body

197

lay beneath the pile of lichen-stained stones? Who had been so carefully laid in eternal sleep with a view of Lake Superior, in all her magnificence and many moods, spread out before them? Misty tendrils of fog wound in and out of the trees. I was terrifyingly captivated, hopelessly drawn toward the cross.

The bleached planks had each been carved, but the wind and rain and sun and snow had done their work, and I had to bend down to make out the markings. I ran my fingers across them. They read quite simply, 'Elizabeth Livingstone, May 16, 1925–November 29, 1926.'

It is a strange feeling to stand facing one's own grave. A Dickensian moment, when I think of it now, like poor Scrooge confronting his future in the company of a ghost. I knelt beside the cross, beside the small mound that contained beneath it the body of an infant, born on the birthday Emily and I shared, bearing my name. The gulls screamed. The Lake whispered. I felt painfully, achingly empty.

Yet again, the fog tapped me on my shoulder. I could not afford to linger.

I vowed to return, to ask questions, demand answers, but the events unfolding even as I knelt before the lost grave came to overshadow the mystery of my death. I was left to exist as a ghost.

I returned to the boat to find Emily there, sitting on a rock as though she had been waiting the whole time. We pushed *Sweet Pea* into the water and crept along the shore, keeping land in sight to avoid being turned around in the fog. We crossed Walker's Channel and worked our way south toward the light. Pa had started the horn, and the sound bounced eerily against the invisible cliffs of Hardscrabble. The gulls, too, could be heard squabbling among themselves, calling out as they flew unseen above our heads. Emily and I rowed, the silence suffocating when it was not broken by the intermittent sound of the horn.

When we arrived, we found Mother sitting in Pa's chair. She had a letter in her hand. It was from Maijlis. The Winnipeg Grenadiers had been stationed in Hong Kong, she wrote, and on the same morning as the bombing of Pearl Harbor, the Empire of Japan had also attacked the British colony. Fighting was bitter and lasted several weeks before the Commonwealth forces surrendered. Peter was missing, possibly captured, known to be wounded. Presumed dead.

Mother didn't move all day. She didn't get up to make dinner, to sweep the floor, to add wood to the fire. I remembered how she looked at Peter the day of his wedding, straightening his tie, brushing off his uniform. She was so proud of him. I wondered if she realized then that she was saying good-bye.

I boiled eggs for supper and served them with thickly sliced bread, but neither Emily nor I were able to eat much of anything. When it grew dark, I slipped out alone, sat on the mist-shrouded point, and allowed my tears to spill onto the damp stones. I wept until my body ached, until exhaustion began to eclipse the anger and hate, until Emily came and led me to bed, tucking her small body against my back, wrapping her arms through mine, and we grieved as one.

Pa didn't come back into the house all night. The foghorn ran for twenty-four hours, calling out across the Lake in a haunting, mournful voice.

Charlie visited the island that week. He had enlisted. My mother begged him not to go. He was still a child. She couldn't risk losing another son, she said.

I shared Mother's feelings. I wanted to add my pleas, to convince Charlie that he needed to stay. But I understood why he wanted — no, *needed* — to go. He managed to arrange a ride back to Port Arthur on a fishing tug that had stopped in at Walker's Channel. We all stood on the headland, watching the boat rise and fall on the choppy waves, white spray surging off the bow as it rounded the point and then headed west toward the foot of the Sleeping Giant.

Emily and I stood close together, our hands clasped.

'He'll come back.' My voice conveyed a confidence I did not feel. 'You'll see, Emily. Charlie will come back to us.'

When we could no longer see the tug, Pa climbed the stairs to the lamp and sat there without saying a word.

War and death can silence the strongest of men.

36

Morgan

She's quiet. I know she's thinking about her brothers. It must be especially painful not knowing what happened to Charlie. In an odd way, she received the same message about both of them, decades apart; missing and presumed dead.

'Did you find out what happened to Peter?'

'Peter was confirmed dead that fall. His body is buried in a military cemetery in Hong Kong. His ID tag was delivered to Maijlis, along with a letter from the commander of Peter's unit. He conveyed the deepest sympathy of the Ministry of National Defense and gratitude for the sacrifice Peter made for his country and for freedom.'

'But Charlie came back.' It's a stupid thing to say. I know he came back; he's the reason we're sitting here with these old books. He came back, but now he's lost again.

'Yes, Charlie came back, as you know, years later. But not the Charlie who left. Not the Charlie that took us out sailing in *Sweet Pea* or happily read stories to Emily when it was hard to tell if she was even listening. That Charlie died, somewhere far across the ocean, with a gun in his hands and his heart full of hatred and revenge.'

'You said there were three deaths?' I almost don't want to ask.

'Yes. Yes, there was one more.'

37

Elizabeth

It was before the opening of shipping season, late in March of the following year. The Lake was free of ice past Porphyry Point, and we had had several days of warm winds from the south. Our radio was able to pick up the signal from Michigan, and we gathered around to listen to a concert from Carnegie Hall and an episode of *Fibber McGee and Molly*. A fire roared in the stove, and for a brief moment, using precious battery power sparingly, we connected with the outside world. We listened and laughed. We heard the news, and after that the weather report. Pa never paid much heed to forecasts. He was much better at predicting the weather, having spent years watching the sky and the waves and tracking the wind direction. A barometer hung on the wall next to the chart of the Lake, and the pressure was marked in his logbooks every day, even in winter. He knew the storm was coming, and he didn't need the announcers on the radio to tell him it would be a vast and vicious one.

Overnight, the sky grew heavy. The dark clouds that usually hovered over the open water at the center of the Lake began to build, sending gusts of wind to rattle the shutters and set the trees hissing. We filled up the woodbin and kerosene lamps and brought in buckets of snow to melt for water, settling in to wait out the storm. The winds increased steadily, pushing massive mountains of water that rolled and tumbled and crashed against the rocky point, sending a horrendous shower that reached as far as the light tower and our little home beneath.

The storm raged for days, building layer upon layer of water that froze like icing on a wedding cake and dripped enormous icicles that hung from the lighthouse gallery and roof. Our stove struggled, gasping for air as the water froze and smothered the chimney, until we could no longer get it to draw. We huddled around the smoky fire, the room dark, and the wind howling as waves collided against the obstinate land and cast themselves over us. In the end, Pa had no choice; we were being entombed by the Lake in our own home. With an ax he loosened the frozen grasp on one window, chopping through the pane and sheath of ice to the outside world. By then the storm was fading, replaced by clear blue skies that only made our ice-encased island seem more unearthly, an enchanted land of wizards and witches.

Pa climbed to the roof, ax in hand, to free the chimney while Mother watched from below. In all the years he had prevailed over the Lake, finding his way through blinding fog, charting safe passage around lurking rocks and hidden shoals, and weathering wind and waves, in the end it was the Lake herself that reached ashore and took the lightkeeper. He slid on the frozen water that clung to our home and died instantly when he hit the ground.

I can see him still. Emily and I stood at the broken window, the world outside glazed white and calm, seagulls wheeling overhead in the cobalt sky, the sun shining, and Pa crumpled, crooked, broken, a stain of red seeping across the ice.

★　★　★

I am not growing weary. I am finding the telling of it makes me stronger. These words that spill out of me and shape the story, that lead to us both being here, now, in this room, have been waiting for their life. It frees me and lightens me to share them. What an odd couple of conspirators we make, this girl and I.

'What did you do?' she asks, filling the pause in my narration.

'The only thing we could do,' I reply. 'We survived.'

★　★　★

The ground, solid as it was, prevented any sort of burial. Mother dragged Pa's body to the fuel house, and we covered him with a wool blanket. For days we chipped away at our tomb, aided by the warming spring sun, until the doors opened and the sunshine reached through the windows. We polished the light's great lens and filled the reservoir with kerosene. We oiled the wheels and replaced the belts that were cracked and waited for the arrival of the *James Whalen*. When the boat came, Mother wrapped Pa's body in one of *Sweet Pea*'s tattered sails. They took him and buried him in the cemetery in Port Arthur. We did not go. We did not see Pa's bones laid to rest. There was a light to keep. I would have buried him on Hardscrabble Island next to the grave marked Elizabeth. I would have kept him closer to me, closer to the island and the Lake that he loved. But Mother did not think of those things.

People deal with loss and death in so many different ways. I did not see Mother grieve, not in the traditional sense. I don't believe it was something she would allow herself, having little tolerance for idleness and self-pity. Perhaps Pa's death coming so soon after Peter's was simply too much for her. In an effort to provide, to care for her family, to bring back a semblance of normalcy and cope with the harsh reality we faced, she confused hardness and strength. At a time when we needed each other more than ever, she became increasingly distant and pragmatic. And I missed Pa's gentle nature and tenderness more than ever.

My mourning was done in private. When I could find a moment, I climbed up into the rafters, out of her sight, and sat amongst Pa's newspapers, flipping through them until my fingers were black from the ink, letting my tears spill. Mother began to lose patience with Emily and all her oddities. Her words — *You should have let her die. Emily will never be right* — weighed heavily on me. It had been my father who was always quick to defend, to encourage his wife to accept my twin as she was. He didn't

206

understand her, not like I did, but he loved her. And now he was gone. Emily needed me more than ever.

It was 1943. Canada was still very much at war. Young, capable men were fighting in the trenches of Europe. And while the conflict conspired to steal my family, at that point, it worked to serve our need. Mother had for years been listed as assistant keeper, first with the Department of Marine and Fisheries, and now with the recently formed Department of Transport, and with few proficient men available to fill the position of head keeper, she assumed the role by default. It suited her well. It had been her vision to have the mantle pass from father to son. We would do it, she said, for Charlie. We would light the beacon and carry the fuel and paint the buildings until he returned home to us, stepping again onto the shore of the island and assuming his rightful role as lighthouse keeper at Porphyry Point Light Station.

Her promotion left vacant the assistant's position. I was eighteen, barely old enough, but still, I applied. I highlighted my experience growing up on Porphyry, my knowledge of the Lake, my familiarity with the great Fresnel lens. I explained my expertise starting up the diaphone foghorn and glossed over my abilities as a sailor. I never heard from the Department of Transport. They chose instead to award the position to a veteran, a young man whose only qualification was the debt Canada owed for his time in service and the German bullet embedded in his hip.

We had never needed an assistant keeper's

dwelling before, but sharing our rooms beneath the light would not be acceptable. The department was required to provide accommodations, and before the new assistant arrived, the bush was cleared back of the main building and a simple two-room home constructed.

Your grandfather stepped onto Porphyry Island at the beginning of June, and Emily and I went to meet him.

He stumbled off the *James Whalen*'s tender with a fiddle clutched beneath his arm, his skin pale and his hands soft, his mouth tinged green from the residue of motion sickness which had plagued him on the crossing from Port Arthur. He wore gray flannel dress pants with a white shirt and tie, still tightly fastened about his neck, and a fedora perched on his head. And he had a cane. He leaned on it heavily as he clambered across the rocky shore to where his gear had been unloaded.

'Well, hello there, you must be Elizabeth and Emily,' he said, with just a faint trace of Scottish accent, hooking the cane over his left arm to free up his right hand to shake ours. 'David Fletcher. It's a pleasure to meet you.'

I looked at that cane and up into his gaunt face and dark, nervous eyes. I did not see a man who had fought horrific battles, who had been gunned down in the heat of combat while his friends died around him, who had then resumed his fight, to live, to walk again, while the war that almost claimed him continued to rage. I saw what I wanted to see. A young man, crippled, defeated, vulnerable. He was out of his element,

208

incapable of meeting the physical demands of the job and the mental stress of a life of isolation and hardship. This is whom the department had chosen over me. I resented him with every fiber of my being. I resented his newly constructed dwelling, which changed the landscape of our island home and disrupted the life Pa had so carefully constructed. He was weak. And he was an intruder.

I didn't take his hand. Without a word, I grabbed his bags and headed toward the light.

'Here, allow me,' he said, hobbling along behind, attempting to relieve me of the load.

I ignored him, silently mocking his obvious inability to complete even such a simple task as he struggled with his cane and violin case on the uneven ground, and continued at a brisk pace. He turned to Emily, who had fallen in step beside me. She had gathered a posy of flowers and walked looking down at them, not at her feet nor ahead at the trail. When I think of it now, what a pair the two of us must have made, Emily being Emily, and me tangled up in righteous anger and misplaced resentment, storming through the woods.

'Lovely flowers, those,' he said. 'What are they?'

Emily did not respond. She did not look at him. It was not a choice for her as it was for me.

'Right then. Deaf and dumb, are we? Shall we walk on, then?' His voice was colored with annoyance.

I did not pause then to respond, but I could feel the flush start at the back of my neck and trace its way up past my ears. I dropped his bags in front of the new dwelling and turned to look at him. 'This'll be where you stay,' I said, and then added, my voice low so that Emily could not hear, 'Don't you ever mock her again. Ever.'

We heard his violin for the first time that night. The Lake was still, muttering softly along the shore, the trees quiet. Emily and I lay together in bed, the window open so the spring air washed across our faces, the music mingling with the songs of the chorus frogs. It was beautiful, achingly beautiful. It made me think all the more of Pa and Peter and Charlie. I was determined not to let his songs soften me, to melt the resentment and anger that had settled on my soul. I tried, but somehow his playing touched a place inside me, and I let my tears fall freely. I would not let him see. I would not let him know. But Emily knew. She wiped my face with her sleeve, and then took my hand, leading me out into the moonlight, and we sat, staring at the yellow square of his window until it went black and the frogs were left to sing the refrain unaccompanied.

★   ★   ★

There is little hierarchy between keeper and assistant. In practice, the one does not have superiority over the other, and while some keepers lord it over their helpers, that was not the case at Porphyry. The work was shared equally, your grandfather learning quickly, always ready to step up to the task at hand in

210

spite of the limitations placed by the piece of lead lodged in his hip.

Mother was much more accommodating than I. She showed him how the light worked, how we wound the clockworks and oiled the cogs and where we recorded the fuel levels and the wind direction and names of ships that had passed within view of the light. When Mr. Niemi took him fishing on their tug, and returned him to shore horribly green, my mother brought him tea and had me complete his tasks at the light until his world stopped bobbing up and down and he'd been able to wash the odor of fish guts and vomit from his clothing. She accepted him on the island, encouraged him even, when we had for so long kept the outside world apart, and this puzzled me. For a time. She and I were just as capable of running the light station without anyone, let alone a man crippled and soft, to help. Perhaps she saw Peter in him, thought of him wounded imprisoned in a foreign land, dying with unfamiliar stars overhead. Besides, she said, the island was no place for the weak. By this I knew she meant Emily, and it infuriated me. Her plans for Charlie did not include her daughters; daughters whose pencil drawings of bumblebees and pennycress did little to keep the light burning, the horn sounding, and food on the table. I wondered then if my application to the Department of Transport had even passed from her hands to the crew of *The Red Fox*.

I, however, made it clear that David was not welcome in our home, around our table, sitting in Pa's chair with a pipe in his hand listening to the news on the radio traveling across the expanse of the Lake from Michigan. He was not Pa. He was not Peter. And he was not Charlie. I was not susceptible to his boyish grin and playful attempts to engage me in conversation. Our relationship revolved around the operation of the light.

He learned to handle *Sweet Pea*, preferring the little outboard to the sails or oars, and ventured farther with each excursion, sometimes returning with an extra trout or partridge, knocking at our door with the offering and leaving without waiting for thanks or even an invitation to share in its cooking and eating. I grudgingly had to admit to his superior mechanical skills. He could fix anything. While I struggled with the greasy parts of a stubborn motor, he quickly disassembled, repaired, and reassembled everything from the kerosene-fueled steam engine to *Sweet Pea*'s 9.9-horse-power Johnson.

He grew stronger as the season progressed, his hair bleaching in the sun and his face becoming burnished and brown, crow's feet forming at the corners of his eyes from squinting out across the water. He never lost the limp, but within a few months the cane remained on his porch when he walked the pathways to the lighthouse or wheeled the cart from the boat harbor with provisions. Visitors to the island loved him. He chatted with the boaters about fishing and fog and the best bays to anchor in, and gave picnickers from Silver Islet tours of the light. He made occasional trips to Port Arthur on *The*

Red Fox and brought back little brown bags full of candies that he gave to Mother, intended, I'm sure, for Emily and me. Emily began to wait for his arrival, collecting her bag of sweets when the ketch docked briefly in the harbor so that he could disembark, but I never gave him the satisfaction.

Emily and I lay awake many evenings, listening to his playing. Some nights, the notes crashed as fierce and strong as the waves that chased each other, rolling and tumbling like great leviathans born on the Keweenaw Peninsula to die, splayed on the black volcanic rocks of our shore. Other nights the music was sweet, soft, and gentle like the rabbits that leaped beneath the lilac bush and dined on Mother's garden. More than once, when Mother was busy with the light, and the moon beckoned mischievously, Emily and I danced, two white gowned faeries in the shadow of a beacon, our feet keeping time to the rhythm and the rhythm keeping time to the fireflies.

I would not give him any sign of approval. My interactions with him remained minimal; only what was necessary to convey the most recent weather report or note the expected date for the next delivery of fuel.

Emily, however, was more easily charmed. Or perhaps, unlike me, she saw things for what they were. She began to slip her drawings beneath his door. Flowers, butterflies, and yes, even the image of the two dragonflies, found their way onto the assistant keeper's stoop.

He came up to me one day as I was hanging our washing on the line to dry in the fresh

August breeze. He had a picture in one hand, a detailed drawing of a raven, meticulously rendered in pencil, breathtaking in its realism.

'These pictures of Emily's are really very good.'

He startled me, appearing as he did between the tea towels and the pillowcases. I pinned another cloth to the line.

'You think I don't know that?' I snapped, though I didn't, really. They were lovely, but I did not have a frame of reference for the great art of the world. Not yet. And of course the sketches that Emily had given to Millie had been published with her research about orchids.

'No, I don't think you do. She has a remarkable talent, a gift. People would pay a lot of money for these. You could leave this island. Make a life someplace else.'

'You've got a lot of nerve.' I dropped the clothespin I was holding back into the basket and turned to face him. 'What makes you think we want to leave the island? That we want some other life? What's wrong with the one we've got?' I had thought of it sometimes, when the nights were lonely. When I missed Pa. But Emily and I were together. She had the freedom to be herself on the island, and I wouldn't allow myself to consider anything else. 'You don't know me. You don't know Emily.'

'I know she adores you, Lizzie.'

I bristled. He had not earned the right to call me Lizzie.

'Elizabeth,' I responded tersely.

'She adores you, Elizabeth. She would follow

214

you anywhere. She will be happy anywhere you are. She lives for you.'

He had it wrong. I lived for her. I protected her.

'She's safe here.' I said. 'People don't understand her in the city. They won't let her be. It's too noisy and too crowded, and she wouldn't be free to make her drawings. It would kill her.'

'And what about you, Lizzie, what do you want?'

This time I didn't correct him. I just picked up my basket and walked back to the house.

A few weeks later, the bears came.

We had been careful with our refuse, burning what we could and burying table scraps and vegetable peelings in the garden. We cleaned our fish on the beach, tossing the waste to the ever-present gulls that fought over bits of guts and attempted to fly off with oversize pieces of skin. But sometimes it wasn't enough.

Emily was sitting on a wooden deck chair, facing out toward the Lake, the woods behind her. Mother had gone to town on *The Red Fox* and wasn't expected back until the next day, so David and I were sharing duties at the light. A passing freighter had captured Emily's attention, her umber hull sitting low in the water as she headed southwest, cargo holds full, trailing a plume of gray smoke from two white stacks.

I was hauling water to the henhouse. We had ended up with a rooster in the mix this year, and Mother decided to allow one of the hens to hatch a clutch. The little yellow chicks peeped and darted between my feet as I entered their

215

confines. The rooster had since made his way into a stew. I stooped to collect the brown eggs in my apron while the hens complained.

He ambled across the grass between the assistant keeper's house and the light. He did not notice Emily at first, still and silent as she was, but wandered erratically in the clumsy appealing manner of the young, pausing to sample the pansies growing in a garden near the step. I knew he was a yearling; he lacked the size of a full-grown adult, but was much too large to have been born the previous winter. From where I stood, I could smell the pungent odor of his fur, dank and sour, and see the sharp claws on his oversize paws. He had inadvertently positioned himself between my sister and me.

Emily felt his presence, turning, and the animal startled. I had hoped he would run into the woods. He didn't. He reared, sniffing at the air, looking back and forth between Emily and me.

'Emily.' I spoke calmly and clearly. 'Don't move.'

The bear dropped to all fours, swinging his head back and forth, grunting and chuffing. Emily looked at me. I did not read fear in her eyes, but I sensed it from the bear. He was trapped, and trapped bears were unpredictable. I moved slowly, stepping sideways, one hand grasping my apron full of eggs, the other waving above my head as I tried to bring his attention back to me. He reared again, and then lunged toward Emily, pulling up at the last second, circling around, facing her again.

216

The shot whistled past my head, clattering into the metal pail that hung beside the coop, knocking it noisily to the ground. The volley echoed, a sharp crack, disappearing over the Lake, and the bear bolted into the bush.

I turned toward David.

'What the hell!' I hollered. 'Can't you shoot a goddamn gun?'

From where I stood, his aim had been off a good two feet, clipping the tools hanging on the shed instead of finding its mark in the head of the bear.

David looked at me. His eyes, usually soft and slightly amused, were instead dark and brooding. With his gun still in hand, he turned and walked past me, heading toward the woods without saying a word.

Emily came over to me. I was shaking, a combination of anger and relief trembling through my body. She looked at me, defending him with her eyes, admonishing me in silence.

'Don't look at me like that, Emily!' I replied. 'You could have been hurt, or even killed.' I did not trust my sister's mysterious connection with wild animals to extend as far as calming a panicked black bear, even if it was young and small.

Emily bent down to the ground. She opened her delicate hand, splaying her fingers wide, but still they couldn't fill the imprint in the soft soil beneath. These were not the imprints of the yearling. The sow that made them must have been standing only six feet away from me. She would have been twice the size of her cub.

He had been faced with an impossible choice, Emily or me. Instead, he had aimed with precision, startling both bears into flight with the tumbling, clanging collision of metal pail against the ground.

He returned a few hours later, going directly to his cottage without a word. There was no music that night, no dancing in the moonlight. And each time I rose to take my turn at the light, he was there, sitting on the step of the assistant keeper's house, his gun across his lap.

It was on nights like those, when death loitered in all her mysterious forms, that I thought of the baby, only eighteen months old, lying beneath the mound of cobblestones on Hardscrabble Island. I did not think of her often, but that night, I did.

★ ★ ★

'Did he kill them?' Morgan asks.

'No. Mr. Niemi told us he saw them swimming across Walker's Channel a few days later. Only then did your grandfather let down his guard. And at that, only some. He became very protective, which both thrilled and annoyed me, checking on us frequently, watching for Emily and I to arrive back in *Sweet Pea* when we took the boat around to other islands to fish or pick berries or set snares. I was surprised when in early December he boarded *The Red Fox* for Port Arthur.'

'You didn't go? You still stayed on the island through the winter?'

'We had no place *to* go. If we had, I don't know that Mother would have. And we managed, although it was so much quieter, without Pa reading the newspaper to us in the evenings, his deep voice singing along to the radio and his hearty laugh rolling around the room. He left a void in my life bigger than the Lake herself. I cut down a tree at Christmas and decorated it with yarn bows and popcorn garlands. We baked honey-sweetened bread and listened to concerts broadcast on the radio. When the ice froze in late February, we snowshoed to Silver Islet to collect supplies brought out for us by the Richardsons. I saw Arnie then. We had not seen much of each other in the years since the cemetery. He was going to school in Kingston, studying to be a lawyer. We stopped in for a mug of cocoa at his place, but it was an awkward visit, our stilted conversation lacking the familiar comfort we had grown used to as children.'

'And you never found out who was buried on Hardscrabble?'

'No. Pa was gone, Charlie was away at war. And I could get nothing from Mother. I asked her about it, working up the nerve one stormy winter night when the wind was howling like a pack of wolves and we were tucked up snug with our knitting. She simply replied, 'Some graves are better left unmarked.''

'It's what you hoped to find in your father's journals.'

I had hoped, I suppose. I know there is a child, a child with my name and my birth date, dead

219

and buried. It is not me, as much as at times I feel like an apparition floating through life at Emily's side. We were like one. Elizabeth and Emily. Emily and Elizabeth. The presence of that wooden cross and pile of stones cannot change that. It is only now, when my side grows cold, when I am trying to learn how to be just Elizabeth, that she once again haunts me.

'It matters little now,' I reply.

'Doesn't it?' the girl asks. The yearning again. She tries to sound indifferent, but it is in her voice. 'Don't you think that when you know your past, it can make a difference to your present? And your future, too?'

She is no longer speaking of me. 'Your grandfather did have a hard time staying away.'

38

Elizabeth

I was out on snowshoes on a clear day in early March, checking snares. Our supply of meat was diminished, and I set rope traps along well-traveled caribou paths around the island. There was warmth in the sun, but the air was desperately cold, so that I stopped frequently, swinging my arms to warm my fingers. The islands in the distance, Trowbridge and Pie, as well as the Sleeping Giant, were mounds of indigo, sitting on the horizon across the mottled blue-and-white expanse of the Lake.

At first I thought it was a moose, a black silhouette between Porphyry and the islands off Silver Islet. But the motion was wrong. Moose had begun to move into the area as the caribou dwindled, and would take advantage of the bridges winter builds between islands, crossing them to new foraging grounds. But this black figure did not have their loping, long-legged gait. I returned to the light, pointing out the approaching image to Mother. She grunted, and put on the kettle. I climbed the tower, and from this vantage point watched. As time passed, I could make out the shape of a man on snowshoes towing a toboggan. By the time the sun disappeared as a fiery orange ball over Thunder Bay, your grandfather was unbuckling his snowshoes at Porphyry.

Mother lit the fire in the assistant keeper's house. I did not notice the smoke trailing from its chimney as I whiled away the afternoon in the lighthouse. But the chill was gone from the main room, and a pot of bean soup was bubbling on the stove. She had known.

David brought with him a peace offering for me — books. I had read and reread the volumes on our shelves so many times I could recite portions of them by heart. It was difficult to suppress my gratitude. But I did. I took them and casually placed them on the ledge beside Pa's desk, masking my excitement with polite thanks. I wasn't about to give him the satisfaction of knowing that I would burn precious kerosene in the lamp for the next few nights devouring every sweet, magical word.

He also brought Emily a gift; little cakes of watercolor paint, a selection of horsehair brushes, and paper. He patiently showed them to her, mixing the pigments together to create new hues that he washed and layered across the page. And then he stood back and watched the enchantment as Emily took the brush into her own hand and her paper came alive, singing and dancing with color. These were her first real paintings.

For that I was grateful. I told him so as he left the warmth of our sitting room and headed out across the darkness to his own quarters, where his stove crackled defiantly against the cold night. He stopped and stood beneath the sky, alive with flickering green aurora borealis, and he told me again, 'She's really very good.'

'I know.'

And I turned back into our cottage and shut the door, leaving him standing in the black night.

It was too cold for him to play the fiddle on those evenings. I imagine he could do little more in his drafty wood-framed building than huddle beneath blankets with his feet tucked right up against the grate and the fire blazing, radiating heat only a short distance from the flame. But he began to play on the evenings he spent with us, and as the days passed, there were more and more of them. He played for Emily. And when his foot started stamping as his bow danced on the strings, Emily clapped in time to the rhythm. I couldn't help but smile. David couldn't help but notice.

And I wondered if he really played for me.

★   ★   ★

June is when the Lake is cold but the air has captured the heat of the sun. More than any other, June is the month that breeds fog. I was completing the daily ritual of polishing. Each night, the light blinked white, illuminating the darkness that stretched wide in every direction. And while the intent was to inform passing ships of our location, it also inadvertently served to attract a host of winged insects, some as large as my hand, and set them fluttering against the hypnotic lure of its panes. Emily found inspiration in the forms — some still clinging to

223

the glass, others expired in clusters on the ledges and planks of the gallery. She climbed with me, pencil and paper to my wash bucket and rag, and sat and drew while I wiped. From my vantage, I could see across to Isle Royale, a low-lying gray headland beneath darker gray clouds, and to the west, a steamer passing Thunder Cape, her course bearing out beyond Black Bay toward the downbound shipping channel. I noted her position, intending to monitor progress and mark the name and time of passage in our logbook when she reached the point.

I checked again some forty or so minutes later and could not see the ship. I could see the gray Lake, flat and dull, lazily pulling at the rocks off the point, and far in the distance, the mesa on Pie Island. Between, water merged gray and indistinct. My rag hung for a moment while the images settled. A fog bank, low and thick and dark, had formed. The ship was wrapped in the center of it.

My rag dropped and lay where it fell. I descended the tower, calling to Mother and David to let them know that the horn must be started.

The fog station at Porphyry was just steps from the dwelling and light tower. Two six-horse coal-fired steam engines ran compressors that produced the air for the signal. We only fired them up when the keeper or assistant could no longer see Passage Island or Trowbridge Lights. Our station had a distinct sound pattern — one long blast lasting two and a half seconds, repeating every minute. It was a loud whistle, deep and round, which tailed off in a distinctive grunt at the end of each descending blast. Ships knew it was us.

David and I met at the door of the building, and we quickly set to work.

Mother had slowly been shifting responsibilities of the light to me. I was no less capable than she, and the events of the past year had seen her health decline as her slight frame collapsed in on itself and walking became more difficult. Most days she shuffled about stiffly in carefully masked pain, her movements restricted but her determination unbending. She remained sharp, her hands never idle, her expectations for order, routine, and propriety undiminished, her praise and affection understated.

She appeared on the front porch, one hand raised to her forehead, shading the nonexistent sun, in an attempt to discern the approaching menace. It crawled across the water, and by the time David and I had the engine fired up and the steam pressure sustained, the bank had swallowed the outlying islands and the mysterious world of Superior in fog. She nodded her approval and disappeared back inside to note the time in the logbook.

I climbed the tower and gazed back over the Lake. I could see the freighter now. She was five miles off, steaming east in the shipping channels, only her derricks and the top of her funnel reaching above the low-lying cloud that stretched for miles and miles in every direction. It appeared as though the surface of the Lake had risen, creating new islands from the tops of others and channels where there had been none before.

As darkness approached, David took the night watch and lit the lamp, adjusting the mantles on the four burners until the flames were steady and bright, winding the gears and setting in motion the weights and pulleys that would turn the reflectors, creating the illusion of the light blinking on and off. Mother, Emily, and I sat in our home beneath the tower, listening to the familiar sounds of the light's clockworks and the intermittent calling of the horn.

I woke just after midnight to silence. The gears above me continued to turn, but I could no longer hear the horn. I pulled on my clothes and headed outside, expecting to be greeted by starlight, expecting the moon to shine a path on the water off the point. I did not expect to still be wrapped in dense, impenetrable fog.

David was already hard at work on the diaphone. He was stripped to the waist, lying on the floor, reaching around the boiler, struggling with a flywheel. There were tools and parts scattered about around him, and I could hear him cursing at the motor beneath his breath, his accent thick and strong and uninhibited.

'How long has it been out?' I asked.

He started, banging his head against the boiler as he slid out from beneath the machine. 'Good lord, Lizzie! You scared the daylights out of me.' He wiped his forehead with an oily rag, leaving a streak of black. 'Not more than twenty minutes. The flywheel's cracked. I'm trying to reach the bolt to see if I can jerry-rig something together.'

226

And he slid back under.

I knelt down beside him, looking up at the motor. My skills, while certainly adequate, could not match his.

'It's thick out there,' he said. 'We've got no choice. We need to fire up the hand signal.'

Together we hauled out the antiquated equipment and set it up outside on the rocky shore. It was an old ship's horn, packed in a wooden case, stored and not likely used for decades. I checked the leather bellows for cracks, hoping that the brass bearings had not corroded, and then pressed the lever. It was a pitiful substitute, a peculiar resonance, whining and harsh, a sad sequel to the satisfying signal of the diaphone. But it would suffice. It would reach out a mile or more from the rocky point to say, *We are here.*

'I'll take the first watch,' I offered.

I settled on the shore next to the horn, marking the time, setting a rhythm that was regulated by the cranking of the brass handle and the sound rushing from it out into the misty night. I had to imagine the islands around me, the shoals and rocks and channels. The ships. I knew that they were out there, listening, listening. Ghosts drifting past. So I called out to them, and I too listened for them to answer.

Dawn hovered below a nonexistent horizon, and the world grew just a little bit brighter in advance of the approaching sun. As the birds around me woke and called out greetings, stretching their voices, I caught an echo of my horn.

Between sounding the horn, I tuned my

227

listening, ignoring the muttering of the Lake, the conversations of the warblers, and the frogs cavorting in the bog.

It came again, its direction indistinct but its pattern defined. Three short, three long, three short. Three short, three long, three short. The signal was unmistakable. The vessel was in distress.

I cranked the reply from our horn, two more cycles, straining to hear each time, getting a better bearing on the vessel. As soon as I completed the third blast, I ran, banging on David's door to wake him, and then did the same to rouse Mother. I was back at the horn before the minute had elapsed, and didn't miss sounding one signal.

Mother and David appeared, their approaching presence heralded by the feeble yellow glow of kerosene lamps. They stood on the rocky point gazing out at the murky wall of cloud that swallowed the light's sweeping beam, straining to catch the call from the vessel hidden in the midst of it.

'She's off course,' Mother said. 'And not far from the shoal, by the sounds of it.'

'I can head out in *Sweet Pea*,' David replied. 'See if I can help. She may have run up on the rocks.'

'Elizabeth will go, too. It'll take the both of you to find your way back.'

I knew the water around the islands better than anyone. David was a better boat handler.

Mother settled herself next to the horn. 'Best get on.'

228

David and I rushed to launch *Sweet Pea*. The water was calm, a flat, oily surface that dimly reflected the glow of the lantern. The little Johnson motor sputtered to life, and we nosed our way out onto the Lake, keeping the shore off our port side. I sat in the bow, the lantern held above my head, weakly illuminating a small world for us to move in. We could see the light and hear the steady sound of Mother on the horn, and we used this to guide us. David held a compass in his hands and continued to glance at it, even while we were in sight of land, taking bearings. We rounded the point to the east side of Porphyry, carefully avoiding the rocks that lurked below, slippery creatures barely breaking the still surface of the Lake. Dreadnaught was only a half mile offshore, a small island, not more than a large rock with a few scrubby trees clinging to it. With one last glance at the black beach on Porphyry, we adjusted our course and headed out from shore, the fog quickly dropping a screen around us.

Partway across, David cut the engine. We bobbed in the mist-shrouded dimness, our eyes straining and our ears grasping for the entreaty of the vessel in distress. I could hear Mother, sounding the horn with precision. I could hear nothing else. No other horn. No motor. And while I knew that the steam-powered turbine could propel the freighter in relative quiet, I wondered if perhaps she had really been a ghost ship. But no, Mother and David had heard her, too. David took to the oars, and we crept along, slowly, cautiously. I noticed the water change;

the swell, barely discernible, had begun to shift, and I knew that we were close to the island, the shore sending the surge back out to us.

'Dreadnaught is off our beam.' I pointed my arm toward a blank wall.

We drifted, the oars dipping, pulling, the water tapping against *Sweet Pea*'s hull, stalking the ship. There were voices — I heard them, spinning, refusing to settle in one place. They came from in front of us, behind us. They swirled like faeries. David and I followed them, first one way and then the other. The oars dipping.

I called out, my voice a signal reaching across the water like the light, like the horn, but they did not hear. When I finally heard her engines, the deep, pulsing, barely discernible reverberations that traveled through the water, climbed aboard *Sweet Pea*, and settled in the pit of my stomach, I knew she was close. Too close.

She broke through the fog less than thirty yards away, a specter, rearing like the cliffs of the Sleeping Giant, massive and gray, bearing blindly toward our little wooden boat. We were a tiny cork bobbing on the blanketed surface, far beneath her decks, invisible, and right in her path.

'David!' I screamed.

David was in the stern already, straining with the outboard. He yanked; it sputtered and failed, once, twice, before roaring to life. I cowered in the bottom of little *Sweet Pea*. The steel hull of the freighter towered over us, and as David turned out of her path, I could hear the tapping of the water as it parted for her prow.

'They think they're in the shipping lanes. They think that the signal coming from Porphyry is another ship.' David was yelling over the sound of the motor. 'We have to find some way of signaling them.'

I looked about the bottom of the boat. We had little of use — our lantern, some rope, a life preserver, a jerry can of gas, our oars. We didn't carry flares, not on *Sweet Pea*. The only portable horn was already calling out from Porphyry, where the great booming diaphone sat useless and silent.

David leaned forward to where I sat, reaching one hand out to grab my arm, the other still on the outboard. 'Are ya feelin' brave, Lizzie?'

I looked up into his face. His eyes were bright, mischievous, his hair a mess of disheveled curls. That freighter would be up on the rocks in a few minutes if we didn't do something. My heart was already racing, my senses heightened. Damn him! I nodded.

'Come here. Take the motor.'

I sidled to the stern and took hold of the throttle.

'Pull up alongside, close as you can get. Hold her steady.'

'What are you going to do?'

David knelt in the bottom of the boat and grabbed the lantern. 'Send them a message.'

We ran parallel to the ship, her great massive hull rising meters from the surface, and I worked to steady *Sweet Pea* in the wake coming off the bow. We were a mosquito, tiny and buzzing, pestering a giant.

231

'Steady . . . steady!' David leaned over the port side, and *Sweet Pea* complained, listing abruptly with the shifting of his weight. I pulled away from the ship's hull, turning too sharply and sending David tumbling against the gunwales. I barely heard the curse. 'Come on, Lizzie, you can do this. Nice and steady, now.'

I approached again, running *Sweet Pea* abeam of the freighter, close enough to be visible from the deck but far enough to be seen by the bridge.

David held the lantern in one hand and picked up the oar with the other. He trained the feeble beam toward the wheelhouse, using the oar to intermittently cover the light. Quick. Long. Flashes. Dashes, dots. Letters. Words.

'Porphyry signal out.'

Again he repeated the message. I couldn't hold it for a third, and we drifted away from the hull, only 'Porphyry' having been completed. David sat in the bottom of the boat, breathing heavily from the exertion.

'It's a shot in hell they saw that,' he panted. I cut the engine, and we watched all 250 feet of her slide past, heading toward the rocks. There was nothing more we could do.

Without warning, she altered course. A light trained down, searching the water.

'David! David, look!' The light blinked. Dashes, dots.

'I'll be damned!' David grabbed our lamp again. Dashes, dots.

She altered course again. We sat there, watching as her stern slipped behind the curtain and she disappeared, the thrum of her motors faintly audible, churning toward the great open expanse of the Lake.

We started to laugh, both of us giddy with relief, collapsing to the bottom of *Sweet Pea*.

I kissed him first. It surprised me more than it did him. He had known, for a long time, he had known.

39

Morgan

'You loved him.' I hug my knees to my chest. It's almost like she's talking about different people, when I think of her, and him. They loved each other. A lifetime away.

'Yes, I loved him,' she replies. 'I have never stopped loving him. And yet I wish it had never been so. Had I not loved him, I could have saved Emily, I could have protected her.' I think about what it would be like to have a sister, to have someone like Emily, and I can't. I think, too, about Derrick. I wonder what it is I feel for him. I wonder if it's love. I want it to be. 'Love is not blind, as they say, Morgan. Love blinds us. It is a thief.'

These seem like such harsh words. 'How can you regret love?' I ask, my voice softer even than I intended. It's the emotion of it all. It's getting to me. 'Better to have loved and lost than never to have loved at all.'

'You speak the naïveté of youth with Tennyson's words.'

I am about to ask her what she means when she interrupts me with a question of her own, one that surprises me. 'Tell me about your grandmother.'

I think back to the world he and I shared, to the happy days we spent, just the two of us. He spoke of my mother rarely, and my grandmother even less. 'I . . . she . . . I don't know. He never said much about her.'

'You don't need to protect me, Morgan. I'm not a fool. Life goes on.'

'Honestly, Miss Livingstone, all I know is that my mom and I both look like her. He said we were a lot alike. I . . . ' I don't know what to tell her. I don't even have any pictures. I have nothing but the violin and the drawings, Emily's drawings. Instead I ask her a question. 'What happened between you and him?'

40

Elizabeth

The sadness breathes out of me as a sigh. I can see David's bright eyes shining out from his sun-burnished face. I can feel the softness of his lips against mine, taste the freshly picked wild raspberries that stained our tongues. I sense his hands, coarse but gentle, tracing my hip, my waist, my breasts, as we lie naked on a bed of moss, surrounded by a guard of trees that mottle a ceiling of azure sky.

'It happened late that summer.'

★   ★   ★

When we arrived back at Porphyry, I was surprised to discover that Mother had returned to our dwelling, where she had put coffee on to boil. She was no longer operating the horn; Emily was. The fog still hung above the water, although the rising sun desperately reaching to touch the earth had tinged it orange. Emily was crouched beside the wooden case, cranking the brass handle with precision. Emily, who had never managed to complete a single chore at the light, had remained to work the signal, guiding us back to the point, guiding us back to her. She stood when your grandfather and I approached. Her face was difficult to read; it often was. She looked between the two of us, and I knew that she knew, and I was the one to lower my eyes. I felt as though I had betrayed her. But she walked to me and touched my face. It was as though she were thanking me. I could not imagine what she could be grateful for.

The fog cleared later that day when the sun was high enough to burn away the mist; the wind joined in to chase any lingering filaments across the choppy waves of the Lake. A few weeks later, *The Red Fox* brought news of the *Palisade* and her harrowing night drifting in the fog off Isle Royale. The timely actions of the lightkeepers at Porphyry Station were to be commended for saving the ship from grounding after becoming helplessly lost, surprisingly far from the shipping channel. There were whisperings of drink on the bridge, of the first mate falling asleep, but they were only whisperings.

The Red Fox also brought news of Charlie. He was stationed in Great Britain, he wrote, but would be deployed soon. He didn't say where or when. He sent his love, thanked Mother for the package she sent him at Christmas, and promised to kill plenty of Germans for all of us. I wonder if it ever occurred to him that Mother's greatest fear lay in one of those Germans claiming another of her sons.

While the war seemed so very far away, it also crept past our lonely island, sleek and gray. At first there were a few corvettes, followed by minesweepers; *Middlesex, Rockcliffe, Oshawa.* Through the binoculars we kept on the hook in the light tower, I watched them pass, saw their identification numbers painted in large, bold block letters on their hulls. They slipped into the water amid celebrations at the Port Arthur Shipbuilding yard, to be cradled by the Lake and sent out to fight distant battles in foreign seas. I sent wishes across the waves, asking them to carry with them even just a small drop of Superior, clinging to their hulls, to remind Charlie of home, to bring him back to us.

Mother spent more and more time sitting in her chair, her back bent and painful. She sent me to gather the stems of the big-leafed devil's club from the Indian cemetery, and, carefully avoiding the sharp spines that protected the healing roots, I brought them to her. She peeled the outer bark and mashed the pulpy insides to a paste and had me spread it on her back. She drank tea made from the tender shoots of poplar, and on cold nights I heated up rocks on the woodstove and wrapped them in cotton, tucking them beneath her covers to keep her warm. I urged her to go to town, to see the doctors in Port Arthur, but she stubbornly refused, just as she refused to inform the Department of Transport that her health had declined to a point where she was unable to complete her duties. Instead, she let me take on more of the responsibilities. We were biding our time until Charlie returned, which suited me fine. When he came home, we could stay on the island, Emily and I, and we would be a family again.

And then there was David.

I fooled myself into thinking that Mother didn't know. It was part of her greater plan, I expect. She said nothing, asked no questions, but noticed our love as it bloomed discreetly, tender and hesitant, like the first buds of spring on the lilac.

At first I refused to allow my feelings the freedom to grow. David was a new, unexpected contemplation that left me confused and conflicted. He was patient with me. We continued the routine of lightkeeping, our stolen kiss hovering unspoken between us while we whitewashed buildings, took delivery of kerosene, repaired the foghorn, and planted the garden. But evenings in our home grew rich again, filled with music and laughter, blooming into a happiness I had not felt since before Pa died.

David was kind and gentle with Emily, and I knew she trusted him, maybe loved him even, like she did Charlie. Like she did Pa. She told him so by slipping paintings beneath his door; it was the only language she had. There were few people Emily seemed truly comfortable around. David understood her. She accepted him. And because of that, it became harder and harder to deny the fluttering of my heart when David smiled at me, or the tingling of my skin when our hands accidentally brushed.

One morning toward the end of summer, I climbed the light tower, rag in hand, to polish the lens. It was early, the sun not yet fully above the horizon, and I took a moment to look out over the Lake, to watch the world waking up. There was a light breeze blowing, and I turned my face toward it and closed my eyes. I didn't hear him come up, but I felt him. He stood beside me, and I kept my eyes closed, feeling the wind, the chill from the Lake, the warmth of his body close to mine.

'Do you ever think of more?' he whispered quietly, as though speaking aloud would break a spell.

I thought of the island, the only home I had ever known. I thought of the chores of the light, of Mother and Charlie, of the baby Elizabeth buried on Hardscrabble Island. I thought of gardens and chickens and the changing of the seasons. But mostly, I thought of Emily.

'I hadn't,' I answered. It was the truth.

I could feel the sun now. It was reaching above the horizon, sending fingers of orange warmth to caress my cheeks. I hadn't thought of more.

I opened my eyes and turned toward him. We lived a lifetime in that moment, sharing our breath, the wind and the Lake and the sun wrapping us together so that there was nothing else, nothing else in the world except the two of us.

'Elizabeth!'

We moved apart as Mother's voice climbed the stairs and summoned me. The spell was broken, but the magic hovered still as David took the rag from my hand and started to clean the great Fresnel lens of the light.

'Coming,' I answered.

I paused before descending and turned back toward David, standing awash in the light of dawn. 'I hadn't thought of more,' I said, 'but I do now.'

Throughout summer, we continued to welcome visitors from as near as Silver Islet, as well as from Port Arthur and Fort William and occasionally, on yachts traveling the Great Lakes from as far away as Chicago. Emily did not wander often, and at that, it was never far. She tended to shun the boaters who dropped their anchors in the bay or moored at the wooden dock, and for their part, the young people who arrived with their picnic baskets for day trips avoided her. Although the night at the cemetery had faded to distant memory, there were stories about the reclusive woman who ran the light at Porphyry and her strange daughter who didn't speak, but wandered through the woods like a ghost, enchanting animals. I was comfortable that Emily kept to herself, content with her pencils and papers and paints. Perhaps that was why I felt I could let down my guard to slip away that late summer day, shrugging off the bond that clasped us so tightly together, to satisfy my reckless young heart.

We had not planned it, although we leaped at the opportunity to venture off alone. Mother was salting fish that David had brought back as payment after a day helping the Niemis lift nets. Emily was sitting in a wooden deck chair, overlooking the cobbled beach near the point. The waves were not large, but they paraded toward the shore and then disappeared, hissing, between the stones. I knew she would be absorbed for hours watching the patterns shape and reshape themselves as the water stained the dark ground and the sun battled to dry it. David and I set off in *Sweet Pea* with instructions from Mother to check the snares and bring in a basket of new potatoes from our garden plot on Edward Island. He brought along his shotgun, hoping to find partridge bathing in dusty bowls of dirt or foraging in the shrubbery.

As we headed out from the boat harbor, we could see a vessel approaching from the west, and recognized it as the Richardsons' boat. It did not surprise me in the least; I had expected the cottagers from Silver Islet to visit on the last few weekends of summer. School would be starting soon, and the leisure of holidays and excursions to the islands would come to an end as young men headed back to Queens or McGill or the University of Toronto. I watched them pull into the boat harbor as David guided *Sweet Pea* into Walker's Channel and around the point to where Pa had dug a root garden many years ago. I waved at Arnie. His cousins were with him, Everett and Jake; they often returned to visit for a few weeks before the routine of autumn settled in. I had not spoken with them for years. I had no desire to.

We grew a variety of vegetables at the point — tomatoes, beans, peas, squash — but the soil was too shallow for much else. This place was much better suited to potatoes, beets, and carrots, but its relative isolation also meant the rabbits were able to readily feast on the plants. As we beached *Sweet Pea*, we flushed a partridge, and David headed off in pursuit while I checked the snares near the garden. They were empty.

The sun beat down, surprisingly warm for the end of August. As I worked, digging the rows of potatoes, the sweat began to prick my neck and trickle between my breasts. Inspired by Millie, I had taken to wearing pants a few years back, finding them much easier to move in, but that day I longed for a flowing cotton skirt that allowed the freedom of the wind. I harvested judiciously, loosening the soil beneath each mound before reaching my hand in to select one or two potatoes from each plant, leaving the others undisturbed to continue drinking in the rainfall and drawing nutrients from the earth for a few more precious weeks. By the time my basket was full, my hands were caked with soil, my blouse was sticking to me, and my face was flushed, streaked with dirt and sweat. I gazed longingly at the blue-black water.

In the heat of the midafternoon, I gave in to its deceptive allure, stripped off my clothing, and slid into the cool embrace of the Lake.

I tried to tell myself afterward that I did not think of David. It isn't true. I did. I thought of him watching me floating on the grounded sky, my black hair fanned about my head, my skin pale against the darkness of the water. It is easier for me to say that I did not think of him. That I did not plan it. That it had not been my intent. But I did. I thought of him, and felt his eyes on me. And it is what I wanted.

When I emerged, my skin tingling and my bones aching, gasping from the cold, he was standing there, a lone partridge dangling by its feet in one hand, its wings slightly agape, and his gun resting on his shoulder. I stood shivering, water dripping from my hair and running down my back to slide into the Lake like a spring stream. He laid the gun on the grass, the hen beside it, picking up my blouse and pants and holding them out to me. I looked up into his face; his eyes were twinkling with amusement that hadn't touched his mouth, his brow furrowed in mock reproach. I reached for my clothes with one hand, the other remaining wrapped about my chest, but he drew back, beyond my reach. I did my best to scowl at him, taking a step out of the water, and he responded by stepping farther away, the grin breaking free, dancing about his cheeks. I darted toward him, snatching at my clothes, but his grip on them was firm. He dragged me to him until I was wrapped in his arms, warm with the heat of the sun against the damp water of the Lake still clinging to my skin. I shivered, not with cold, breathing in the smell of him, the tang of his sweat, the remnants of gunpowder, a hint of tobacco. My clothes dropped forgotten to the ground.

We spent the afternoon beneath the trees, the warblers and vireos serenading us, drinking water straight from the Lake, eating late-season wild raspberries, and dozing beneath the cloud-dusted canopy of blue. It was the first time I felt wholly and completely free.

We returned home at twilight. I lied to my mother, telling her that we had been unable to start the outboard motor and that David had spent most of the afternoon taking it apart and putting it back together again.

'Where's Emily?' I asked, placing the basket of potatoes on the floor and heading upstairs to prepare the light.

'I haven't seen her for many hours,' was her reply. 'But I'm sure she'll be home before the light is shining. She never stays away long now.'

'Now' was since our evenings had been filled with music. 'Now' was since David and I had left the island in *Sweet Pea* to rescue the freighter. I was not worried; it was not unlike Emily to disappear for a short time. I proceeded to trim the wicks of the lamp and set it in motion, as I had so many times before.

The partridge was plucked and fried with a little salt pork and served with the new potatoes, boiled in their skins and slippery with butter. And still Emily had not arrived. I began to feel uneasy. The moon, not yet half full, peered in and out between clouds that scudded across the night sky, providing just enough light to find my way to the assistant keeper's house. David grabbed his gun, and we began down the path that led to the boat harbor. I carried a lamp, but didn't light it, relying instead on the faint illumination from above.

My eyes strained at every shadow, my ears started at every sound, and I struggled between anger, frustration, and worry. Emily knew this island intimately. She knew every beach, every path, every fen, and most of the trees and plants within them. And while the water fascinated her, she did not go into it. It was futile to call out. She would not answer. She never did.

There were no boats anchored in the bay or tied to the dock in the harbor. Only a few orange coals glowed in the fire pit, and an empty whiskey bottle was propped against a stump. Arnie and his cousins must have left hours ago, heading back to Silver Islet, to their warm beds, before darkness descended. I could see no one about. The wind rustled through the trees, causing them to whisper and sway, and I started several times at the snapping of twigs beneath real or imagined feet. It was not like me. David opened the boathouse, and I lit the lamp and trained the yellow light into the dark corners. They were empty.

We made our way across the clearing to the short path that took us to the beach across from Dreadnaught Island. As we stepped out of the woods onto the shore, I saw her, a crumpled mound of white cotton dress, her black hair, so like mine, trailing loose and free. She was lying on the ground, the moon an eerie lamp above her. She was not moving.

'Emily!'

I rushed to her, dropping to the rocky shore beside her limp form, my eyes taking in her torn dress, the gash on her arm, her bloodied face and swollen lip, her closed eyes. I cradled her head in my lap. 'Emily!' I whispered, the tears already beginning to fall. 'Emily, it's me!'

David was beside me. I could hear him swear. He turned away and swore again, and I knew that rage boiled within him as strongly as guilt tore through me.

And then I heard footsteps. This time, it

246

wasn't the imagined tread of a hungry bear or the ghostly wanderings of transient souls. It was the steady footfall of a man walking through the trees and stepping on the loose lichen-coated rocks of the shore.

David heard them, too. He spun around and raised his gun, training it into the darkness. I saw it then, the canoe pulled up above the reach of the waves. I did not recognize it.

'Who's there?' I heard the soldier in David's voice. Authoritative. Demanding. But I also heard the tremor, the emotion that touched his heart and reached all the way to the tip of his finger, resting on the trigger.

There was no answer.

A dark shadow removed itself from the trees, and took the shape of a man. It paused for a moment before moving across the beach toward the canoe.

'I said, who's there!' David cocked the gun. Emily stirred and opened her eyes, struggling to sit up.

The shadow reached the canoe and looked in our direction, hesitating. And then the world stopped spinning. The Lake sighed along the shore, barely making a sound as it tapped against the hull of the canoe. The trees held their breath while the moon slipped behind a cloud and then blinked out again on the other side, bright, illuminating. The shadow turned abruptly and came toward us. I saw a hand reach beneath a deerskin cloak. I caught a flash of metal; a blur of darkness, and then a shot rang out. It echoed against the trees, back and forth, trailing off into silence. The shadow merged with the ground.

Emily pulled herself from my arms and crawled over to the body that lay half in and half out of the water beside the canoe. She leaned over and traced her fingers along his creased and weathered face, the scars barely concealed beneath a full gray beard.

The shot had caught him clean between the eyes. Eyes that had looked at me through the trees while a pack of wolves disappeared across a frozen Lake. Eyes consumed with guilt, refusing to meet mine, over the pelt of Heathcliff. Eyes my father called haunted when he wrote about assistant keeper Grayson in his journal all those years before.

It was still clasped in his hand: a satchel. A satchel with a metal buckle that contained freshly gathered roots from the devil's club, strips of willow bark, clumps of dried sphagnum moss. Medicine of the woods. Medicine for Emily. He had been trying to help her, to tend to her wounds.

David collapsed onto the shore beside them, his rifle cradled over his knees. 'Oh god!' he whispered. 'Oh god, what have I done?' He buried his face in his hands.

I touched Emily's shoulder. She flinched, pulling away from my hand.

'Did he do this to you?' I asked. 'Emily, did he hurt you?'

She looked up at me, her gray eyes so unlike my own. I saw in them fear and sadness and shame. She shook her head.

And then it came over me like a cold fever. He

had been an obnoxious boy; had he grown into a vile man? Fueled by drink, had he wandered away from the fire, stumbling to the beach? She would have been vulnerable. She would have been alone. After all those years of festering hatred, he had finally found a way to get back at her.

'Everett.' I barely whispered the name. Emily dropped her gaze, pulled her legs up to her chest, and began to rock, back and forth, back and forth.

Everett.

David carried her home to the light and laid her in our bed. Her dress was torn down the front. I burned it, first stoking the fire until the flame blazed hot, spilling heat into the room. Angry purple bruises marred her face and breasts, and a deep wound ran ragged across her arm. It had been wrapped, tied off with a strip of cotton. I knew there would be a matching piece missing from Grayson's shirt. By the light of a kerosene lamp, I bathed her, washing away the dirt and tears and the blood that ran fresh between her legs. I brushed her hair until it shone and sat with her until her eyes closed and she drifted to sleep, the light above turning, turning, turning.

Mother kept vigil in her chair. Every four hours she struggled up the wooden stairs to wind the pulleys and then returned to sit. We spoke not at all.

David appeared in the dark hours that stretch between midnight and dawn. I stood with him in silence, the moon having slipped below the horizon; our only light a projection of orange thrown by the open door of the cottage and the reflection of the beam, stretching out far across the night.

Crickets took up the conversation where our voices failed, speaking comforting nonsense in their familiarity.

'How is she?' he finally asked.

I turned to him, the light catching his features, sharp, tense, and I wanted to reach out to him. Wanted to have him wrap me in his arms. I just shook my head, letting the tears fall again, silent.

'Hey, hey,' he whispered, reaching for me, his hand beneath my chin, his thumb wiping away the salty droplets that clung to my chin. 'It's not your fault.'

I bristled, stepped back, knocking his hand away. He knew. He knew I cried as much for the blame that sat hot and hard and heavy in my chest, that stole my breath, clutching at my heart and holding it tight. Had I not been with him, this would not have happened. Had we returned on time, Emily would have been at the light. Emily needed me, and I had failed her. She was my life, and I was hers. I could not have both. I could not have Emily and David.

I turned and walked up the wooden steps and into the warmth, the closing door consuming the rectangle of light he was standing in, leaving him to the songs of crickets and the intermittent beam of the light sweeping overhead.

I never saw your grandfather again. He knew. We both knew. He had killed an innocent man. And while never one to hide from the consequences of his actions, to do otherwise would have meant compromising Emily. She would not have survived it. He loved her too much to do that to her.

And he loved me too much to stay, to make me choose between them. The morning after he killed Grayson, before the sun was full in the sky, the body and canoe were gone.

And so was he.

Part Three

Sisters in Flight

41

Morgan

I'm lying in my bed. I've been awake for hours but I don't feel like getting up and facing people and making stupid conversation. It's Saturday. I usually sleep until noon on Saturdays, after a Friday night out. But I haven't been out for days. Not since Derrick and I split and I got drunk and made an ass of myself. Not since the night I spent at the old folks' home. Not since I learned about Grandpa shooting Grayson.

Not since I was grounded.

Miss Livingstone was about to keep going with her story. There was more, I think, that she was going to tell me, even though she never saw my grandfather again. But Marty showed up, his bushy eyebrows dancing up and down his forehead as he looked back and forth between us. He didn't say anything, even though I'm sure he had all kinds of questions. I think that's how he is; doesn't poke his nose into other people's business. Instead he looked at me and told me someone was there, asking for me.

At first I thought it was Derrick. I wish I could say I didn't hope that it was, but I did. Damn him! I quickly pulled on my boots and hurried down the hall to the entrance. But it was Laurie, sitting in one of the leather chairs next to the fireplace, her face all scrunched up with worry and frustration and disappointment. And probably exhaustion. *Shit!*

We just looked at each other. She didn't ask me for an explanation. And I didn't give her one. I have a feeling someone had already. Marty.

'I'll be right back,' I told her, then returned to Miss Livingstone's room.

Elizabeth had settled herself in the bed. She looked small and tired and somehow vulnerable in a way I'd never seen her before. I realized it must have taken a lot for her to relive her past to tell me about Grandpa. And I realized, standing there in her room, looking down at her where she lay on the bed, eyes closed, that we both loved the same man.

'I gotta run,' I said. 'I . . . uh . . . '

'It's not the boy, is it?'

I couldn't help smiling. She is so fucking observant. 'No. No, not him. My foster mom. She must have been worried about me.'

'It comes with caring.'

I just nodded my head, forgetting that she couldn't see. She was trying to tell me more with those words. She knows about worrying and caring. I looked at the journals on the table and wanted to straighten them into a pile and wrap them up again, but I left them. They didn't hold the answers to her questions, and I was disappointed for her. I tapped my foot against the doorframe. I wasn't used to the feeling.

'I'm sorry you didn't find what you were looking for in your father's diary. That you didn't find out who was buried in that grave or why Charlie went out to the island to find the books.'

She pressed her lips together. 'Makes little difference now.'

'I'll come back later.' It was a statement, but almost a question. I wasn't sure she wanted me back again, now that there were no more journals to read.

'I would like that.'

I turned to leave.

'Morgan,' she continued. I paused and looked back at her. Her eyes were open, unable to see, looking instead on the past. 'He was a good man. A very good man.'

I stood quietly for a moment in the doorway, remembering Grandpa the way I knew him. When I looked back at Miss Livingstone, I didn't see a fragile old woman. Instead, I saw Elizabeth, the young woman who had loved a good man. A very good man. It made me feel happy for her, but in a sad kind of way. I turned and walked down the hall, away from the memories, hers and mine.

Marty held out my violin as I passed his office. He also handed me a doughnut wrapped in a napkin and a paper cup filled with hot liquid that smelled of ginger and honey.

'Thought you might need this.'

It helped, but not enough. The conversation with Laurie was awkward during the short car ride between the home and high school, something about calling and always there to talk to and some other shit. I mumbled an excuse for an apology before slamming the door and heading inside, late. Derrick wasn't there, and I was glad I didn't have to face him. I had a hard time staying awake through history class and left as soon as the last bell rang. I was dying for a cigarette, lighting up as soon as I entered the path that ran along the river toward the retirement home. I stopped on the bridge to finish the last few drags before flicking the butt into the brown water, watching it swirl and twist as the current carried it out toward Lake Superior.

Marty intercepted me in the hallway, outside Miss Livingstone's room, where the door was closed. He shook his head.

'She's needing her rest.'

I tried again the next day, but she wasn't even in her room, so I did what I had to for Marty and then left.

I've spent the last few evenings alone in my basement room with my violin. It doesn't hurt so much anymore when I play it. I think it helps that I know more about him, that there's someone else who shared his songs. The music made me remember, and remembering made me feel lonely, and scared, and small.

I can smell coffee. And bacon.

Derrick hasn't called me. I haven't called him either. We're both too proud. I want to, but then I don't. What a fucking mess.

There's a knock on my door.

'Hey.' It's Laurie. She's got two mugs of coffee, and she hands one to me and sits on my bed. 'I thought you were awake.'

I sit up and take it from her, blowing on it before I sip. It's rich, with lots of sugar and cream. Just the way I like it.

'You okay?'

'I'm fine.' I don't know what she wants from me. It isn't any of her fucking business, really. What does it matter to her, anyway? I doubt I'll even be here long. I'm never anyplace for long.

'Marty from Boreal Retirement Home called the other day. He told me you've been doing a great job with the painting.'

I shrug my shoulders. I guess he has to keep Laurie and Bill in the loop as part of the whole restorative rehabilitation crap.

'He also said that you've been spending time with a woman who knew your grandfather?'

'Yeah.' I know he told her more than that. I was grounded.

We sip our coffee. Silent. I can hear the TV in the other room. Noise from the kitchen.

'They were lovers,' I say.

'Oh.'

'Before he met my grandmother.'

'Is that right?'

I take another sip of coffee. 'I don't remember my grandmother.'

She looks at me, her eyebrows crinkled together, and I can tell she's thinking about something.

'You never would have met her. She was never in your life.'

'How would you know?'

'Well, before you came into our care, we had a meeting with your social worker. She told us about your family, whatever they knew.'

Somehow this pisses me off. A room full of people who are practically strangers, who don't really give a shit about me, sitting around talking about me like I'm some fucking object, writing notes in a file, passing judgment, making decisions about my life, and I don't have any say in any of it. But it makes me wonder what else she knows.

'Oh yeah? Maybe someone should think to fill me in.'

She puts her mug down, empty. 'What do you want to know?'

'About my grandmother.' Not my mother. Not my father. I want to know about my grandmother. Because of Elizabeth.

She pauses for a moment. Maybe she won't tell me anything after all.

'Your grandfather never married. He didn't have any other children. He had only been living in Nipigon for a few years before you were born and was semi-retired, but sometimes worked on a commercial fishing tug. He'd lived in southern Ontario before that, but the file doesn't say much more about where or what he did. There was a little bit about your mother, which you already know.'

I do. But she's only a name on a piece of paper: Mother; Isabel Lambton. Father; unknown.

'She was from Toronto. Maybe your grand-mother was someone your grandfather met when he lived in that part of the province.'

She doesn't say it out loud, but I can hear the suggestion that whatever the relationship was, it didn't last. Obviously they didn't stay together, whoever she was.

'Your mother was older when she had you,

and on top of that, she was diagnosed with ovarian cancer after she found out she was pregnant. She was dying before you were even born. Apparently she tracked down your grandfather from the information on her birth registration. Sometimes people who have lost touch with their family feel compelled to find them and reconnect when they're pregnant or really sick, and she was both. I suspect that your grandfather didn't even know he'd had a child until she showed up in Nipigon.'

The thing about never knowing your mother is that you get to imagine her and make her whatever you want. When I did that, my mother was always strong and young and beautiful. And she had Grandpa. They shared the same things we shared. The nights by the fire. The music. The stories of the Lake. Now, just when I'm starting to pull together the fibers of my life, the fabric is being ripped apart again. I realize that the only person I ever called family might have been a stranger to my own mother. I didn't know that the threads that linked me to my past were so fucking fragile.

'Your grandfather raised you after your mother died. She had named him as your guardian. It must have been a lot for him to take on at his age, but he did a remarkable job. He obviously loved you very much. They told me he taught you to play the violin and that you played beautifully. I' — she pauses and looks at me — 'I didn't realize just how well you played.'

I can't imagine she looks at me and sees a

remarkable job. I haven't exactly made life easy for her.

'Why haven't you told me any of this before?'

She sighs. 'You've never asked before.'

She stands up and walks over to the window. I didn't put the screen back properly last time I snuck out, and she snaps it back into place.

'Sometimes people say things with their actions that they can't find a way to say with their words,' she says, one hand resting on the windowsill, her back to me. 'If you have any other questions, I would be happy to help you find the answers.' I don't say anything. She's not talking about my family anymore. She knows about the window.

She comes over and stands beside my bed, looking at me. 'At some point, we all ask ourselves, Who am I? The thing is, it's not about who you are or who you were, it's about who you can be.' She takes my empty mug from me, heads out the door. 'Pancakes are ready.'

*   *   *

I spread newspaper on the sidewalk and set the paint can down, prying open the lid with a screwdriver. The day is mild, mild enough, Marty said, to finish up the last little bits of painting that have to be done, and then I'm free to go, my obligation to Boreal Retirement Home, my 'restorative rehabilitation' for my thoughtless act of vandalism, finished. Anne Campbell, RN, Executive Director, will sign off on the papers, and I will never have to come back again. I pick

262

up a wooden stir stick and mix in the skim of oil that floats above the white paint until it's smooth, then set it down to rest on the lid of the can. I'm moving slowly.

The day is nice enough that several of the residents are outside. Mr. Androsky is here; his son and little Becca have brought the weekly milk shake, and a brightly colored plastic princess with oversize eyes and unrealistic hair is busy exploring the rock garden around the pond. I have not seen Miss Livingstone.

My phone rings, but I don't pick it up. Derrick has left three messages already. He wants to talk things over. He doesn't say that he's sorry, and I can't tell whether he wants to see me or make sure I don't cause any shit for him. I'm still pissed off. And it pisses me off even more that I still want to see him.

'Whatcha doing?' Becca has wandered over to where I'm working on the fence. She reminds me of a girl at the first foster home I lived in. I was twelve, she was four. We shared a room, and sometimes she crawled into my bed in the middle of the night, just lifted up the covers and climbed in next to me. She was always gone by morning, usually leaving behind a wet spot that I got shit for. I never told them it was her. I didn't care; they could do what they wanted to me, it wouldn't make a difference. I was quickly learning how to not feel anything. But I knew she cried at night, I knew she missed the warmth of her mother. I was glad when they switched her to another home. Not because I didn't want her around, but because I heard that the family was going to adopt her. So I was glad, and only a little jealous. I was learning not to get attached to anyone.

'I'm painting,' I answered.

'Why?'

Because the cops caught me tagging and thought it would be a good idea to teach me a lesson by giving me a load of fucking useless work to do.

'To make the fence pretty.'

'White isn't pretty.'

I dip the brush into the tin again and squish it along the board. 'White is the prettiest color.'

Becca squints at the fence. I can tell she thinks that's a load of shit.

'Nah!' She laughs. 'White isn't even a color! How can it be pretty?'

I sweep the brush back and forth. The old peeling paint has left a texture on the wood beneath that I can only see if I look closely. The spray paint patterns have been covered, the bright colors of my dragonfly. They're in the past. They're still there, but now all the scraping, all the sanding, all the priming, has made a blank canvas. I step back and look at the work I've done. I'm starting to see what can be. 'Well, white's the prettiest color because it's really all colors; it's magic.'

She looks at me like I have two heads.

'If you look real close, and if you believe in magic, you'll see them all in there. They're enchanted, just waiting to break free. Red and orange and yellow, green's in there, and enough blue to fill the sky. Even purple, like Marty's

264

flowers.' I shake my head at her. 'White is the prettiest color because it can be anything.'

She leans toward the fence. 'It's magic?'

'You bet,' I reply, dipping my brush back into the tin.

The little girl stands watching me for a moment. She turns and walks back to the picnic table, where her little backpack lies propped against one of the legs, and I think that I've lost her. But she opens the zipper and drops the plastic princess inside, closes it up, and snaps the buckled strap over the top. She turns back to me and reaches for the paintbrush.

'My turn.'

42

Elizabeth

The faint smell of cigarette smoke drifts in my window. I can hear Marty whistling as he walks through the courtyard.

'See you found a helper,' he says.

'It seems little girls, like boys, will also covet a thing when it's difficult to attain,' is the reply.

I actually laugh out loud. Damn, she's as smart as I thought. It feels good to laugh.

I can hear Marty, too, enjoying her reply, his laughter robust and full and round. 'I think Tom Sawyer found better helpers. Yours has managed to get more paint on herself and the ground than on the fence.'

Her reply is simple. 'Shit!'

The whistling resumes and then fades.

I slide the window shut and wrap myself in a woolen cardigan before opening the door of my room and stepping into the quiet hallway. The wolf follows. As I expect.

43

Morgan

I put the lid back on the paint can and hammer it shut. It's getting dark. I've cleaned up most of the mess and fixed the drips of paint that pooled at the bottom of the fence, but Becca is another story. She managed to get a few spots of 'magic' on her clothes, and her hand and arm won't be clean anytime soon. It looks like she's wearing a white glove. Mr. Androsky seemed to think it was funny, and his son just sighed and shrugged it off.

The paint can leaves a ring of white on the newsprint when I pick it up, and it circles an old photograph of a ship. The black print stares up at me, the headline reading, 'Divers Find 1926 Wreckage of Steamer off Edward Island.' I put down the paint, my hand brushing across the faded image, the word *Kelowna* and the year 1921 scrawled in one corner. I know Edward Island. I sit on the sidewalk and read.

Thunder Bay — A group of sport divers from Minnesota discovered the long-lost wreck of the steamer SS *Kelowna* southeast of Edward Island on Porphyry Shoal Saturday during a search for another more recent wreck reported in that area. The *Kelowna* disappeared during an early winter storm in 1926.

The divers, Jack Huffman and Terry Fraser, are part of a group cataloging the shipwrecks of Lake Superior and Isle Royale. In an interview with the *Chronicle Journal* on Sunday, Huffman described their surprise at discovering the *Kelowna*.

'She went down without a trace almost 80 years ago and was believed to have run aground off Isle Royale,' said Huffman. 'We've spent years looking for the wreckage, and it was only by chance that we were diving near the spot where she lay, looking for a more recent ship that ran aground on Magnet Island in the fifties.'

The *Kelowna* was built in England in 1921 and was owned by the Chicago-based shipping company Larkin and Sons. The freighter was designed for use on the Great Lakes and was powered by a thousand-horsepower steam engine, but also rigged with two masts. She carried diverse freight from Montreal up the Great Lakes to Thunder Bay.

'Story was they were making one last trip of the season, and got caught,' said Huffman. He explained that the *Kelowna* passed through the locks at Sault Ste. Marie on December 4 with a mixed cargo of papermaking machinery, fencing wire, shoes, foodstuffs, piping, and tar paper. Unfortunately a massive storm began hammering Lake Superior the next day, and the freighter was last seen steaming toward Isle Royale, heavily coated with ice. Neither the boat, nor any of the 22 passengers or crew, were seen again.

Huffman and Firth plan several more dives on the wreck over the next few weeks, hoping to discover the cause of the sinking and to document the wreckage.

The newspaper is dated September 18, one week before I first came to Boreal Retirement Home. Only days before Miss Livingstone's brother disappeared and his boat washed ashore near Silver Islet, near Porphyry. Near where the *Kelowna* went down. This doesn't feel like a coincidence.

I tear the article from the page, fold it, and tuck it into my pocket.

★ ★ ★

The black Honda is idling in the parking lot. I hesitate. I can still hear the last thing he said before ditching me: *You're nothing without me, you're nobody*. It pisses me off. It really does. But mostly it hurts because it feels like the truth. He dared to put into words my own fears; the whispering doubt, the loneliness that's been building. Derrick made me feel alive again. Then I think of the drug deal, and I realize that I'm pathetic.

I almost lost the music. I'd let it go. Put away the violin and Grandpa's songs. Silenced his voice. And then she made me remember. Miss Livingstone and her stories. I remembered what

269

it felt like to really be loved. And even though it hurts and it's hard and it's messy, inside all of that I was somebody to someone. Who am I? Really? I have no fucking idea. But I know what I'm not. I know what I don't want to be.

I thought I wanted to see him. I thought I wanted him to want me back, but suddenly I don't want to be around him anymore. I turn and walk away from the car.

'Hey!' His feet crunch the leaves that litter the sidewalk. 'Hey, come on, you never returned my messages. Can't we at least talk?'

'I think you've said enough.'

'Hey, Morgan.' He grabs my arm, and I turn to face him. 'I'm sorry. I . . . Look, I didn't think it was a big deal. Nothing happened.' He rubs my arm up and down, caressing me, intimate. 'Nobody got hurt. Nobody got in trouble.' He's using that voice again, the one he saves for his nervous clients.

I look at his hand on my arm and take hold of it, wrapping my fingers through his so our palms are together, as much to stop him as anything else. 'You're wrong, Derrick. Something happened.' I look him right in the eyes. And it's hard to hold his gaze. I drop his hand and turn, spreading out my arms to take in the expanse of the sprawling seniors' complex nestled behind us in the trees. 'This, this is shit. This is nothing. It's kids' play.' I turn back and look at him. 'You know what I do in there? I sweep the fucking floors and put white paint on a fucking fence. The other day, if I'd been caught, it wouldn't have been a bunch of old folks I was keeping company. It wouldn't have been some fucking reconciliation and rehabilitation program. It would have been a hell of a lot different. And you know what? I don't need that shit.' I look into those green eyes, and I can't tell what he's thinking. I can't read what's behind them. But they remind me somehow of the bags of powder sharing space with Grandpa's violin.

I'm not angry anymore. I'm just tired. And a little sad.

'And I don't need you.' I'm not saying that to be spiteful. I'm really not. But for the first time, I realize that he doesn't define me. I'm not nobody without him. I never was.

I can feel the folded newspaper in my pocket.

'Good-bye, Derrick.'

Derrick clenches his jaw. I can see him working it through. He isn't used to rejection. I think he's surprised I didn't come crawling back to him. I think I'm surprised, too. He adjusts his jacket collar and turns his back on me. I watch him walk to his car, see the black Honda kick up small stones and leave black marks on the pavement as he peels out of the parking lot. For the second time in a week, I'm standing alone, feeling small on the side of the road, watching the taillights as the car drives away.

This time is different.

★ ★ ★

There is only one computer for all of us to use. It sits in the dining room on a desk cluttered with papers and empty candy wrappers and other shit people can't be bothered to pick up. Some of the kids have their own laptops, but I've never cared enough to find a way to get my own. It's late by the time I get on it. The TV is on in the other room, and everyone else has collected there, so at least I will have some privacy.

I enter the name of the ship, *Kelowna*. Turns out that's a city in British Columbia, and all the hits that come up have nothing to do with the ship. At least not the one I'm interested in. I put the paint-splattered newspaper article beside me on the desk, flattening it out so that I can see the picture of the two divers and the old photo from 1921. When I add 'shipwreck' and 'Lake Superior,' I find what I'm looking for — a listing of ships that sank on the Great Lakes. I click on the link. 'The *Kelowna*, a steam-powered cargo ship, disappeared during a winter storm in late 1926. She was traveling to Thunder Bay with a full load and twenty-two people on board and was last seen, heavy with ice, passing Whitefish Point Light. An early winter storm ravaged Lake Superior' — God I love that word, *ravaged*, makes it sound so violent and passionate at the same time — 'and it was assumed that she had succumbed to the waves and foundered near Passage Island. The wreck was never found.' There is the same photograph of the ship that's in the newspaper, black and white, the rigging for the two masts adorned with flags and the caption beneath it noting the date the boat was launched: July 7, 1921.

There's a link at the bottom of the page for Larkin and Sons, the company that owned the ship when it disappeared. It's a nice website. The company is still in business in Chicago. They've obviously changed over the years, but they're still in shipping and seem to be doing very well. I click on the 'about us' tab.

It's an odd place to find a reference to the sinking of the *Kelowna*. I expected more business type of history. But there it is. December 1926. *Kelowna* was making one last trip of the season, carrying goods from Montreal to Port Arthur, when it disappeared in the storm. Robert Larkin, one of the 'and Sons,' was on board with his wife and two young children, traveling to Port Arthur to spend the winter with family. The ship was lost with all hands.

★ ★ ★

The house is quiet as everyone heads off to bed. Except Laurie. She's in the kitchen, loading up the dishwasher like she does every night. She comes up behind me, and I know she's looking over my shoulder at what I'm doing on the computer. I get it. But it bugs me.

'Homework?'

'Yeah,' I lie. It will make her happy.

She gathers up the candy wrappers, and while she's doing that, sees the newspaper article and picks it up, reads it. 'How tragic,' she says. 'I can't imagine being out on Lake Superior in November in a storm. I can remember it being bad enough in July.'

She puts it back, grabs an empty coffee mug, and heads back toward the kitchen.

'You used to boat?' I ask.

She opens the dishwasher, puts the mug in, turns it on.

'Every once in a while, when I was a kid. My uncle used to take us out sometimes; Thompson Island, Sawyers Bay, Loon Harbor, Porphyry Island. Most of the time it was great, but when the wind and waves picked up, it scared the hell out of me. But that was a long time ago. I haven't been for years.'

'Porphyry?'

'Yes. Right near where that shipwreck was found. We always liked to hike up to the lighthouse and say hello to the lightkeepers. I can remember the rabbits all over the place. Hundreds of them. We'd chase them but never caught one. And the burned trees at the point, even decades after the fire, the trunks were still scorched and black.'

'Fire? What fire?'

'My cousin told us that there was a woman who stayed on there as lightkeeper during the war after her husband died. Apparently her daughter went crazy, burned the place to the ground, and the mother died in the fire.'

Oh my god! Emily!

'Of course then we thought the place was haunted. It made for great campfire stories.' She turns out the light in the kitchen, looks at me. 'You okay? It looks like you've seen a ghost.'

There is more to the story.

'I'm fine. It's just . . . '

She looks at me for a minute, and I don't say anything. The silence starts to feel awkward, and

274

Laurie is waiting for me to talk.

'It's just an interesting story.'

She has one hand on the railing, one foot on the stairs, and I think she's about to say something else. But then she doesn't. She just tips her head to one side, smiles.

'Good night, then.' She turns and heads upstairs. 'Don't stay up too late.'

All the rooms are dark. The only light is the glow of the computer monitor. I enter more words in Google. Emily Livingstone.

There are pages and pages of hits and a banner halfway down the screen with images — her paintings, vibrant, rich, and bold — and a picture of a young woman, black and white, grainy. I click on it, and it links me through to a website.

It's a gallery in England with a page devoted to Emily's work. There's a short bio: born in Canada, the daughter of lighthouse keepers, raised on the shores of Lake Superior, which provided inspiration for her body of work. It was rumored that she spent time confined to a psychiatric institution before being sponsored by the renowned biologist Alfred Tanner, who was apparently some kind of lord or something, with a shitload of money, and his wife, Mildred. They relocated Emily and her twin sister Elizabeth to England and helped introduce Emily to the art world by promoting her work at a London gallery. It goes on to say that Emily 'achieved critical acclaim and commercial success in the 1970s in spite of the fact that she never had any formal training and she never made public appearances. She was reclusive, and that only seemed to make her work more desirable for collectors because new pieces rarely come onto the market.' She was last known to be living in Italy. Only one gallery was allowed to sell her work. They hadn't had anything new in almost ten years, but there were lots of people buying and selling her old pieces. Apparently, they're still popular with collectors.

I look at some of the paintings. They're familiar, yet not. The prices are listed in pounds, and I don't understand their value, but there are a lot of zeros after the numbers.

There's a picture of the artist. I click on it so that it fills the screen. The woman is young, her dark hair pulled back and piled on top of her head, and she's wearing a simple, high-collared blouse. She's sitting in a chair, one hand resting on her cheek. I'm looking for Miss Livingstone — Elizabeth — in the face. There are similarities, I suppose, if I look hard enough for them, but they're not obvious. It's the eyes that captivate me. They aren't at all like Miss Livingstone's. They look right through me, like they can see deep into my soul. They're unsettling.

When I can't stand looking at them any longer, I shut the monitor off. The darkness swallows me.

44

Elizabeth

I am alone in the sunroom. They have, considerately, given me my privacy. The last shafts of sunlight stretch across the room, wrapping me in warmth, consoling me. I still hold the object in my hand. It is shaped like a barbell, cool and smooth along the middle and on one of its spherical ends. It is engraved, but even my inquisitive fingers cannot discern the letters etched into the metal. The other end is bumpy, ornate with pattern. I imagine it is tarnished, the black settling into the grooves between filigree swirls that run along its circumference, framing the heart-shaped perforations that tinkle with just the slightest movement. I don't need to see it to know what it is.

I know it, but it is not familiar. I only glimpsed it once, and then oh so briefly, as it escaped from an old cookie tin, falling to the floor of the assistant keeper's house. Beyond that, it holds no meaning. I had thought it might. I had thought that holding it would somehow tie everything together, make me complete and whole. But it hasn't.

The book on my lap is familiar. I recognize the musty smell of its long-forgotten pages, and the raised letters on the leather cover. It is heavy, its paper drunk with the waters of the Lake, bloated as in the death of the drowned. I know the dates that are entered on the yellowed sheets and the hand that wrote them without anyone having to tell me.

They left more than an hour ago. But still I sit. I am not surprised at their news. I knew as soon as they walked down the quiet hallway, their shoes squeaking formality as they trod across the wooden floor, that Charlie's body had been found. An autopsy will be performed, they tell me, to determine cause of death. They also tell me that his head showed signs of trauma. They think the boom caught him unaware as it swung across the cockpit, perhaps flung by a rogue wave or an unexpected gust of wind, that he had been knocked unconscious and fallen overboard. Presumed drowned.

He is not as nimble as he once was.

The Lake knew that. How unusual for her to give up her dead. I wonder what she's trying to tell me.

There are other footsteps now. Not the efficient tread of staff nor the hesitant pace of visitors.

Morgan.

45

Morgan

I wonder if I'm disturbing her, but she lifts her head when she hears me, so I sit down across from her, the warm sun on my back. Marty told me what happened. I know there are things you're supposed to say when you learn that somebody died. It's really kind of stupid because it's not like it's my fault. I don't really have anything to apologize for, but I don't know what else to say.

'I'm so sorry.'

'The Lake took him,' she says. She's calm. I don't think this surprised her at all, but knowing it makes it final. There's no more time, no more hope. It means saying good-bye.

'It is fitting, I suppose,' she adds. 'It is how he would have wanted it.'

She doesn't say anything about the journal. I know right away what it is. And I know what years it covers. I pick it up and carefully open it, my heart racing, thinking about the information it might have in it.

'It is no use,' she says. 'I have already asked Marty to look. The water has not been kind to the ink. Whatever words my father penned on those pages have been washed away by the waves. I will perhaps never know the reason Charlie had to exhume these relics from their decades-old grave. Whatever secret they keep, the Lake has claimed, along with Charlie's life.'

I run my fingers over the first page. She's right. The writing is smeared. The pages themselves are stuck together, and as I try to separate them, they start to tear and fall apart.

We sit silently. I figure it's better to say nothing than to say something stupid and useless. I notice that she's holding something in her hand. 'What's that?'

She lifts up a rattle. It looks old and is made out of silver but has turned dark and dull. It tinkles delicately. 'It was in the pocket of his jacket.'

'May I see it?'

Miss Livingstone hands it to me. I've never seen anything like it before, and I turn it end to end. It's engraved. There's a name on it. Anna.

'Miss Livingstone,' I shake the rattle, 'who's Anna?'

'Anna?' She leans toward me, reaching out, frantically grasping at emptiness, until I put the rattle in her hand and she brings it close to her chest, her fingers running over the etched letters. 'It says Anna?'

46

Elizabeth

I feel as though I am floating. Everything that keeps me grounded has become an apparition. I am no longer sure what the truth is. I am swimming. Elizabeth. Emily. Anna.

It makes me ache. It cannot be hers — I know it isn't — and yet . . . I clasp the rattle to my chest, not because I find connection through it, not at all. It is because of the name.

Anna.

'There is, perhaps, more of the story you need to know.'

* * *

I began to suspect the pregnancy in November.

Emily needed time to heal and kept to her bed for several weeks. The light in her had faded, but I could see it flickering and tried to encourage it by bringing sketchbooks and pencils and cakes of paint to her bedside. She had no interest in them. This worried me more than the bruises that turned purple before fading to green and yellow and finally disappearing from her skin. I knew that the marks that didn't show would be the ones to last the longest. By the end of September she was spending small amounts of time outside, but only venturing as far as the chicken coop or the rocky point. More often than not, I found her sitting on the stoop of the assistant keeper's cottage, her head leaning against the door, her eyes questioning. I explained to her that he had to leave. For her sake. She did not understand. I'm not sure I did either.

I longed for him, but knew that it was best. I could not have devoted myself to Emily had he been there, and she needed me. What happened was evidence of that. They divided me; I had to choose between them. But I missed him. I missed his comfortable presence. I missed our conversations. I missed the music. I missed what could have been.

We heard nothing about Grayson's death until the following spring. He was a hermit, known by only a few, as he spent months at a time out on the water in summer or along his traplines in winter. He was not reported missing until after the close of shipping season, when he failed to collect an order he had placed at Sewchuck's Brokerage. It was assumed he had capsized and drowned or been attacked by a bear or some other calamity consistent with living in the wilds of northern Ontario. There were whisperings, rumors suggesting that he had encountered the group from Silver Islet and chased them back to their boat and off Porphyry Island at the end of his gun. And further speculation about the disappearance of the assistant keeper from Porphyry Light at around the same time. But the gossip shared over cups of tea in the old miners' homes along the waterfront road in Silver Islet, or conversations held on the wharf, went no further. No one from that group who came to the island that late August day breathed a word of it. Not even Arnie Richardson. At first, I wasn't sure he was even aware of what Everett had done, but I suspected that he did when he didn't bother warning us about their encounter with Grayson. There was a reason he didn't feel a need. He knew the lone wolf was not a threat to us, that he had chased Everett away from Emily and the group of them off the island. It angered me that he hadn't found some way to protect Emily in the first place, but I was oddly grateful for his silence. I knew she could not survive exacting justice for what had happened. It would have been her silent word, the word of the lightkeeper's eccentric daughter, and that of a dead hermit, against those of young, educated men from well-off families.

Emily seemed to be more like herself by October. I assumed it was because we heard from Charlie that he was coming home. He did not elaborate. All he said was that he would be returning to Porphyry Point Light in the spring. This was welcome news on many fronts, not the least a logistical one. David's sudden departure had left the Department of Transport in a quandary. Mother and I managed, and it was so near the end of the season that they did not make any changes to staffing. Once again, we were able to stay on.

Before winter set in, I took a trip into town to stock up on supplies. Emily and Mother stayed behind. I stopped in to see Peter's wife, Maijlis.

She had remarried, to a man almost ten years older than she who worked in the bush camps outside town, harvesting the forests of pine and spruce to be sent to sawmills and made into lumber. I sat in her kitchen drinking strong black coffee and eating her freshly baked cake. She was the picture of domesticity, and I found myself a little jealous of her snug house and electric stove and blond hair. I was dressed in the pants I had become accustomed to wearing, my straight black hair that spoke of my heritage pulled back and loosely plaited so that it hung in a thick rope down my back. I felt coarse and awkward next to Maijlis. She was expecting a baby, her belly round, her breasts full, her cheeks flush with the glow of motherhood. As we talked, her hands moved absently to the child growing within her, caressing it through the flowered fabric of her dress and the flour-dusted cotton of her ruffled apron.

It was weeks later, as we whiled away the late November afternoon indoors, with the rain coursing down the windows and the sky hanging low and dark, that I first saw Emily do the same.

She was standing, looking out the window, out across the water to the space where the rain and Lake merged into one. Her hand traveled unbidden to rest on her belly. I caught the movement from the corner of my eye, and raised my head from my book to look at her. It took me a moment to register what it was that pulled at me, and then I remembered Maijlis. Realization crept up my spine; my skin became hot and my mouth dry. I looked at Mother. She returned my gaze, but did not follow it to Emily, instead holding my eye long enough to speak the truth before turning her attention back to peeling potatoes.

Emily felt my scrutiny and turned to me, her eyes the color of the sky, the color of the Lake. The light was back in them. She knew. Within days, she began to paint again.

Mother and I did not discuss it except one time, in the middle of February, when Emily began to swell so that we could no longer deny it. Emily was outside, wrapped warmly in a coat, standing in the great expanse of white that had embraced our world and quieted the Lake. Mother watched her through the window. Just watched, her hands unoccupied.

'There is a plant,' she said. 'We could brew a tea.'

'It is too late,' I replied.

'The child will be a burden on all of us.' Her hands still idle.

'We've borne worse before.'

She picked up a rag, began to dust the barometer on the wall, wipe the kerosene lantern sitting on the desk. 'This one is not ours to bear.'

She had never been an affectionate woman, never warm; it was not her way, and Pa's death had further extinguished what little sentiment she managed to hold. But to hear her speak this way about Emily's baby, no matter who the father was or how the child was conceived, saddened me, as much for her as for Emily. This was her grandchild.

'We will find a way,' I replied. 'We always do.'

And we spoke of it no more.

We did not consider bringing Emily to town to see a doctor. At that time of year there wasn't a way, except for a grueling journey by snowshoe across to Silver Islet and, from there, by dogsled to the city. Mother managed to find tasks to keep her busy and out of sight whenever anyone visited the island, which wasn't often. I realized that she was concealing her from prying eyes and speculating tongues, especially those who knew your grandfather's departure was shrouded in mystery. It was not acceptable in those days for girls to have babies before they were married, no matter the circumstance, and it appeared our family was no exception. We were protected by the isolation of winter, but spring would soon arrive, and with that, the child. And a child could not be kept secret, even where we were, removed from the world on our small island in the middle of a great Lake. I should have given that more thought. It was a dangerous threat, looming, and I did not see it.

I worried that Emily would be frightened by the child forming in her body, resentful of its existence, a reminder of the terror she had suffered. I needn't have. One night, as we lay together in our bed, she took my hand and placed it on her belly, holding it against the warmth of her skin until the baby moved beneath. My heart quickened. There was a new life blooming inside my sister, and after all the hardships and all the death that had surrounded us, it was good, it was wonderful, and it filled me with hope.

I did not anticipate Charlie's response.

He returned to the island in April, after the ice had loosened its grip enough to allow *The Red Fox* passage. We watched the vessel approach from the north, sails set to ease the tossing of the waves. I could picture my brother standing on the deck, the wind howling through the rigging, bracing against the heeling of the boat, spray flying into his face, already at home out on his beloved Lake. It was too rough for them to land near the light, and I noted that their course was set for the boat harbor. Restless with anticipation, we could not wait for him to walk the path to the light station, and hurried to meet them there. Mother and I even ventured out onto the wooden dock to catch the lines tossed from the boat and secure them to the cleats, so that he would reach us sooner. Charlie leaped off before they were fast, enfolding me in a strong embrace and kissing Mother happily on both cheeks. Emily, as was her way, held back on the shore, hovering inside the boathouse. He headed toward her, his grin fading as he noticed what he could not help but notice, his eyes seeking mine in question even as she endured his tentative hug.

We did not speak of it on the walk to the light.

At first our little party was animated, catching up on the years spent apart, hearing stories about his time in England and the other men he met there. When Charlie wrote to us, he had not spoken of an injury, but his arm was in a sling, his hand contorted awkwardly. When I questioned him, he shrugged it off. 'It's nothing.

287

Really.' I learned later that the injury was not a wound carried from the front, but had been sustained only a few nights before, in a dark alley at the back of a tavern. It was a symptom of a new Charlie. As we neared the light, our conversation ceased. We were listening instead for the voices of Peter and Pa. Charlie had not been back since Pa died, and we allowed the silence, filling it with our memories.

That evening, Charlie cornered me down by the fuel shed, away from Emily, away from Mother.

'What the hell's going on?' he asked. I was surprised to smell liquor on his breath. Pa rarely drank, and had kept brandy only for the times when a body needed to be warmed from the inside as much as the outside. Even then, it was never around Mother. She still maintained the strictness of her upbringing and would not allow any alcohol in her home. I had not expected Charlie to bring drink with him out to the island and consume it in such a casual manner. 'Whose is it?'

How does one tell such a tale? I tried. I fumbled my words until I could put them into sentences and told him what I could. I told him about Everett, about finding Emily, beaten and bruised and bleeding. I did not tell him about the trapper, about David and shooting Grayson. I did not explain the assistant keeper's sudden departure, and he didn't ask.

'And where the hell were you?' he demanded when I had finished speaking, his eyes hot and accusing, his mouth working sluggishly to form

288

the words. 'Why in god's name did you not keep that bastard away from her?' I had asked myself the same question a thousand times, but to hear it coming from him was unbearable. He leaned his face in close to mine. I closed my eyes, hiding from the scorn, feeling the spit landing on me as he spoke. 'You allowed her . . . you allowed them to bring shame on us.' I lifted my face to his, feeling my own anger rise. How dare he lay any of the blame at Emily's feet? I glared at him, but this didn't stop the torrent of indignation that spilled unchecked. 'Why the hell didn't you get rid of it? Between the three of you, you could have figured out how.' He might as well have slapped me. He started to walk away, but stopped and turned back. 'Look at you. Look at you, carrying on like nothing's wrong, like nothing's changed. Like Peter isn't gone. Like Pa is going to arrive the next time 'The Red Fox pulls into harbor and sit back in his chair and light his pipe like the whole goddamn world was just waiting for him. It isn't going to happen, Lizzie.' He shook his head. 'And now this. How could you let this happen? What are you going to do now?'

At that he turned and walked a meandering path back to the light, and the door slammed shut behind him. I stood for a moment, watching where he had gone. As I was about to return to my work, he emerged again, struggling to carry Pa's chair the short distance to the assistant keeper's cottage, where he disappeared inside. He didn't come out again until the next day. It was as though he had never come home, leaving

Mother and I to complete the tasks at the light as we had done now for so long without him, and a deeply unsatisfied yearning in my soul for the man my brother had been.

I realized then that the Charlie who had left so long ago, not much more than a boy, bent on avenging his brother, had not come home. That Charlie had died. Instead, this new Charlie brought the hatred and prejudices that had festered in the trenches of Europe home with him, and placed them on his own doorstep. Something had changed between us, between him and Emily. Perhaps it was the war, or the drink. Perhaps he could simply no longer tolerate the differences that made her . . . her. And that is what made it so hard for both of us.

Within a few days he seemed to grudgingly accept our new reality, shouldering his share of work as best he could with his damaged arm, sharing meals in our room beneath the light, but creeping off in the evenings with a bottle of whiskey to sit alone in the drafty building that was there to house the assistant keeper. It lulled me into a false sense of comfort.

Emily's pains began on a warm spring day in the middle of May. The season always arrived a little later out on the Lake. Some years, patches of white snow remained hidden in the shaded hollows in the woods while plants struggled to poke their way through the soil to reach the sunshine, and this year was no different. Emily and I were checking the wetlands for fiddle-heads. She was moving slowly, her tiny frame weighted by the bulk of the child.

It caught me off guard. We were walking together along the path that runs from the light to the boat harbor, cutting through a bog, which was home to the sprouting fern plants. She stopped as a contraction gripped her, pausing to lean against the trunk of a tree while the spasm coursed through her body. She did not cry out, and I was a few yards down the path before I noticed she was no longer at my side. When I turned to look at her, to see why she lagged behind, I knew her time had come, but still I asked.

'Is it the baby, Emily?'

She nodded.

I came alongside her and took her by the arm, intending to support her as we walked back to the cottage. I was counting on Mother to know what to do. She had birthed before. She knew the miracles that brought new life into the world. She was efficient and practical. But Emily refused to go. The contraction passed, and she straightened, stepping forward on the path, heading away from the cottage and deeper into the dark woods. It occurred to me that the contractions had been coming for some time, that her restlessness throughout the night had stemmed from more than the usual discomfort she had been experiencing lately. Her labor was well established. I told her we needed to go back, that we needed to get her into bed, that we needed Mother. But she shook her head and continued walking.

Not knowing what else I could do, I followed. She stayed on the path heading down to the boat harbor, stopping to lean against the wall of the boathouse as another contraction rippled through her. When it passed, she proceeded across to the beach on the east side of Porphyry, where she sat, looking out at Dreadnaught Island. We spent more than an hour there, the time punctuated by the rhythmic progress of her labor, barely discernible in a quick intake of breath and the clenching of her hands. A small breeze picked up, and while it was fresh and warm, with the promise of milder days to come, I began to feel the fingers of cold working themselves through my coat and prickling my skin. Emily seemed content, but I was restless and again encouraged her to return to the warmth of our home and the skills of Mother.

When she stood, her waters broke, spilling onto the shore and disappearing into the coarse black sand. She turned to me then, turned to me with those dark gray eyes, pleading, begging, but I did not know what she was asking. It was far to the light, too far for me to leave her, to run in search of Charlie or Mother. I was torn, trying to decide how to get her back, how quickly I could get help, when she collapsed onto the beach, deep moans escaping from her as she clutched at the fabric of her clothing.

I knelt beside her. The black sand had captured some of the sun, but this was no place for a child to come into the world. I wanted the woodstove. I wanted the bed, and towels and water and Mother. I worried for Emily. I worried for our baby.

'Look, Emily. If you can make it back to the

boathouse, I can push you in the cart up to the light. We need to get back. We need to — '

She was shaking her head violently as another contraction took hold. This one refused to let go, and she grasped at me, leaning her head back, her moan intensifying, pulling itself from deep within her. Beneath that, I could hear the Lake whispering as it tumbled against the rocks and reached up the shore. I had no choice.

I took off my coat and laid it on the ground, crouching on it and gathering my sister in my arms. She leaned into me, her back cradled by my body, her head resting against my chest. Her screams mingled with those of the gulls overhead. I was terrified, tears streaming down my face as her back arched with each spasm, sure that I was going to lose her, sure that this child was going to rip her apart. But her body knew what to do, and she followed its rhythm. When it was time, she gathered her strength, pulling her knees up, and reached below her skirts to guide our baby into the world with a final rush of water and blood.

She brought the child up to her chest, tucking her beneath her coat, beneath her blouse, against her skin, nestling her between her breasts. I knew enough to anticipate a cry, to watch for the intake of breath, and I held my own, waiting. Finally, I heard her gasp a couple of times, her little chest rising and falling, her fingers and toes turning pink, her tiny cries echoing through the trees. Emily looked at her. She looked at her like she looked at the columbine, taking in every tiny detail, the matted black hair, the dark blinking eyes, the creases in her legs and arms, the shape of her ear. She traced her face with one finger and cupped her tiny head, moving her gently so that her bow-shaped mouth could grasp a nipple and begin to suckle.

I started to laugh. She was perfect. Absolutely perfect and she was ours.

It was then that I heard Emily speak. For the first time, for the only time. And while it was far from clear, formed by a voice that had until then only created sounds, infrequent and undefined, I knew without a doubt what she said — 'Anna.'

47

Morgan

'You're kidding, right?'

I can tell by the look on her face that she's not kidding. I don't think she's one to kid about something like this.

'It is an interesting coincidence, is it not?' she replies. 'Oh, Morgan, it was so long ago, I wonder at times if my mind is playing tricks on me. But to think that this' — she picks up the silver rattle and shakes it gently — 'belonged to a baby of the same name, well, I . . . ' Her voice trails off. 'I don't know how we came to possess it. Perhaps it was given to Peter, or Charlie . . . '

She doesn't say it might have been given to her. She knows it isn't hers. She would have remembered it. Maybe she's right, maybe it was a gift, but why would someone give them a silver rattle with another baby's name on it? Or keep it all those years, hidden away even, if it was some hand-me-down toy?

Never mind. Emily had a baby. It doesn't matter what her name was, the old lady has a niece out there. That's fucking interesting.

'Where is Emily's baby . . . Anna, now?'

She has grown quiet, as if remembering is too painful. She puts the rattle back down in her lap, on top of the waterlogged book.

48

Elizabeth

As romantic as it sounds to give birth on the volcanic sands of an island next to the cleansing waters of the Lake, beneath the pastel blue of a spring sky with gulls wheeling overhead, the reality quickly became something different. Emily began to shiver, her body spent, the fresh breezes coming off the water unrelenting. I knew we could not stay where we were. Anna was snug and content, her head resting on her mother's chest, listening to the heartbeat that had been her constant lullaby for months, warmly tucked beneath the layers of Emily's coat and mine. Emily was weak as I helped her stand, and she leaned on me as we crossed back to the boat harbor. From there, I helped her and our baby into the cart and began the journey back to the point and the warmth of the cottage, back to Mother and Charlie.

As soon as the white buildings came into view, I called for them, my voice carrying with it a mixture of effort and urgency. Charlie arrived first, pausing only briefly to take in our appearance; me, coatless and shivering, a look of concern overshadowing the excitement I felt at the arrival of the baby, Emily, wrapped in both my coat and hers, riding in the box of the cart. He hurried toward us and gathered Emily into his arms. Mother appeared in the doorway of the cottage. She saw Charlie with Emily's tiny frame, took one look at the fresh blood that stained her skirts, and shuffled back inside. Charlie laid Emily on the bed, Mother pushing forward, reaching out with knowledgeable hands, lifting the folds of her skirts, scowling at the blood that soaked her clothes and seeped fresh between her legs. She did not realize that the child had been born, did not see her tucked away, hidden beneath the layers of coats. She could not have anticipated that Emily, in spite of all her odd ways, had chosen how and where to bring our baby into the world, and summoned a strength that none of us could ever have imagined.

The tiny sounds of the newborn stilled Mother's exploring hands.

'It's arrived?' she asked, startled, and pulled the coats away from Emily so that the babe could be seen.

'*She* has arrived,' I answered. I began to shiver, my legs weak from emotion as much as from the effort, and it was all I could do not to collapse onto the floor. 'Her name is Anna.'

Mother looked at me, and I read pity and judgment in her eyes, as if this were all an unfortunate incident we could have avoided. She quickly tied a knot in the cord and cut it, removing the afterbirth to a bowl, then reached to take the child from Emily. My sister resisted.

Mother was not pleased. She was not touched by the miracle of Anna's birth as I had been. She did not see the beauty and hope in the tiny perfect little body. Instead she appeared annoyed, disappointed when she looked at the fragile form of her grandchild resting comfortably in the arms of her daughter.

'Give her to me.' Her voice was soft but firm. Emily's grip tightened, and she shook her head.

Charlie stepped out of the shadows and peered down at Emily and the baby. And then he left. He turned away from all of us and walked out the door, letting it slam shut behind him.

Mother dropped her hands to her side and stood silent and exasperated, hesitant, considering, and I worried that she would pry the child from Emily's arms. I stepped into the space between them, and leaned down to remove the coats and replace them with a quilt. I turned and busied myself lighting the stove, my hands shaking as I struck match after match until one flared long enough for me to hold it to the tinder and twigs I had piled on the hearth. When they finally caught, I stoked the box so that warmth spilled out to fill the room, then set the kettle on to boil water. Still my hands shook.

Mother eventually shuffled away from the bed, eased herself into her chair and returned to her knitting. I bustled about the kitchen, listening to the clack of her needles, a steady rhythm.

Over the past months, as Emily's belly grew and the days lengthened, when the nights were filled with jobs to pass the time, Mother had knit socks to send to soldiers. Her needles framed a box, four sides, neat, even painstakingly crafted stiches, a turn for the ankle, casting off to shape the toe. Mother made socks. She did not knit blankets. There were no layettes lying in wait. No sweaters. No jumpers. She had not instructed Charlie to fashion a cradle or me to stitch sleepers. Mother, whose experience I counted on to direct the matter of birth and babies and motherhood, whose hands always sought a purpose, had done nothing to prepare for the birth of Emily's child.

As her needles continued to click, a creeping coldness gripped me. A growing awareness, lit by the flames of the stove that warmed a room where a girl nursed her newborn child while her mother sat separate, distant, apart, knitting socks.

Mother had never intended for Emily to hold her baby.

Emily, who had always seen more than I had, had understood what was not there. She knew. She knew enough to shun the comfort and warmth of a bed, the wooden walls of the cottage that stopped the wind. She knew what I did not: that there would be no refuge in the experienced, knowledgeable hands of our mother.

You should have let her die.

Emily knew. And now, the baby had been born. The baby had a name. She suckled at her mother's breast.

After a time, Emily let me take the child from her. I bathed her as best I could in a basin, gently wiping away the remnants of birth that clung to her before wrapping her snugly in flannel towels. I bathed Emily, too, removing her skirts and blouse and soaking them in pails of water, scrubbing them until they were clean and hanging them outside to catch the breezes of the

Lake. She refused to dress, instead lying naked on the bed, washed by the orange glow from the stove, with Anna nuzzled up to her breast. I watched them fall in love.

When night fell, Charlie was the one to light the lamp. I heard his heavy footfall climb the stairs and scuff about on the wooden floors of the gallery. When he was done, he trudged back down again and out the door, without a word or even a glance. Mother prepared dinner in silence. We ate in equal silence.

I fashioned a cradle out of a drawer from the dresser, emptying the contents into a pile on the floor and then lining it with a folded woolen blanket and the clean, soft cloths that we used to polish the lens. I placed it on the floor beside our bed and laid the sleeping Anna, tiny and perfect, inside. Exhausted, Emily and I fell asleep, lulled by the rhythm of the light and the familiar chorus of frogs singing in the bog.

And while I heard Charlie enter a few hours later and climb the stairs to the light, I did not hear him pause by our bed on his way back out. Nor did I hear the buzzing of the outboard motor as *Sweet Pea* eased away from shore, heading toward the sprinkling of lights that defined the little hamlet of Silver Islet, with the tiny bundle of our baby tucked in her makeshift cradle at his feet.

49

Morgan

What a prick. What a fucking prick. I can see why she hasn't spoken to him in sixty years.

'Anna,' she says the name again. 'Such a coincidence. Such a sad and tragic coincidence.'

I'm not convinced.

★ ★ ★

She doesn't notice that I take the book with me when I leave. I walk with her back to her room and pretend like I'm putting the journal on her table with the other ones, and make sure the rattle is really noisy when I set it down. She told them that she won't be going to the dining room for dinner — that she wants to be left alone. They all know what happened. I tell her again that I'm sorry. It seems like the right thing to say. And then I leave her, sitting in her father's chair in her room.

The instructions say to put the book in the freezer. I was going to put it in a big bag of rice, like Laurie did when she dropped her cell phone into the sink while she was doing the dishes. But when I googled 'how to dry out a wet or damp book,' the University of Michigan library website said to freeze it right away. The book isn't dripping wet. It's just damp and puffy. I wonder when it was they found Charlie's body and the book and rattle in his pocket. It could have been yesterday, or even before that. I can see that there's already a bit of mold growing on the cover. So I do like it says and I put it in the freezer. While it chills in there next to the Pizza Pops and vanilla ice cream, I have time to find the other things I need.

I have to do it in stages, so I set myself up in my room, clearing off the top of my dresser so that I can work there. I put down a layer of newspaper and get my hair dryer and a roll of paper towel ready. I have no idea how long it takes to freeze a book, and I check it so much I'm starting to annoy Bill. I guess once it's hard, it's ready, so I take it down to my room as quickly as I can. The cover opens fairly easily. I gently train the hair dryer on the first page inside and fan it back and forth to dry the thawing moisture as it rises from the top sheet. I smooth my hand across it, hoping to hell I'm doing it the way I'm supposed to. I figure I can't be doing any more damage than the Lake already did. And besides, Miss Livingstone will never know. Once the book has thawed enough that it feels wet again, I lay a piece of paper towel between the dry pages and the wet pages and put it back into the freezer. I have to wait until it freezes again to do any more.

Laurie and Bill don't let me smoke in the house. They aren't so stupid that they don't know I smoke, and I don't think they really give a shit, but they make me go and sit outside on the back deck or front steps anyway. I actually don't mind, most of the time. It gets me out of the house and away from the noise of the TV that's always on, and the bickering of the other kids. While I'm waiting for the book to freeze again, I decide to go outside and light up. It's one of those nights when you can smell winter coming. There's an aroma, not like flowers or dog shit in spring, or wet, moldy leaves in the fall, but you can just tell that it's going to snow by how the air is, by what it smells like. I butt out my cigarette before I'm finished, just so I can take it in.

★　★　★

It takes me a long time to get the book to dry. A lot longer than I thought it would. I'm patient, though, and the pages are slowly starting to come apart and I can make out some of the writing, even though the ink is smeared. I read it as I go along. There is the usual stuff the lightkeeper wrote about. All the ships and things he did to keep the light running. He mentions Charlie a few times, and Peter. Talks about taking them fishing, about trips around the island and hunting caribou. I finally come to the part where Miss Livingstone and Emily are born.

Saturday, 16 May 1925 — Lil delivered today, a month before her expected date of confinement. We did not have time to get her into the city, so she birthed on her own with incompetent, and therefore somewhat limited, help from me. We have been doubly blessed — surprised by twins! Two tiny little girls with dark hair and dark eyes. They are small and seem so fragile, being born early, but it does explain their hurry to come into the world. Lil is doing well. We will keep careful watch over them and hope for the best. Have named them Elizabeth and Emily.

I learn that the twins not only survived, which I know already, but that they thrive, feeding frequently, becoming squawking and demanding of their mother, so that they all become exhausted, and that little eight-year-old Peter is able to help out his father with the chores. He says that the twins are inseparable; that the little one, Emily, cannot stand to be away from her sister for even a moment without kicking up a fuss. I guess Emily needed Elizabeth even at such a young age.

The date of the mysterious grave marker on Hardscrabble Island is November 29, 1926. The sinking of the *Kelowna* was in December 1926. There are still many, many more trips into the freezer before I reach those pages.

I'm going to need another pack of cigarettes.

★   ★   ★

It's long past midnight. The house is quiet. I repeat the process — freeze, blow-dry, blot, freeze, blow-dry, blot . . . I'm halfway through the book, but still months away from the sinking of the *Kelowna*.

The lightkeeper describes an idyllic life. The girls grow. A year passes, and they reach all the baby landmarks of rolling over and smiling and learning to crawl, while mantles are replaced and kerosene is delivered and repairs are made. Their winter is uneventful. He teaches Charlie to read that year using newspapers that arrive in bundles, several weeks at a time. They hunt caribou and deer. Shipping season opens late, and thunderstorms are frequent and violent. They mark the twins' birthday, although there are no gifts or cake, just a simple notation in May 1926 that they are now a year old. He seems to be taken by his daughters more than he was the boys, as he mentions the actions of the twins much more frequently. Especially Emily. She is most obviously his favorite.

Wednesday, 16 June — Took delivery today of a little gaff-rigged punt that will replace the old, leaky tender we have been using. She's a lively little thing and will be excellent for traveling about the islands and for fishing. Named her *Sweet Pea*. The twins are toddling about now. Elizabeth is much stronger and larger than Emily, but Emily has picked up more words and uses them at times with tiresome frequency. She has become my shadow, following me about on my chores when she can, but never going far from Elizabeth.

Something must have changed. Miss Livingstone claims Emily never spoke. Ever. Except one word, the name of her daughter. Anna.

Saturday, 10 July — Have had no rain now for almost three weeks. I am making almost daily trips to the potato garden to water. Charlie is always eager to accompany me and particularly enjoys adventures in *Sweet Pea*. He is shaping up to be a strong sailor.

Monday, 9 August — The berries are not plentiful this year, but we have spent several long days on Edward Island picking. The girls amuse themselves, playing for hours with sticks and leaves while Lil harvests, filling their mouths with the purple fruit until their lips and cheeks are stained. They are inseparable, and seem to share a bond and language all their own. Emily is certainly the brighter of the two, crawling into my lap, demanding stories, pretending to read along using incomprehensible language, mimicking my actions in a most adorable fashion.

I drift off around three in the morning while the book is doing a turn in the freezer. I sleep longer than I want to. When I wake, I'm still dressed in my clothes, and the lamp on my desk is glaring accusingly at me. It takes me a while to remember what I was doing, and why I'm lying like a passed-out drunk on top of my covers. It's dark outside, even though it's late in the morning. Everyone must be out because the house is quiet; even the TV is silent. When I look

306

out the window, there's no car in the driveway, and I'm relieved I have the place to myself. The sky is low and heavy, and the wind is tossing about tiny specks of white. I return to my task. It isn't long until I discover the secrets the book holds. But they're not the ones I expected.

Thursday, 18 November — An illness has found its way to our home. Peter and Charlie have both been suffering from fevers. They have been confined to bed, alternately shivering beneath piles of blankets and kicking off the covers as the heat overcomes them. They are in capable hands. Lil has been steeping concoctions for them from the herbs hanging in the pantry, and I am confident they will recover soon.

Sunday, 21 November — The boys both show signs of improvement, their fevers have broken, but they remain lethargic, barely sipping broth. I am reading them a story by Jules Vernes called *Twenty Thousand Leagues Under the Sea*. It keeps them amused, although they are asleep more than they are awake. My concern has switched to the girls. They have both become listless, and I fear they will be the next to succumb to the illness.

Monday, 22 November — Both Elizabeth and Emily are now quite ill. Their faces are flush with fever, and they are refusing to take any nourishment Lil offers them. I am most concerned about Emily. She does not have the strength of her sister. She is so small and fragile.

Freeze, blow-dry, blot . . .

Saturday, 27 November — It has been five days now that the girls have been ill with this fever. They grow more and more lethargic. Unlike the boys, they are now covered head to toe in an angry, red rash. The weather has become irritable or I would pack them all into *Sweet Pea* and head to Port Arthur in search of a doctor. Lil is doing all that she can, and the strain of this illness, first the boys and now the twins, is beginning to show. I am helping as much as I can. My concern grows.

Sunday, 28 November — Emily's fever broke last night. Her tiny body has rallied, bolstered by Lil's herbs. Elizabeth still suffers, her body gripped by seizures, her breath coming in short, rasping gasps.

Monday, 29 November — Elizabeth died this morning. She took her final breath a half hour after sunrise. I have removed her body from the cot, from the side of her sister. Emily is inconsolable.

I've been reading the pages while I'm blowing hot air from the hair dryer over them. But when I read these words, I turn it off. The silence is loud. It doesn't surprise me. It happened a long, long time ago. But still, it touches me.

I peel the next page back and insert paper towel between it and the dry one, then turn the hair dryer back on.

Tuesday, 30 November — Lil has taken to her bed. She assures me that it is nothing more than exhaustion, that she is not ill, but I have my concerns. I am fashioning a simple wooden coffin for Elizabeth and will bury her near the boathouse. Emily continues to cry. She refuses food, taking in very little nourishment in spite of Lil's encouragement. I cannot bear the thought of losing another daughter. I will not dig two graves.

Thursday, 2 December — A winter storm is working itself across the Lake. The wind has whipped the water into a turmoil, and I hope to God there are no ships attempting a late-season journey, but I light the lamp regardless. Emily continues to weep. Her cries match those of the wind, tearing at my heart. Nothing can be done to console her. We have tried everything. It is as though a part of her has died. I fear for her life, too.

I've moved my project to the kitchen table so that I'm closer to the freezer. I'm using an empty tuna can for an ashtray, and it's almost overflowing. I don't give a damn if I catch shit for smoking in the house.

Freeze, blow-dry, blot . . .

Saturday, 4 December — I wonder at the orchestration of life, at the fortunes of chance, of the blessings within tragedy. A most unusual occurrence, and I am fraught with guilt, all the while relieved. She is a gift from the Lake. She has brought life. I cannot bring myself to undo what I have done. I will lay the story on this paper and turn the page to think on it no more.

My heart beats fast. It's the date I've been looking for. The script here is much more difficult to read. I can tell the lightkeeper was writing quickly, forming the words with large looping letters that run together. I have to read slowly when I just want to rush to the end.

I was driven from the comfort of my home by the cries of my only daughter, my precious Emily, out into the depth of the most horrendous storm I have seen in my many seasons at this light. Or I was drawn, perhaps, by the wolves — I don't know which. Between the howling of the wind and the laments of my only surviving daughter, I heard them conversing, so I took my gun and walked the east shore under the pretense of searching for them. As I clambered over the slippery rocks, I spotted a tender being driven toward the shore. It appeared empty, but I still waded in, the icy water mixing with the driving snow so that I was chilled to the center of my being. I caught the bow, turning it to the shore and guiding it up onto the beach, fighting with the waves. I was able to pull it far enough from the water's reach that it was no longer at risk of splintering, and it was while I struggled with it that I noticed the body inside. It was a woman, wrapped in a stiffly frozen woolen blanket and curled in the bottom of the boat. Her eyes were open, haunting dark eyes, staring blankly, her auburn hair framing her beautiful but ghastly pale face, her lips purple-blue. I did not question for a moment that she was dead, that she had been floating for some time, tossed by the waves, driven by the wind toward Porphyry Point. I quickly scanned the beach and waters, looking for signs of a wreck, for other boats, but there was nothing. I knew I couldn't leave her there, exposed to the elements, so I climbed into the craft and gathered the form in my arms, intending to lay the body to rest in the woodshed until the storm abated. As I lifted her, I heard a cry, feeble, smothered. At first I thought I had been mistaken, that life yet coursed through the woman's veins, and I laid her back against the gunwales, but her blank, staring eyes confirmed her state. The cries came from beneath her coverings, and in them I heard an echo of my own dear Emily. I hastened to remove the blankets. It was a child, perhaps two years old — small and delicate, barely alive, with hair the color of night. I quickly gathered her up, tucked her beneath my jacket, and returned to the light. Peter and Charlie were asleep. Lil has contracted the fever; her glazed eyes opened briefly when I entered the cottage, but registered nothing. Emily was in her cot, her cries reduced to exhausted whimpering, and I feared she too hovered near death. I knew I had to warm up the tiny body I carried, and I knew too that the reaper hovered outside in the howling wind. I removed the child's damp clothes and laid her in the bed, laid her beside Emily, in the place so recently occupied by Elizabeth. Within moments, Emily's cries had ceased. Fearing the worst, I returned and peered in at them. I saw their two bodies curled together, Emily's hand grasping a clump of the other's hair so like her own dead sister's, her eyes closed, sleeping peacefully. But the eyes of the other stared back at me. She did not cry, this child, but her eyes spoke volumes. I fear I have stolen the life of one to give life to the other.

It all makes sense. Oh my god, it all makes sense. Elizabeth is dead and buried. Of course.

But something's not quite right. I can't quite put my finger on it. The book is back in the freezer, but I've lost my patience. I hover in the kitchen, waiting.

Tuesday, 7 December — Both girls are thriving. They are feeding well. The boys continue to gather strength; Peter has even ventured from his bed. I have been scouring

312

the shores for signs of a wreck and have found nothing. The tender is not marked. I can only assume that the ship from which it issued has foundered in the area. It may be many more days before we receive a report. I have buried the woman's body at sea. I wrapped her in canvas and weighted her with stones. I am not sure why I have done so. I have buried Elizabeth too, but not as I intended. I took her instead to Hardscrabble Island. She lies beneath a cairn, away from any paths that would lead someone to stumble upon her marker, where she can look upon the Lake for all eternity, where the light will sweep across her bed, where she will sleep and not be found.

What is written next comes as a complete shock. It is all I can do to read to the bottom of the page before quickly grabbing my things and heading out into the storm, the journal stuffed into my backpack and my violin tucked beneath my arm.

I have to tell Miss Livingstone.

She isn't Elizabeth.

50

Elizabeth

I stand beneath the shower, hands gripping the chrome bars fastened to the tile walls. Water rains down, trickling like a thousand streams across my body. I close my eyes and lift my head, allowing the drops to flood my face and mold my hair until it hangs, sleek and thick, a snowy river dripping puddles that collect at my feet and disappear down the drain in the floor. I can feel the wolf, prowling. He is becoming more persistent, visiting almost daily now. He is patient. He sits, watching, waiting. I wipe my eyes, but they fill as quickly, and I don't bother clearing them again. I reach out a hand, exploring the wall until I find the tap and turn it fully to the right. I gasp when the cold water stabs at me, as cold as the Lake. My eyes flash open at the shock, but still they see nothing. My skin prickles. My pulse quickens.

51

Morgan

My god, it's snowing. The wind is an icy hand reaching right through my jacket. The snow is wet and heavy, blown into my face and down my neck. Already it's piling up on the streets, making them a slippery, slushy mess. It's hard to walk. Cars are skidding around corners. It's always like that the first snowstorm of the season. People forget how to fucking drive. But even I have to admit; this is a good one, especially for this time of year.

My heart is racing. I want to get to Boreal quickly, but the buses are running late, and I have to wait outside in this fucking weather for what feels like an eternity before one finally shows up. There aren't many people on the bus, and the driver drops me right in front of the building. I manage to thank him as I rush out the door.

When I get close to the entrance, I can tell that something isn't right. I press on the buzzer and stand there, shivering, while the snow whips around my head. Nobody answers. I try the door, but it's locked. Of course it is. It always is. But there's also always some garbled voice to speak into the intercom, and pass judgment on anyone asking for access. Why aren't they there now, of all times? I press my face against the

315

glass, peering inside. I can see some of the staff way across the lobby. They're in a group, talking, one of them waving her arms around and pointing at the door. But they don't see me.

'Hey! Hey!' I bang on the door to get their attention, but they've all headed off down the hallway, and I'm still left standing outside. 'Shit!'

I make my way around to the back of the building, past the fence I spent so many hours painting. It blends in, now, with the storm raging around it. White on white. I try to open the door that leads from the sunroom to the garden, but it's locked too. I knew it would be, but I had to try it anyway. When I press my face up against the glass, I can see Marty inside. My banging and hollering gets his attention.

Marty doesn't ask why I'm there. He just opens the door, and I step inside, out of the wind and swirling snow.

'Now isn't a good time, Morgan,' he says.

I set my violin down and brush the snow off my coat. It's dark in here, hushed and cozy, but there is a tension beneath that. I can feel it more than anything. Only a few lights are on, dim and feeble. Marty is putting his jacket on, getting ready to head outside. There's something else going on.

'What's up?'

'Miss Livingstone's wandered off.'

I stop my brushing. I feel a thousand questions fighting to find a voice. But I think of what has happened, and I think, too, of my last conversation with her, and I don't ask any of them.

He does up his jacket and pulls a toque down until it almost touches his bushy eyebrows. 'Power failed. Iced-up tree branch fell on the lines. Sometime after it went dark, she slipped out the door. Alarms didn't go off.' This is more than Marty usually says, and it makes me think he feels responsible.

'What can I do?'

'Not much except go out looking.' He glances out the door at the blanket of white blowing around outside and then adds, under his breath so I can barely hear, 'and on a goddamn night like this.' He shrugs a couple of times, and without another word heads out into the storm.

I look around. There're cops at the front door now. Anne Campbell is there, letting them in. I slip out the back and follow Marty's prints. They're already disappearing, swallowed up by the wind and snow.

★   ★   ★

The bus is completely empty when I get on it. I'm surprised the driver even saw me to stop and pick me up. He tells me that this will be his last run, that the roads are getting so bad they've decided to cancel service, and I tell him that I'm not going far. He's got a radio playing eighties rock music, and between songs the announcer comes on and gives a list of all the events that have been canceled. A concert at the Lutheran church, swimming lessons at the Complex, even an AA meeting. The forecast is calling for a foot of snow overnight and then more again

317

tomorrow. Snow and blowing snow with reduced visibility. They've already closed the highway to Nipigon.

I sit staring out the window. We're quite a few blocks away from the home when I spot her. She's walking up a side street, wrapped in a dark coat. Her head is bare, and I can see her long white hair flowing free.

'Stop! Stop right here, let me off here!' I hurry to the doors, trying to pull them open before the driver has even stopped the bus.

Beneath the drifting snow is a layer of ice, buried, hidden, waiting. I don't expect it, and it steals my feet from me when I jump down. I land in a drift and curse, almost sliding under the bus. I have to pull my legs back to keep them from being run over. Stupid fucking weather. By the time I manage to get to my feet, the doors to the bus have closed, and I hear the brakes huff as it pulls away.

I don't even realize that I've left my violin on the seat.

She's walking away from me, bent into the wind, stepping slowly and carefully.

'Miss Livingstone! Miss Livingstone!' I run up behind her and grab her shoulder. 'What the hell do you think you're doing? It's fucking freezing out here! Everyone is looking — '

She flinches at my touch and turns toward me. My words catch in my throat. Her hair, the color of snow, falling around her shoulders, is the same. But that's where the resemblance ends. It's not her. It's Miss Livingstone, but it's not her. Vibrant gray eyes look back at me. I have

318

seen them before, in a photograph. They are haunting. They are the color of the Lake.

It's Emily.

★ ★ ★

She looks at me with those piercing gray eyes, and I take a small step back. She smiles at me, like she recognizes me, like she knows who I am. And then she does the strangest thing. She reaches up with one hand and touches my cheek. She traces a finger around my eyebrows, down my nose, and over my lips. I want to pull away, but I can't. She cups my face in her hand and makes a noise, but her mouth does not form words.

A car pulls up next to us. It's a cop car. Still I stand there. We both do. The snow swirling around us flickers in the headlights, like the sun sparkling on the surface of the Lake.

52

Elizabeth

They say the girl found her. That she was
wandering around in this god-awful blizzard that
tears at our building and throws itself at the
windows like a pack of hungry wolves. She is
back, now, in her room, warmed beneath
blankets, but I can tell that she is not well. I am
surprised she had the strength to climb from her
bed, to find a coat and navigate the chaos
brought on by the power outage, to find the
doors and slip out into the storm. Whatever
possessed her to do so?

I am sitting by her bed. Her breathing is
ragged, and the hand that I am holding is dry
and hot. Too hot. Morgan is here with me. She is
standing, silent, near the door, but I know she is
here.

'You don't need to stay,' I tell her.

'No, I . . . I want to.'

I am glad of her company. I am more glad still
that she wants to be here.

She didn't know that Emily shares the same
building; that her room is just down the other
hall from mine in an area that restricts comings
and goings and where there are nurses with
watchful eyes and keen ears. Emily needs more.
More than I am able to give her. She is prone to
fits. I can manage them, most of the time. But I

320

am old. And tired. When I found that the Lake was calling us back home, drawing us from our reclusive life in Tuscany, it was partly because I could no longer give Emily the care that she needed. This place offered us the privacy I wanted, and the proximity to the Lake that I craved. The world does not know where Emily Livingstone is. They could not accept her as she is, I am sure of that. So I hid her. I protected her. I have spent my life doing that. It is my purpose.

The girl moves a chair to the other side of Emily and sits down. I can hear her fumbling with her bag.

'There's something I need to tell you,' she says. 'Something I think you should know.'

I can smell the mustiness of the book. I know it is the journal. She has found something in it that the Lake tried to steal. I'm not sure I want to know what it is. But she begins to speak, and I cannot stop it. It spills from her, my father's words, like waves rolling toward the cliff, crashing and hissing when they arrive, and then slithering off to disappear into the depths, only to be followed by the next, and then the next.

They are mesmerizing.

53

Morgan

The book is in layers, paper towel alternating with the pages so that it's even bulkier than it was to begin with. I open it carefully, flipping through the damp sheets until I find the part where Elizabeth and Emily were born. I'm not sure how to start.

Miss Livingstone . . . Elizabeth . . . is holding her sister's hand. Emily is frail. She isn't breathing well, and she hasn't opened her eyes since we brought her back to her room. I rode with her back to the home. In a cop car. Not how I ever thought I would end up in the backseat of a cop car. By the time we managed to make our way through the ice and snow and pull up at the front doors, Emily was shivering, her eyes glassy. Even then she didn't want help from the nurses when they tried to take her to her room. But she is calm, now, peaceful even. Elizabeth and I are here.

Her room isn't like Elizabeth's. The quilt covering her is similar, but that's all. The walls are plastered with paintings and drawings, and there are pencils and papers and paints lined up on a desk beside the window. The paintings are all of the same thing; a baby, a newborn baby. Intricate, detailed. No one has to tell me it's Anna.

I take a breath and begin.

The old woman listens as I read her father's words. He speaks of the babies, twin girls, born too soon. He talks of the illness, the days spent caring for first one and then another of his children, cut off from the world as fevers consumed them. And then, the death of Elizabeth.

She doesn't say a word. Nothing. Her face shows no emotion. So I continue. I read of the boat, floating ashore in a storm, of a woman with red hair, of the child wrapped in her cloak, who the lightkeeper placed in the cot beside Emily. And there, in taking on the warmth of her body, gives life to them both.

The story isn't finished. There's more. I'm about to turn the page when she interrupts me. Her voice is quiet, trembling.

'I know,' she says. 'I have always known.'

54

Elizabeth

I can hear Mozart playing. Marty would have put the music on. It is soothing. I take a deep breath and run my fingers through my hair, sweeping it from root to tip. I know it is completely white now. The color of snow. It tells me I am old, but it lies. Inside, I am not.

The child, Elizabeth, I can feel her. Cold and buried beneath rocks, tugged at by the wind and washed by the rains. Is she lonely? I am with her. I have walked with her along the shores of the Lake. She has lived with me, been with me always. She is me. We are one.

Emily and I, we complete each other. We are threads woven together as a single piece of cloth. We share a life just as the baby Elizabeth and I share a death. She could not have survived without me. I lived for her. It is our truth.

I begin to speak. It will fill the room with more than Emily's labored breathing, words that will chase around the walls and up to the ceiling and hover in the corners. Perhaps it will keep the wolves at bay.

'There is part of the story I have not told you,' I say.

★ ★ ★

The morning after Anna was born, I woke before Emily did. The day was so new that night hung desperately to its edges, gray and silent, unwilling to let go. It was still; the birds had not even begun their warbling, withholding their songs until the sun peered tentatively over the eastern horizon to nudge at the darkness. There was just enough light to see. Emily was curled beside me, her dark hair splayed across the white sheets, one hand trailing off the bed, resting, I assumed, on her child's makeshift cradle. I sensed immediately that there was something wrong. It was too silent. Too still.

The light.

In all my years on Porphyry, throughout all the storms, amid illness and adversity, not once, *not once*, had we let the light go out. Until then.

I slipped from the bed, pushing past the shadows that hung in the room and flitted around my heart. I knew what they had done. I knew it before I had fully swept the cobwebs of sleep from my mind, but I could not bring myself to embrace it. It was unthinkable. It was beyond cruel. I could not fathom Charlie, even the Charlie who had dragged himself home from the war, his heart and mind wounded deeper than his flesh ever was, that he could be capable of doing something so despicable. And Mother, who had suckled us at her breast, how could she conspire to this end?

I saw her then. Sitting in the chair. Mother was awake, watching me as I knelt on the rough wooden floor where our baby — where Anna

— had been, my hands futilely searching, lifting the quilt, moving the basins I had used to wash Emily, opening the curtain that hung around the other bed, the bed she and Pa had shared. She was looking at me, her eyes sad, pitying, but her chin firm, her lips set in a tight line. And then I remembered. I remembered a late-summer night, the year that Charlie went to school in town, when the light blinked about the room and my parents' voices floated unbidden to me: *We have damned them both. Emily will never be right.*

I can see now. Emily mourned her twin. She mourned Elizabeth, buried beneath a pile of lichen-clad stones. She was incomplete, one foot in the land of the dead. A spirit in the world of the living. And me, a poor substitute, a sacrificial offering from the Lake. All those years. How could I not have seen it? The times that Emily had wandered away, roaming the island, prone to all its dangers of cliffs and water and wild creatures. And men. Boys.

You should have let her die.

Mother would never have accepted Emily's child.

'What have you done with her?' I tried to whisper, but the anger in me boiled over and the words were rough, catching in my throat and choking me. Emily stirred, her hand moving. Searching.

'She will be better off.' Mother's voice was flat, dismissive.

'Better off without her mother?'

Mother grunted. 'Her mother is not capable.

She cannot care for herself, let alone a child.'

'She is mine just as much as she is Emily's, as much as Emily and I are one. How could you take her from me?'

She stood, slowly, painfully.

'She is not your child.'

She turned her back to me and moved toward the stairs, climbing them deliberately, methodically. It was done. She had decided it was time to tend to the light, for the few short hours until the sun rose, to resume her dutiful nature, to be vigilant, responsible. Her footsteps shuffled.

I had not moved. I was still crouched on the floor, beside the bed. Her tread thumped, climbing higher and higher. Up to the light.

'You're wrong.' I did not whisper this time. 'She is ours, mine and Emily's. You have no right.' Emily was awake. She sat on the bed, her eyes searching, seeing me on the floor and Mother climbing the stairs, hearing the silence of the still light, feeling the muted warmth from the glowing embers in the stove. And knowing that Anna was gone. She pulled her knees up to her chest and began to rock.

Mother continued to climb. 'Where is she?' I was screaming now, my voice cutting through the dawn, echoing off the cliffs, drifting across the Lake. Still she climbed.

I rushed the stairs, taking them two at a time. Mother's shuffling gait was quicker than I realized. She was already at the top when I reached her. She was priming the light; the fuel was open, and she poured some into the reservoir. Her back was to me. She set the can

327

on the floor and took the box of matches from the shelf.

* * *

I pause in my speaking. I don't even know if the girl is still in the room. She is silent. Listening? I have never given these words life before; speaking them makes them real, and I am afraid to. I have let them lie, hidden in the dark recesses of my mind, buried, dusty, and silent — I cannot deny them if I give them shape and form and sound. I have told no one.

I have thought of that day often. It has haunted my dreams. I have played the scene over and over again in my mind, lived it in the darkness of a thousand nights. I remember. But I am not sure that I remember the truth. It is like a dream from which you wake too soon, a nightmare that leaves you sweating and your heart racing. And then, lying in the darkness, coaxing sleep, you craft your dream until it has an ending that is satisfying, one that does not haunt you, and only then can you return to slumber peacefully and allow the remnants to drift away, like the morning mists. Have I created a truth? One I can live with? Have I relived the moment so many times that my fiction is now my truth — the truth that I want it to be? I have to be honest. I do not know. I do not know what is truth. I do not know who lit the match. I do not know how the fuel spilled. I do not know whether I pushed her, or she pushed me. I do not know.

And so I continue.

She opened the box and took out a match and turned toward me. I was shaking from head to foot. My body quivered, and my mouth was so dry, it was difficult to form words.

'Where is she?'

I could hear Emily below. My beautiful silent Emily was making the strangest noises as she stumbled about the room, and I could see her movements as easily as if they were before my eyes, simply from the sounds that echoed up the stairwell; the chairs clattering across the wooden floor, Pa's books tumbling off the shelves, dishes breaking, pots rattling. She was searching, just as I had.

'Where is she?'

I moved closer, taking hold of Mother's arm. She pulled away from me, turned toward the light, and ran the striker head of the match across the coarse paper on the side of the box. I watched the sparks trail along behind, sputtering and flickering until the match caught, welling with yellow light in a bright flash, then settling to a steady glow. Mother was intent on the mantle, her back to me so that I could not see her face. She was dismissing me. It was done. We were finished. We would see to our duties. Charlie would become the lightkeeper, shining the great beacon out over Lake Superior, marking the dangers, lighting the path for all the ships that wandered the waves, just as we had done for a thousand and a thousand and a thousand nights. We would bury our dead and whitewash the buildings and polish the great glass lens. We would fish and hunt and plant potatoes in the garden. And Emily would wander, and I would find her. I would always find her. She needed me.

And I needed Anna. It was not over. I was not done. I would not be dismissed. I grabbed Mother again, grabbed her, and pulled her to face me. I could hear Emily climbing, now. I could hear her on each stair, her tread steady.

'Where is our daughter?' My voice shook.

'She is not your daughter.' Mother had the match in her hand. It glowed, reflected in her eyes, and I held her gaze, strong, defiant. 'She doesn't even share your blood.'

The words struck me. And I knew. I knew it was true. Somehow, I had known all along. And then the match fell. It bounced once, spinning on the edge of the alcohol can, twisting, still burning, landing inside the tin, floating, resting on the fuel. I looked at it for an eternity. Emily reached the top of the stairs. She was beside me. Emily saw the match fall. She saw it dancing on the rim of the tin. She saw it hover.

I saw the flash of flames from below. I saw Mother, a silhouette at the top of the stairs, as I tumbled backward, and then I saw no more.

The flames quickly consumed the dry fir boards that formed the walls of the light tower. They found their way into the rafters, where decades of Pa's newspapers were tucked away, and hungrily devoured those. They burst through the windows and licked at the lilac bushes Pa had planted years ago, before leaping across to continue feeding on the building that housed the fog station. Only the assistant keeper's house was spared the flames' fury.

I remember small, disconnected pieces as I drifted in and out, Emily's face over mine. The roar of the fire and the snapping of the balsam saplings that stood like torches between the rocks. Charlie shouting. The sail of *Sweet Pea* above me, white against the purple-blue sky. The acrid smell of smoke clinging to me, to Emily. In the distance, across the Lake, the lighthouse itself, in its entirety, a beacon, flaming orange in the misty haze of the encroaching dawn. That was the last time I saw Porphyry.

★ ★ ★

'I spent months in the hospital, the pain from the burns on my back and chest so intense I longed for death. They told me I cried out, from the depths of morphine-induced sleep, calling for Emily. I knew, deep in the core of my being I knew, that we did not share the same blood, that we were not twins. But that did not change the fact that Emily and I were very much, in every way that mattered, sisters. And so I lived. I lived for Emily.' I close my eyes, my useless eyes that still cannot help but see the memories that haunt me. 'Charlie had her institutionalized. They put her in the Lakehead Psychiatric Hospital, locked her away.' I pause. 'They blamed her for the fire. They blamed her for Mother's death.' My voice is barely a whisper. 'I never told them otherwise.'

She says nothing, the girl. She does not

condemn nor console.

'By the time I was well enough to leave the hospital, Charlie was gone. It was another year before I wrote to Alfred and Millie and then managed to get Emily released. By then, I could find nothing about Anna — no one could tell me what had happened to her.'

55

Morgan

We sit in silence for a moment, listening to Emily's labored breathing. I can tell it has taken a lot for Elizabeth to share that part of her story. But the lightkeeper had more to say. His story isn't finished. She thinks it is, but it isn't; it's what comes next that I've been waiting to tell her.

'There's something else,' I say. 'There's more . . .'

Just as I'm about to begin reading again, Emily stirs, and the words of Andrew Livingstone are silenced. Those haunting gray eyes open, and while the hand connecting her to Elizabeth remains, her gaze finds me, holds me, and I can't speak any more, not even if I wanted to. Her thin pale fingers seek out my hand. Her eyes grow heavy, and she drifts off to sleep again, one hand in her sister's and one in mine.

I don't read any more.

★ ★ ★

The storm rages outside, just beyond the window, beyond the wall, but so far, far away. We sit there, the three of us, joined by our hands. The journal lies, silenced, in my lap.

Emily takes her last breath sometime after

midnight. It's so peaceful, neither Elizabeth or I notice when it happens.

★ ★ ★

We sit for a long time in Emily's room after she dies. Neither of us wants to take the next step, to get up, move on, leave. Elizabeth tells me about Emily's dementia, that for months, years even, she had been slipping away until there were very few days where she even recognized Elizabeth. As tears run down her wrinkled cheeks, she says it feels like she had lost her a long time ago, but it was still hard to say good-bye.

I sleep in the chair in Elizabeth's room, after the nurses come and cover Emily's face and help Elizabeth to bed. I remember to call Laurie to tell her I'm not going to be home, that I'm going to stay with Miss Livingstone. It sounds lame, like I'm just making up some bullshit excuse to stay out and party. But I've never called before — with or without an excuse — so I think she believes me. She says she's glad I called and to know I'm safe. And she says she'll leave the front door unlocked, just in case.

Marty comes in a few times during the night to check on us. I don't see or hear him, but he covers me with the afghan. By morning, the storm has quieted down. I sit in Elizabeth's room and sip tea.

'In some way,' she says, 'I have always known. But I refused to be haunted by a child's grave, by my mother's dying words — to spend a lifetime wondering, who am I?' She places her teacup down beside the pile of journals. They're all there except for the one I have; the one with the truth. 'It has only been since they found *Wind Dancer*, since Pa's words reached from the grave, that the mystery was brought to simmer at the surface and make me wonder again. But it is irrelevant, isn't it? I know who I am. I've known all along.' She picks up the rattle that sits on the top of the books, and her hand trembles slightly, so the rattle makes a soft sound. 'I am the life I lived. I *am* Elizabeth.'

Emily knew. Somehow she knew. And in her way, she asked me not to tell.

Elizabeth hands me the rattle, and I turn it over to read the name.

Anna. Daughter of Robert Larkin of Larkin and Sons Shipping. She was aboard the *Kelowna* when it went down near Porphyry Island. Her name was spoken to her, sung to her. It was part of her. And she remembered.

'You keep it,' Elizabeth said. 'It means nothing to me; I have no memory of it.'

Elizabeth wouldn't. It was never hers.

★　★　★

It's been four days now since I found Emily wandering in the storm, since the night she died. I'm down at the waterfront, standing on the rocks at the end of Pier 3. The blizzard only lasted a day, and since then, the sun has come out and warmed things up enough that all that's left of the snow is a slushy mess. But it's still cold. Too fucking cold to be standing outside by the Lake. But I'm here anyway.

Marty drove me home, after the streets had been plowed and cars could push their way out from underneath the mounds of snow that buried them. That's when I realized I no longer had my violin.

When I stopped by Boreal Retirement Home the next day, Marty gave it to me. He'd called the bus depot and they tracked it down. He drove there and picked it up. I'm grateful to have it back — the violin. But it's the music that speaks to me most, and I almost lost that a long time ago. I won't lose it again. It's part of me.

Marty asked me to paint the fence. I thought he was fucking with me, but he meant it. He said it might be nice to have some kind of mural — that the white surface seemed to be waiting for color. We went out and looked at it, looked at all the work I did, standing there silent while the wind blew snow around us. The sky was bright enough that I could see the faint lines of my dragonfly — Emily's dragonfly — beneath the white.

'You know,' he said, 'when you paint over something, everything that was there before isn't really gone. It's still there. All the layers of color, the scrapes and dents, even the bare wood hiding beneath, they shape what's painted on top, inspire it even, but they don't define it. That's up to the painter.' He looked at me with those sapphire eyes, twinkling beneath bushy white brows. 'The artist.'

I knew he wasn't talking about fences.

I'm not talented like Emily, but I'm challenged

by the thought of taking her work and letting her story flow through me. I can already see what I want to do. I think I'll paint both dragonflies, one larger, one slightly smaller. *Sisters in Flight.* It seems right.

There's a raven sitting on a piling just off the point, feathers ruffled to keep warm, its thick black beak silent. It spreads its wings, and I can hear them cutting the air as it flies overhead and disappears above the city. Marty and Elizabeth will be here soon. It was Marty's suggestion that we sprinkle Emily's and Charlie's ashes over the water, and I think they would have liked that. I hope the strings of the fiddle will allow me to play at these temperatures.

The water is deep blue today, liquid ice. I have the journal. I open it up to the page that talks about Charlie and his sisters and read it one last time.

Saturday, 11 December — Lil has remained in bed for almost a full week, but her fever has broken, and I know this influenza has now been contained and we are on the road to recovery. She will be back on her feet and managing our household soon, and I thank God there have been no more deaths. I have not spoken to her of the child, nor of the woman I have buried at sea. There will be time for that when she is well. Besides, what is done is done, and I am grateful for the gift that has brought life back to my daughter, completing her, filling the emptiness left by the loss of her twin. Peter

337

knows. I can see it when he looks at them; he knows the small child is not his sister at all. He will say nothing. It is his way. But Charlie does not remember that Elizabeth died. He was still delirious with fever when I took her cold form from Emily's side and when I slipped the life-giving form of another into her place. Oh, they are similar enough, with their raven-black hair so like each other's, their fair skin and delicate features. But even the twins were not so alike, Elizabeth always being the larger and stronger of the two. Now it is Emily who is larger. And so, today, when Charlie ventured from his bed and peered down at the girls, when he spoke to them and caressed their cheeks, as he is wont to do, he has confused their names. In order to keep our dark secret, in order to ensure that a young boy given to casual conversation does not speak of it, I will do what I must do — for Emily's sake. She will take the name of her dead sister and pass her own to the child of the Lake.

I tear the page from the journal. God, it makes so much sense, really. It explains why their mother never really accepted her. It explains so much about who she was, how she never quite belonged, wandering through life caught somewhere in a world of her own creation, silent except when she spoke to the wind and the trees and the animals. I can see how she would have been captivated by the Lake and at the same time terrified of it; it almost killed her. And when the *Hartnell* was wrecked and she spent day after day walking the shore, searching, she was living it all over again. She even gave her own child the name from her past. Emily remembered. She remembered being Anna.

You should have let her die.

Their mother's words haunted Elizabeth; they shaped her life. She became the protector, the advocate, sacrificing everything for the sake of her sister. In the beginning it wasn't Elizabeth who lived for Emily; Emily lived for her.

But in the end, the lightkeeper wouldn't let any of them die; not Elizabeth, not Emily, not Anna. He saw to it that they all survived, somehow, some way. Even if it meant living a lie.

Charlie knew the truth. He must have. That's why he went back for the journals when the *Kelowna* was discovered. He was going to tell Elizabeth, after all those years. He probably read his father's words when he returned to the island after the war. Did he blame himself for the secret? He would have been only about five years old. He had been too sick to see the lightkeeper take the dead baby Elizabeth out of the cot and replace her with another, smaller baby, a baby that had washed ashore in the middle of a storm; he wouldn't have known any better. He would have thought that they were the twins, his sisters. And he would have assumed that the larger girl was Elizabeth. Of course he would. What reason would he have to believe otherwise? And so the child that was born Emily becomes her dead sister, Elizabeth. And the daughter of Robert

Larkin, the little girl named Anna, stolen from the Lake, stolen from her life, becomes Emily.

I tear the page into pieces and toss them to the Lake. They sprinkle across the surface, dancing up and down on the ripples. They don't melt like snowflakes, but eventually they drift apart, carrying with them the truth.

56

Arnie Richardson

He leaves the old dog in the car and walks along the road in front of the CN Station, pulling his scarf tighter around his neck and leaning on his cane. He can see them out on the point at the end of Pier 3, the old woman tucked in a wheelchair. It is Elizabeth Livingstone, he knows. A girl is there, too, playing a fiddle, in spite of the cold wind. It's a subdued ceremony, not matching the publicity that consoles the rest of the world in the wake of the news that the renowned artist Emily Livingstone has died.

He knows her work well. He followed her career as best he could, and even has a small print hanging in his cottage at Silver Islet. It proved too difficult to find her. To find them. It was more difficult to write the letter, and he ended up sending only a note, telling them where to find their belongings from Porphyry, should they one day return. He sent it to Emily's agent, to the gallery in London that carried her work. He knew they eventually received it when the belongings were claimed a few years ago, and that they had returned. He wished he had said more.

The child was not with him long. He held her, briefly, that May night when Charlie banged on their door in the dark hours before dawn, insisting she was his family's responsibility. His mother and father took care of things. They did not ask questions; it was how they were and how things were done. There were reputations to preserve. When they registered the birth a few days later, Porphyry was still smoldering, the baby's mother had been institutionalized, deemed unfit, and in the blank space for the father's name, they wrote David Fletcher, occupation, assistant lighthouse keeper. Arnie did not correct them. She was adopted by a couple from Ottawa. It was his mother who picked the name Isabel. At one point he made some inquiries, officially typed up on the letterhead of his firm. He found out that she died of cancer years ago.

He stands there for a time, looking out at the small collection of people at the point, catching faint strains of the fiddle drifting on the breeze. He considers walking down to them, speaking to Elizabeth. Instead, he sighs and turns, making his way back to the car. The Lab greets him enthusiastically.

57

Afterword: Morgan

The helicopter swoops down, flying close to the surface of the Lake, and I can hear the pilot's voice through the headphones.

'That's Porphyry up ahead.'

The tall white tower is easy to pick out, and the red-roofed buildings, scattered across the rocky point. The Lake is turquoise, blending into mottled green where the bottom rises to shallows near the shore. As we approach the landing pad from the east, I can see the Sleeping Giant, a purple silhouette reclining on the far side of Silver Islet. It feels odd to see it from this angle, like I'm looking from the other side of a mirror.

I know it's not the same. The house and light tower that she lived in are gone, burned in the fire. They built a new assistant keeper's dwelling sometime in the sixties, I think, so that's gone too. But it's what she wanted.

I hold the urn in my lap.

It's been more than five years since we gathered at the waterfront, that cold November day. God, it feels like so long ago.

I couldn't convince Marty to come. He told me he'd said his good-byes and made some excuse about needing to fix a piece of equipment, but I knew the thought of flying in a helicopter scared the shit out of him. Elizabeth arranged it all before she died. We talked about it when I was home from university for reading week. She made me promise, but she didn't need to — I would have done it anyway. I think she knew that.

The helicopter hovers briefly, then touches down on the landing pad at the point, and the rotors begin to slow. 'Take all the time you need.' The pilot fiddles with switches and levers and then helps me to unbuckle. I remove my headphones, pop open the door, and climb down. They don't follow; it's just me and Elizabeth walking across the rocks toward the buildings.

The light was automated years ago, and nobody lives in the houses anymore. But someone has been out to clean things up. Everything's freshly painted, the lilacs are blooming, and the grass has been cut.

I sit on the concrete base below the light tower and look out across the Lake. I can see a freighter in the distance. It's heading toward Thunder Bay, slicing through the cold water and leaving a foamy trail behind it. In the distance, I can see Pie Island.

It's all so familiar, it feels like I've been here before.

I returned home from school a few weeks ago. It was almost like she waited for me to come back, to be done with all my exams, to have some time to sit with her and tell her about my classes and roommates and the band I'm playing in now. She bought me a graduation gift. I saw Marty's hand in it, but she would have told him

344

what to get. A blue electric violin. She said she could never understand the kind of music I played, that an old lady like her could still learn lots of things, but not to appreciate wild screaming guitars and pounding percussion when there was music like Paganini and Bach. I showed her how we layered the classics into our pieces, but she scrunched up her face and shook her head and it made me laugh. I know she was teasing me. I know how proud she is . . . was. The blue violin said so.

Laurie was happy to see me, too. I've got my own place now, but I visit her sometimes at her house or meet her for coffee. She and Bill haven't taken in any new kids. She says they're retired. Between Caleb and me, we probably wore them out. She says no and smiles, but it's a tired smile.

A couple of years ago, Elizabeth got a letter. It was from the estate of Arnie Richardson and had been written a long, long time ago, but never mailed. There were some legal documents in there, including a faded copy of the birth registration for Emily's baby, Anna. They named her Isabel. Elizabeth and I still aren't sure how much of the story Grandpa was able to piece together when she showed up at his door, thinking he was her father. But he would have known enough to figure out what had happened, who she was. So he took her in. He loved her. He loved me. I wonder if he told her stories about her mother, about the time they spent together on Porphyry Island. I wonder if he showed her the picture of the dragonflies, the one she slid

345

under his door when he was assistant light-keeper; the one he kept hidden in the violin case.

Emily knew me. She knew who I was. I don't know how, but she did, I know she did. She saw things that no one else even knew were there. That day, when I found her in the blizzard, it was like it was the other way around; it was like she found *me*. Marty says I look like her. We have the same eyes, the color of the Lake.

It's a long hike to the boat harbor, and the fucking mosquitoes are insane. I almost dump Elizabeth right there on the path to be done with it. The old boathouse is still standing. It's a little lopsided, but it's been painted, too, and the dock repaired. I find the path to the beach on the east side of the island, place the urn on the rocky shore, and sit beside it, looking out at Dreadnaught Island. I didn't bring my fiddle. I didn't need to. The music is here; it's in the waves and wind and the songs of the birds. And in my memory.

While I'm sitting there, I decide that I'm not going to do things like she asked. Not quite.

The door is open, but I'm strapped in. On our first pass, the gulls take to the air in a flash of white wings, and then we bank around and fly over Hardscrabble Island again. I open the urn and lean out, far enough to send the gray dust spilling over the edge. It floats through the air, drifting over the pile of lichen-covered rocks where a weathered cross marks the grave of the baby Elizabeth Livingstone. A gust of wind catches the cloud before it settles on the stones, and carries some of it out over the surface of

Superior. The Lake dances and sparkles like a thousand beams of light.

Elizabeth and Emily. They're together again.

Author's Note

While *The Lightkeeper's Daughters* was inspired by the Canadian men and women who served as Great Lakes lighthouse keepers during the late nineteenth and early twentieth centuries, it is above all else, a work of fiction. As such, I have taken some liberties to tell the story of the Livingstone family.

Porphyry Island is the last in a chain of islands that stretches beyond the Black Bay Peninsula on the Canadian shore of Lake Superior. The light station serves to mark the shipping channel north of Isle Royale, leading to the former communities of Port Arthur and Fort William, now Thunder Bay. It was the second lighthouse constructed on the Canadian side of Lake Superior, and first illuminated the waters near Black Bay in 1873. Andrew Dick, who served as keeper from 1880 to 1910, left behind several personal journals that captured reflections of his time at the light with his Indigenous wife Caroline and their ten children. The journals were discovered years later in the attic of one of the summer homes at Silver Islet, and two volumes are now housed at the Thunder Bay Museum. These journals were inspiration for *The Lightkeeper's Daughters*. The original lighthouse no longer remains, having been replaced around the middle of the century, and while it served as a guideline, I have made some modifications on paper, most significantly from the light being fixed to flashing.

During the early part of the twentieth century, shipping on Lake Superior was lucrative, with cargos of iron ore, lumber, and grain heading down the lakes, passing sister ships loaded with equipment and shoes and tea coming up. These were the days before technology found its way onto the bridges of ships, before GPS and satellites and marine radio. Captains plotted their course on charts, taking bearings on landmarks, using compasses to steer by, and their logs to calculate distance traveled. Their tools were sextants and slide rules and they posted watches whose job it was to scan the horizon for lighthouses and beacons and other vessels.

As much as a lighthouse was there to shine a signal across the darkened waters, it was the sound of the foghorn that most often defined safe passage for unseen vessels creeping along the shoal-filled waters under the shroud of Lake Superior's infamous fog. Here again, I have taken some liberties with the Porphyry Point Light Station since the original diaphone foghorn was commissioned in 1908, not in 1918 as I have indicated.

The nearby community of Silver Islet features significantly in the story, and is itself rich with history, tragedy, and fascinating characters. It was established in the 1870s to serve the needs of the Silver Islet mine, which operated until 1884 when the winter shipment of coal failed to arrive before the end of the shipping season.

Eventually, the stockpile of fuel ran out, the pumps that kept Superior's water from flooding the shafts grew silent, and the Lake reclaimed the mine. With declining silver prices, the mine was never reopened. A few years later, the homes and company buildings that clustered along the waterfront were purchased and converted into summer cottages.

There are many shipwrecks littering the cold depths of Lake Superior and the *Kelowna* and the *Hartnell* appear as compilations of several incidents and have been located near Porphyry Island for the sake of the story.

Lake Superior appears in full iconic truth; temperamental, beautiful, vast, magnificent, and moody. While it has been said she seldom gives up her dead, I am grateful she has been willing to share her stories.

Acknowledgements

No book is created in isolation in spite of the time writers spend in a dark room with only their characters to keep them company. I am grateful for all the support I received while working on *The Lightkeeper's Daughters*.

My thanks to the Ontario Arts Council who supported my creative endeavors through the Writers' Works in Progress and Writers' Reserve grants.

To Jenny Bent, my fabulous agent, (who only laughed when I asked if she was sure she had the right phone number when she called to offer representation) and all her incredible staff at The Bent Agency.

To my dynamic editing team at HarperCollins: Iris Tupholme, Emily Griffin, and Laura Dosky, who worked to pull out my strengths and to help shape my words so that the best possible story emerged, and to Miranda Ottewell for her attention to detail.

To my fellow vixens of Laughing Fox Writers, and all its earlier incarnations, who share a common journey with the written word, for pouring wine, for eating pizza, for reading drafts, for sharing retreats, and mostly for making me take the giant leap to send my work out there, especially Heather Dickson, Donna White, Marion Agnew, Cathi Grandfield, and Holly Haggarty. (As you can see, the manuscript is no longer in my sock drawer.)

To my early readers, Lucy Laframboise, Kristine Dalzall, Darrel Makin, Susan Visser, and Emma Tranter, thank you for your feedback. To my reference sources who helped with everything from lighthouse keeping on the Great Lakes, to graffiti tags, to the types of orchids found on Porphyry Island; Larry and Patricia Wright, Ted Armstrong, Rob Foster, Kim Armstrong, Dave Poisson, John O'Meara, Michelle Beck, Sarah Mason, and Lora Northway — this book is richer because of you.

To my husband, Richard, and my amazing 'kids,' Erin, Colin, and Ryan, who believed in me even when my confidence faltered, who gave honest feedback, and who reminded me to eat lunch.

To my dad, Craig McDonald, and in memory of my mother, Sue, who took me sailing every weekend and summer holiday of my youth, and instilled in me a love of, and respect for, Lake Superior, and to my sisters, Barbara Mitchell and the late Theresa Flatt, who shared those trips and encouraged me on this journey. To Mary Ann Beckwith, for sailing with me again.

And finally, to the lightkeepers whose stories influenced this work, most especially the McKay family who served for generations as lighthouse keepers at various stations on Lake Superior. I had the incredible, incredible good fortune to be able to spend time with Bob McKay, former senator with the Métis Nation of Ontario, who was the assistant lightkeeper at Porphyry Point Light Station from 1960 to 1965, serving with his cousin Cliff McKay. Having spent his youth at his family's fishing camp in Walker's Channel, Bob was able to share with me his early knowledge of Porphyry Island, his personal experiences, his love of lighthouse keeping, his many photographs, his sense of humor, and the respect he holds for his Indigenous heritage and the history of his family. I was also fortunate enough to connect with Cliff McKay's wife, Frances. Cliff was lightkeeper from 1959 to 1979 at Porphyry, and Frances spent many wonderful summers on the island. At the age of ninety-four, Frances read an early draft of *The Lightkeeper's Daughters*, and paid me the greatest compliment any writer could ever receive by saying, wistfully, that it made her feel like she was back on Porphyry again.

To all of you, I am grateful.

THREE THINGS ABOUT ELSIE

Joanna Cannon

There are three things you should know about Elsie. The first thing is that she's my best friend. The second is that she always knows what to say to make me feel better. And the third thing . . . might take a little bit more explaining. Eighty-four-year-old Florence has fallen in her flat at Cherry Tree Home for the Elderly. As she waits to be rescued, she wonders if a terrible secret from her past is about to come to light. And if the charming new resident is who he claims to be, why does he look exactly like a man who died sixty years ago?

DALILA

Jason Donald

Irene Dalila Mwathi comes from Kenya with a brutally violent personal history. Once she wanted to be a journalist, but now all she wants is to be safe. When she finally arrives, bewildered, in London, she is attacked by the very people paid to protect her, and she has no choice but to step out on her own into this strange new world. Through a dizzying array of interviews, lawyer's meetings, regulations and detention centres, she realises that what she faces may be no less dangerous than the violence she has fled . . .

NO GOOD DEED

John Niven

What do you do when the homeless man on
the street you've just given money to thanks
you by name and turns out to be one of your
'closest' friends, one you haven't seen for over
twenty years? For Alan, there's no question — it's only natural that he'd want to see
his old mate Craig off the streets, even if only
for a few nights, and into some clean clothes.
But what if the successful life you've made for
yourself — good job, happy marriage, lovely
kids, grand Victorian house — is one that
your old pal would quite like to have too?
Even if it means taking it from you? Gradually, inevitably, mayhem ensues as Craig turns
Alan's orderly household upside down, threat-
ening to wreck Alan's life for good.

THE COTTINGLEY SECRET

Hazel Gaynor

Cottingley, Yorkshire, 1917: When two young cousins, Frances Griffiths and Elsie Wright, announce they have photographed fairies at the bottom of the garden, their parents are astonished. The girls become a sensation; their discovery offering something to believe in amid a world ravaged by war . . . One hundred years later: When Olivia Kavanagh finds an old manuscript and a photograph in her late grandfather's bookshop, it sparks a fascination with the story of the two young girls who mystified the world. Delving deeper into the past, and the truth behind an innocent game that became a national obsession, Olivia begins to understand why a nation once believed in fairies. But can she find a way to believe in herself?